THE BUCCANEERS;

OR,

THE HIDDEN TREASURE.

BY EDWARD ELLIS.

WITH THIRTEEN ILLUSTRATIONS.

BY F. GILBERT.

LONDON:
JOHN DICKS, 313, STRAND; AND ALL BOOKSELLERS.

THE BUCCANEERS;

OR, THE HIDDEN TREASURE.

CHAPTER I.

COME BACK FROM THE GRAVE.

At length his misery was ended.

It had been a hard struggle—a long, wearisome, and bitter struggle, in which he had striven manfully, fought bravely, persevered, and conquered.

Better days had come; happier times were in store for him. For many years he had been hoping against hope; he had been working on in the dark, with no prospect to help him on the hard and cruel road by which he had travelled.

But there was hope now!

There was a prospect—a bright and glorious prospect before him. He stood upon the threshold of a new world. He held the cup of happiness in his hand. Was it possible that it could slip from his fingers at the last moment?—was it possible that yet another disappointment awaited him, more hard to bear, more bitterly cruel, than any he had yet suffered?

We shall see.

The life of privation and toil which he had led had left its traces upon his face; and though he was not more than twenty-five, there were wrinkles upon his brow, and his hair was prematurely grey. He would have been a handsome man, had not his lips been so thin and so tightly compressed and his grey eyes so stern and cold.

His name was Owen Redgrave. He wore a ragged coat, he had not a shilling in the wide world wherewith to bless himself, and yet he was one of the happiest men in the world. He stood beneath the leafy porch of his mother's house, one calm summer's night, and traced with tear-dimmed eyes the winding road in the valley before him, along which, scarce six hours ago, he had wearily dragged his blistered feet, faint-hearted and despairing—a homeless outcast.

He looked around upon the blue hills, the green woodlands, the shining river, the garden crowded with sweet-smelling flowers—above all, the dear old house, every quaint gable end of which he so well remembered—every nook and corner of which, since those far-off, boyish days, when he had dwelt in it, he had recalled a score of times in his dreams. Happy dreams, how bitterly hard to awaken from, to the struggle of his daily life!

But that was over now. He had returned at last. He had been forgiven. How could he ever have doubted a mother's love? He had sobbed upon her breast; she had softly brushed back his tangled locks, and looked down lovingly into the careworn face. For a few brief moments, time had seemed to stop, the weary work of years to be undone, and they were as they had been once in the happy days gone never to return.

Yes, he had come back, poor, broken-spirited, to seek a shelter in the house he should never have left; and the few brief hours which had elapsed since his return had been so full of bewildering joy and happiness, that he had somehow felt a craving to be alone by himself for a few moments, to ask himself calmly whether it was not some mad dream, like many in his life he had dreamt, and from which stern reality had rudely awakened him.

But no, it was no dream.

Yonder lay the road he had come—far away beyond the world he had left.

He had led a wild life at home and abroad.

He had been reckless, profligate, criminal.

But all that was over now. He had turned over a new leaf. He was going to begin life afresh.

He lit a pipe.

It does not follow as a matter of course, that because he still continued to smoke, his good resolutions were worthless. He had been, among a score of other trades, a sailor; and he had many a time found his pipe a friend and consoler, when friends were scarce and consolation scanty.

His pipe was black and short, and had seen much service. Many long miles had they travelled together he and it, and vast quantities of the fragrant weed had they jointly consumed.

Smoking was such a habit with him that, almost involuntarily, he filled the bowl and struck a match, as he stood there in the honeysuckle entwined porch round which the fast gathering twilight darkened. A rustling of the branches in the hedge-row surrounding the garden suddenly aroused him from the reverie into which he had fallen.

Upon the other side of the hedge lay the high road, which wound through the valley beneath, and further on lost itself among the blue hills. A dirty, travel-stained man came crawling slowly along, and stopped in front of the house.

He pushed the branches on one side, and peered through the hedge at the dwelling, which the shades of evening rendered but indistinctly visible; but he noted the warm light filtered out from the red window-curtains of the cozy parlour, and a grim smile crossed his grimy face.

"A snug enough place, this," said he, to himself. "A warm little nest, I'll warrant me, and well feathered! I wonder whether it's the house I want?"

It might have been; but certainly it was not to be supposed that he was expected. He was not exactly the sort of man likely to meet with a hearty welcome from any respectable family.

He was a sea-faring man apparently, but there was very little of the jolly tar about him.

It is true that one quite as dusty and travel-stained, and almost as ragged, had a few hours before met with a warm welcome from the mistress of the house, but this second prodigal would surely have more trouble in finding an owner.

He was perhaps as ill-looking and ill-conditioned a cur as ever strayed uncared for. When he pulled back his ragged, red hair, and glared with heavy blood-shot eyes through the opening he had made in the hedge, the sudden apparition of his ugly face would have been well-nigh enough to scare any timid person out of their wits; and as, reptile-like, he wriggled his misshapen carcass among the bushes, he was the exact impersonation of some evil spirit come to blast the peace and happiness of the quiet home upon which he gazed with a covetous leer.

Owen Redgrave looked up hastily when he heard the crackling of the dry twigs in the hedge, but it was now too dark for him to discern an object at so great a distance.

He paused for a moment, therefore, holding the ignited match between his finger and thumb; then, as it flickered and failed, he applied it hastily to his pipe, and as hastily inhaled the smoke. The pipe lit, only a faint red light glowing through the gloom indicated its position and the whereabouts of its smoker, and the momentary illumination of his features, as he drew the match into a blaze, was so faint that it would have been almost impossible for any one well acquainted with his face to have recognised him at a short distance, yet the man peeping in through the hedge made a slight start when he caught a glimpse of them, and half withdrew his head from the opening he had made.

It might have been, though, that he feared he had been discovered.

Presently, when he found that the smoker had not stirred from the spot which he had hitherto occupied, the stranger thrust his head further through the hedge, and cast greedy looks around.

"It must be the place I want!" he muttered to himself, when he had effected a somewhat lengthy survey of the premises. "Only, who's the party with the pipe?"

It was too dark for the spy to obtain anything like a satisfactory view of Redgrave's figure, and having in vain strained his eyes to pierce the gloom which enveloped it, he drew back his head again.

"Can't make it out," he said: "there were only the two ladies and a female servant, from what I understood. The old lady does not keep a carriage, so that can't be the coachman: besides, if it was, it isn't likely he would be standing smoking his pipe on the doorstep; unless, indeed, the ladies are away from home. It will be like my luck if they are."

He left his place of observation, and walking as lightly as possible, and keeping under the shadow of the hedge, moved onwards.

Twenty yards or so from the spot where he had been standing, was the gate which led into the garden from the high road. The ill-looking stranger stole a very thievish kind of hand in between the bars, and felt for the latch.

"These sort of gates jingle and clank so as to be heard a mile off," he said. "I must take care not to let it slip. If I could only get inside the garden, though, I should like to have a peep round."

Very cautiously, then, he slipped in that lank, ugly hand of his, and noiselessly opened the gate.

But while so employed, some one, advancing very leisurely up the road, and whose approaching footsteps, hidden by the grass at the roadside, upon which he walked, had been inaudible to the spy, came plump upon, and almost fell over, this stealthy trespasser.

"Hallo!" cried the new arrival.

"Hallo!" responded the spy.

"Who are you?"

"Who are you?"

"What are you doing there?"

"Nothing!"

"You seemed to be taking great pains to do it, then."

"I wasn't doing any harm."

"I don't know that."

"Leave hold of me."

"When I've had a look at your face, my friend. Wait a minute."

It was a tall, strongly-built man, wearing a suit of rusty black and a white neckerchief, who had laid hands upon the spy's collar, and who now, with a powerful wrench and a persuasive dig of his knuckles, which there was no resisting into his throat, dragged him from the spot where he had stood, spun him round, and propping him up with his back to a tree, stared hard into his face.

"Well," said the spy, when they had thus stood silently for a few moments, "are you satisfied?"

"Not over and above!" the other replied, sternly.

"I hope you'll know me next time," observed the spy, doggedly.

"Yes, I shall not forget you."

"That's all right!"

"You're a stranger in these parts?"

"Yes."

"You've not been here long?"

"No."

"A tramp, I suppose?"

"What makes you suppose that?" said the spy, fiercely. "I'm as respectable as you are, I daresay, although my coat's a trifle dusty, and as honest."

"I hope so," said the gentleman in black. "Only I should not have thought it!"

"What was I doing wrong?" the spy retorted, recovering his equanimity somewhat, now that the other's knuckles were removed from his throat. "Couldn't I open a gate to go into a garden, to ask my way somewhere, without being pounced upon and half strangled by you?"

"What did you want to ask?" inquired the other, to whom this explanation did not appear altogether satisfactory. "I can tell you."

"I wanted to know the way," the spy stammered,— "the way to—to Mrs.—Mrs.—I mean to Wakerleigh."

"A mile futher on," said the gentleman, pointing down the high-road, in the direction from which the spy had come a while since; and the latter, having mumbled some inarticulate words of thanks, shambled slowly away, whilst his informant stood thoughtfully watching his retreating form.

"An ugly customer, that," said the gentleman in black; "meant to rob the hen-roost, probably, or steal the clothes off the hedges, or the flowers out of the garden. I wonder what he did want? I shouldn't like to meet him myself in a very lonely spot. Egad! I shouldn't have cared for the interview now, if he had only known what I had in my pocket."

And as this reflection passed through the gentleman's mind, he involuntarily clapped his hand upon his breast-pocket, which, beneath his touch, emitted a sonorous chink.

"A hundred pounds in gold," said he, with a smile, "are enough to tempt a rascal like that to do any one a mischief!"

He was evidently no coward, this gentleman in rusty black, who carried about with him a hundred pounds in gold in his breast-pocket; but the little scene through which he had just passed was calculated in some measure to heighten his pulse, and cause a more lively circulation of his blood. Perhaps it made him just a little bit nervous, for it is very certain that he started violently at the sight of a very seedily attired young man, who, upon approaching the house, he found smoking a pipe upon the doorstep.

"Hallo!" cried the gentleman again. "Is this another of them?" he thought to himself.

Owen removed the pipe from his mouth, and inquired whether the gentleman wished to see his mother.

"Your mother?" repeated the new comer, looking up and down in amazement. "No—I want Mrs. Redgrave."

"She is my mother."

"Bless me! Oh! is she? Ah!"

It was in anything but a complimentary tone that these words were uttered, and they were accompanied by a stare which said very little for the good opinion of the speaker.

Meanwhile, Owen Redgrave silently led the way to the parlour where his mother was seated. She rose as the visitor entered, and gave him her hand.

"I have been expecting you, Mr. Hardstaff," she said; "I wondered what had detained you. This is my dear boy Owen. You do not remember him?"

"No," replied Mr. Hardstaff, still suspiciously scanning Owen's scarcely respectable exterior, through half closed eyes. "Been away a long while, sir," said he; "abroad, perhaps?"

"Yes; I have been away a long while abroad," answered Owen, with a deep sigh.

"Sit down, Mr. Hardstaff," continued Mrs. Redgrave. "This is my solicitor, Owen. You have brought the money, have you not, in gold?"

Instead of replying, however, the lawyer again glanced towards young Redgrave, and uneasily scraped his chin with his hand.

"Have you brought it in gold?"

"Yes, madam. I beg pardon. I have it quite safe. It's lucky I have, too. I might have been robbed just now."

"Robbed?"

"Yes, by an ill-looking vagabond I found trying to open your garden-gate."

"Dear me! Who was it?"

"A stranger to me. A tramp, I should think—a thief, I am certain."

"Owen, dearest," cried the old lady, in alarm, "I am so afraid of some one taking away my favourite fowls. I know they will be lost some day; Mary is so careless about locking the door. Would you go and look about?"

Owen sprang to his feet, and hurried away, without any loss of time; while Mr. Hardstaff, closing the door behind him, drew his chair to the table, and, taking from his pocket a small canvass bag, poured forth the gold.

"A hundred pounds," said he, "and two hundred more in notes. Please to count it over, madam, and tell me if you find it correct."

The lawyer and the old lady bent over the glittering heap, the lamp-light shining brightly on their faces, while greedy eyes were watching them through a crevice in the half-drawn window curtains—the greedy eyes of the spy.

While his mother and the lawyer were thus occupied, Owen Redgrave had left the house, and noiselessly picking his steps, crept round the wall side towards the hen roost. To arrive at it, he was obliged to pass by the parlour window, through which the light poured in a ruddy stream upon the grass.

A dark figure, crouching close to the wall, threw a black shadow upon the pathway, and disclosed the occupation of the spy.

Owen, without a word, sprang forward and secured him.

Then, in each other's grip, they struggled for several yards out into the grass plot, when falling, Owen the uppermost, in a place where the light lay full upon their faces, they paused to pant for breath.

But then it was, with a sudden exclamation, half of wonder, half of terror, that Owen Redgrave released his hold, and staggered to his feet.

"Is it you?" he muttered faintly between his ashy lips. "Is it you, or your ghost come back from the grave?"

"It's me, sure enough," said the spy, rising to his feet, "although I never dreamt of finding you here. I told you we should meet again. How are you? I'm always glad to see an old friend."

"Hush!" cried the other, in a whisper, and casting a terrified look around. "Come farther from the house, that I may talk to you."

And with trembling steps he led the way to a spot at some short distance, where, concealed from view, as far as the house was concerned, they could converse without fear of interruption.

CHAPTER II.

DANGER.

"WHAT has brought you here?" Owen Redgrave inquired at last, after he had for some moments silently contemplated his companion's unprepossessing countenance. "What has brought you here, Jonas Drake?"

The man, thus addressed, plunged his dirty fingers among his ragged red hair, and responded with an ugly grin.

"I might ask the same question of you. Upon my life, I am quite surprised to see you. So spirited a young man to be wasting his time here at this outlandish place, while he might be making his fortune. What are you a doing down in these parts, Mr. Redgrave, if I might make so bold?"

"I live here."

"Do you?"

"It is my mother's house."

"Is it?"

"And under these circumstances," continued Redgrave, with an angry frown, "you will please understand me to be in earnest when I say that if I find you hanging about the premises, and peering and prying as you were just now, I shall take the liberty of breaking your neck."

There was very little doubt that the speaker meant to do his best to make good his words, and Jonas Drake eyed him uneasily. He, however, plucked up courage after a brief pause, and spoke in a whining tone, which rendered him in the other's eyes more hateful, if possible, than before.

"I shouldn't have thought you would have spoken to an old friend this way," he said; "because I am an old friend, Owen, and you can't deny it. We were very thick together once upon a time, though now you may try to make believe to forget all about it. I've suffered a deal since last we met, Owen; I've been near to death's door. I've been many a time half starved. I've not a penny in the world to bless myself with now."

"What do you want?" asked Owen Redgrave, sternly.

Jonas Drake glanced up at the speaker, and wiped his mouth upon the back of his hand.

"I want a little help, that's all," said he; "and I appeal to you as a friend to give it me."

"I have nothing to give."

"Nothing to give?"

"No."

Drake smiled grimly as he glanced around.

"This is a comfortable little place, though, of the old lady's," he observed. "She's pretty warm, too, here, I'll lay a pound. Ask her for something for me."

"I cannot."

"Why not?"

"I have returned here, hungry and in rags, and she has received me with open arms. I would rather cut out my tongue than beg of her."

"Why so? She would only be too glad to give it you; she would never miss it, too. How could she, with the house full of gold?"

"What do you mean?"

"You know well enough. Isn't she counting it over now in that parlour, where I was looking in through the window?"

Redgrave glanced uneasily in the direction indicated, and back again to his companion's face.

"You have no claim upon me," he said, after a pause, and in a determined tone. "Take yourself off. Let us part as we have met. There is no love lost between us; but the world is wide enough for each to go his separate way, without any fear of our meeting again."

As he spoke, Redgrave turned upon his heel, as though he would have gone away, but the other, laying his hand upon his arm, stopped him.

"Not so fast!" he said, between his set teeth; "let's talk reasonable, if we are to talk at all. I will have money, I tell you, and you shall give it me!"

"Shall?"

"Yes; you know you are in my power, and you know how. Do you suppose I have forgotten that affair of the forged bill of exchange, or that I have let it slip out of my fingers. Not likely. Look here, now, Mr. Owen Redgrave; you know me for what I am, and you know I'm not the man to play fast and loose with. What's brought me here, do you suppose? Accident? Not a bit of it. I came to sell that forged bill to your mother; and, as I've found you here, lucky for you, I shall give you the opportunity of buying it in her stead."

"Scoundrel! I——"

The young man made as though he would have taken the other by the throat; but the moment that he made a forward movement with that intent, the sound of a footstep upon the gravel walk, close by the spot where they had been talking, caused him to pause.

It was Mr. Hardstaff on his way home.

"Who's there?" cried the lawyer. "Is that you Mr. Redgrave?"

"Yes."

"Saw nothing of the robber, I suppose? Ah!"

The lawyer started as his eyes fell upon the face of Owen's companion's.

"Bless me!" he said; "you here again?"

"By your leave, sir," replied Jonas Drake, with a low bow. "If you've no objection, I should like to speak to my friend, Mr. Owen."

"Your friend?" repeated the lawyer. "A friend of yours, Mr. Redgrave?"

"No—yes," stammered the young man. "We have met before."

"Oh, indeed! Good night to you."

Mr. Hardstaff stared at them harder than ever; then, turning abruptly, walked away. He stopped fifty yards from the house, and took off his hat to scratch his head.

"Strange affair," he muttered to himself.—"very strange affair! Queer young man, the son! Queer person, the son's friend.—very queer person! Very queer affair altogether!"

He put on his hat again with a bang, and walked away at a faster pace than before, and reached home without being able to arrive at any satisfactory conclusion.

*   *   *   *   *   *

"I hope nothing has happened to Owen."

The table of the cozy parlour was laid for supper; the lamp burnt brightly; the curtains were closely drawn. The night had turned somewhat chilly as it advanced, and the glowing warmth of the little room was anything but disagreeable to those who might enter from the bleak darkness without.

The old lady, in her arm-chair, sat at the table waiting for her son's return; and by her side a fair young girl of nineteen, who was Mrs. Redgrave's niece, and whose beautiful and intelligent face bore a strong resemblance to that of her elderly companion.

Grace Atherton was the orphan child of Mrs. Redgrave's younger sister; and from an early age she had lived under her aunt's roof. From an early age, also, had she been taught to believe that at her aunt's death the greater part of the old lady's property would descend to her; for the poor mother had but faint hopes of her wild son's life, and never dreamt that they would meet again in this world.

"But as he has come back, dear Grace, you will not grudge him a portion, will you? I must see Mr. Hardstaff again to-morrow, and add a codicil to my will. I cannot leave my own flesh and blood to want. Poor boy, poor boy! how he has suffered! How we have both suffered all this weary while we have been parted!"

"Dear aunt," the young girl answered, in a low, trembling voice, "you cannot think how happy that has made me. You shall not add a codicil, though, to your will, but make out a new will altogether, and leave Owen what is his due—all your property."

"And leave you without any, I suppose?"

"He has more right to it than I have."

"But is there not enough for both; and, oh! if it would only happen——"

"What could happen, aunt?"

"He is twenty-five, and you are nineteen."

"Well, aunt?"

"And he's a handsome fellow, and I'm sure you'd soon love him; and——"

"Well, aunt?"

"And you used to be lovers, you know, when you were a little boy and girl; and——"

"Well, aunt?"

"And I daresay he will love you when he comes to know you."

"Oh, you think so?"

"I'm sure of it!"

"Then let me tell you something."

"What is that?"

"It's a secret, mind!"

"Certainly."

"To be told to no one?"

"Of course not."

"Well, then, he does."

"Does what?"

"Loves me."

"Who says so?"

"I had it upon the best authority. He told me himself."

And then a blushing face was hidden on Mrs. Redgrave's shoulder — a beautiful, blushing face, smothered in silky-brown curls, through which two brown eyes, that tried to be roguish through their tears, peeped coyly out.

While they were speaking, a footfall in the passage without assured them of Owen's return, and Grace rose, smiling, to meet him.

But he only pressed her hand very slightly, and averted his eyes as he took his seat at the table.

"How long you have been, my dear!" his mother said.

"Have I?"

"Yes—a long while. I was getting quite nervous. You saw no one, I suppose?"

"Yes—no, no—I saw no one."

"Is anything the matter?"

"The matter, mother?"

"Yes; you seem thoughtful and sad. Has anything happened ?"

"No, dear mother," the young man replied, with a forced laugh; "nothing to be afraid of. I have been thinking of my past life—a subject not too cheerful. Thinking what a fool I was to be a tool in the hands of others—to do what I have done. That's all. I won't think of it any more. Ha, ha, ha!"

There was something strangely harsh and grating in his tone as he said this—something strangely unnatural in his wild laugh, which seemed so out of place, and jarred discordantly upon his hearers' ears.

His mother was the first to speak. She rose, and threw her arms around his neck, and sobbingly implored him to think no more of those things—to look upon those dreadful days as gone for ever—irrevocably passed away, and to live only in the future.

"The future !" repeated Redgrave, in a gloomy tone, as he covered his face with his hands.

A moment afterwards he started up, and burst into a fit of almost hysterical laughter; and throughout the supper his merriment was loud and boisterous.

When the hour arrived for the little family to repair to their several couches, the mother parted with her son with some emotion, evoking a blessing upon his head as she pressed him to her breast.

"Heaven bless you, my poor boy, you need rest ! Thank heaven for its great goodness in bringing us together ! May we never part again !"

The son retired to his room—the room which had been his years ago—and was not long before he had thrown himself upon his bed.

It was not long before the other inmates of the house were slumbering. The moon rose in the heavens, and shone down upon their peaceful home. The great clock upon the staircase ticked loudly in the death-like silence—a silence which anon was broken by the stealthy footstep of the midnight robber, creeping upwards by the creaking stairs to the room where the money lay; and the happy mother slept, unconscious of the danger threatening her from the assassin's knife.

CHAPTER III.

NEXT MORNING.

AT an early hour next morning, Mr. Hardstaff, the lawyer, walked over from the village where his house and office were situated, and made a call upon his neighbour, Mrs. Redgrave.

He had passed a sleepless night, a prey to every kind of uneasy reflection. For the life of him, he could not contrive to banish from his mind the recollection of the previous evening's adventure.

Had he acted wisely to leave the money in the old lady's charge ? Would it be safe under her protection ?

Was the son a trustworthy person ? If so, how about the son's friend ?

More than once during the night, as he rolled to and fro upon his restless pillow, the lawyer felt inclined to get up, dress himself, and go down to Mrs. Redgrave's house. But then came the reflection—if all should be safe, how ridiculous must such a course of conduct appear to his client ?

No, he at length determined, he would wait until the morning. At last, as day was breaking, he fell into an uneasy slumber, from which he was awakened suddenly by what he fancied to be a piercing shriek.

He sprang upright in bed, trembling violently—the cold sweat of terror upon his brow, and listened intently

But all was still : it must have been imagination.

As, however, he was lying down again, worn out and weary, determined to go to sleep, another voice without disturbed him—the sound of hasty footsteps —of a man running through the village street below.

There was a twist in the road some thirty yards or so beyond the lawyer's house. When he had had time to spring out of bed, and run to look out of his bedroom window, the running man, whoever he was, had turned the corner, and his footsteps were faintly audible in the distance.

He had come from the direction of Mrs. Redgrave's house, and had gone on by the road leading to the nearest market town—a town through which the railway passed.

If he were a robber, and had robbed Mrs. Redgrave's house, he would have plenty of time to escape by the first train.

But why should it be supposed that such was the case ?

When the lawyer came to reflect upon the matter, he saw that the supposition was wild and extravagant in the extreme.

The occurrence, however, had thoroughly aroused him, and effectually banished all hope of sleep.

He rose, therefore, and betook himself to his office, and tried to settle his mind to work.

This was, though, as difficult a task as to get to sleep; and by the time that his usual hour for rising had arrived, he had got through such a very small quantity, that he might, for all the good he had done, have remained quietly in bed.

When the servant came to clean the room, and lay the cloth for breakfast, she was not a little surprised to find her master waiting for her.

"How early you are, sir !" she said.

"I could not sleep."

"I was awakened in the night."

"Eh ? How was that ?"

"Some one was running by the house."

"Was that all ? Did you hear nothing else ?"

"I thought I heard a cry as well. Did you hear anything, sir ? I hope no one is hurt."

Mr. Hardstaff would not wait for breakfast. He put on his hat, and, early though it was, set off to Mrs. Redgrave's house.

In the garden he saw Grace.

"Good morning, Miss Atherton ! How is your aunt this morning ?"

"She is not down yet, sir."

"Have you seen her ?"

"She does not rise so early. Do you wish to see her ?"

"No—yes. I think I should like her to know that I have come."

"I will call her."

"How is Mr. Owen, to-day ?"

"He has not yet left his room."

The lawyer went into the parlour, and took a seat.

Presently he heard a loud tapping at the door of the room overhead. Then he heard the door opened.

Then a moment's pause, and a piercing shriek.

Springing up-stairs, he rushed in the direction of the sound.

Grace Atherton met him at the door of her aunt's bedroom, with an ashy face.

"What is the matter ?"

"Go in."

As he had thought : there had been robbery.

The contents of the drawers and cupboards lay strewed in all directions upon the floor, and upon the bed lay Mrs. Redgrave—cold and dead.

"Where is her son ? Which is his room ?"

"There !"

The lawyer flung open the door of the room indicated.

It was empty. The bed had not been slept in, the lawyer saw at the first glance, although somebody had lain down upon it for a short time, marking it with the impression of his body.

And Owen Redgrave?

He was nowhere to be found!

The servants were called up, and interrogated. They knew nothing, and stood confounded, scarcely able to comprehend the full horror of the situation.

"Go to my house," said the lawyer to the gardener. "Run as quickly as you can. Tell nobody a word about what has happened, but bring back my horse."

While the man was gone, the lawyer walked to and fro thoughtfully in the garden. Then he came upstairs, and locked the door of the room where the body lay, taking the key with him.

When his horse arrived, and he was about to mount into the saddle, Grace stopped him.

"Oh, sir!" she cried, turning towards him a wan, tearful face, "what are you going to do?"

"I am going over to the magistrate, to lodge an information."

"Information! Are you—will you accuse any one?"

"As yet," replied the lawyer, sternly, "we can accuse no one—we can only suspect."

"Suspect! Oh, for heaven's sake, tell me, sir, do you believe Owen Redgrave to be guilty?"

Mr. Hardstaff was silent for a moment; but just as he was about to speak, the sound of footsteps, and the clamour of voices in the road without, caused him to pause, and look up in the direction from whence came the sound.

A loud ringing at the bell announced that the newcomers, whoever they were, had stopped at the gate; and presently the gate was heard to open, and a crowd of men approached.

Four police officers were distinguishable in the midst, holding between them two prisoners.

The first Mr. Hardstaff readily recognised as the spy of the previous evening.

The second, dusty and blood-stained, with flushed face, tangled hair, and torn attire, there was no mistaking him.

At the first sight of his well-known face, poor Grace gave a wailing cry, half-shriek, half-groan, and would have fallen to the ground, had not the lawyer caught her in his arms.

But the weakness was but momentary. Commanding her feelings with a mighty effort, she drew near to her betrothed husband, and pressing her cold lips to his forehead, whispered in his ear, "Dear Owen, I believe you to be innocent; but oh, heaven, grant that you may be able to clear up this horrible mystery!"

One of the policemen advanced towards Mr. Hardstaff, with whom he was personally acquainted, and drew him upon one side.

"A nasty job this, sir."

"What is it?"

"Found these two having a scuffle among the brushwood at the top of the railway cutting, over there by Squire Thornley's."

"Yes—yes; I know the place."

"The elder man—the red-headed one—had got the other down, and would have strangled him, if me and my mate had not dropped upon them providential."

"Yes, yes!"

"As soon as we came up, and before the young one had time to speak, the other out with the grievance. They had just robbed this place together, and had quarrelled about their shares. The worst of it is, that the young man seems to be the son of the party that has been robbed."

"Yes, unhappy young man, it is the case."

"He contradicts the other's tale, though."

"What is his statement?"

"That he was following in pursuit, and that he had overtaken the other, who is the real thief, and whom he was endeavouring to secure."

"And you—you believe him?"

"We must look into the matter, sir, before we can say what we believe. They're certainly pals, these two, or have been."

The lawyer was silent.

The recollection of the scene in the garden flashed upon him.

How was it possible that Owen Redgrave could be innocent?

CHAPTER IV.

GUILTY, OR NOT GUILTY?

THE assizes were being held in Carlingford, and the morning of Owen Redgrave's trial had arrived.

Without the gloomy county gaol, and the quaintly-fashioned but monstrously inconvenient court-house, all was bustle and confusion, eager expectation and intense anxiety. A noisy, gabbling crowd filled the market-place, and ebbed and flowed ceaselessly in all the adjacent streets. Every hotel, tavern, public-house and beer-shop was doing a brisk trade, and bursting with liquor-consuming customers.

Barristers in wigs and gowns, with briefs, bustled, full of importance, in and out of court. Barristers in wigs and gowns, without briefs, bustled in and out of court with more importance still, as though they had the weight of all the State's affairs upon their shoulders.

In harsh, discordant voices the local newsmongers were bawling out all sorts of spurious confessions supposed to have been made by prisoners whose trial was about to take place, but which in reality emanated from the prolific brains of the hack writers attached to the printing-offices down in crooked lanes or noisome alleys in the poorest part of the town.

At ten o'clock the court was opened. With no small difficulty the local police forced a way through the unruly crowd to allow for the passage of the civic functionaries bound for the court-house.

The crowd rolled noisily to and fro as these worthies passed through, and struggled vainly to penetrate within the imposing portal which guarded the stern and frowning gaol.

There were several cases which had excited great local interest; but among them, that which enlisted the greatest share of public attention was the trial of Owen Redgrave. The vaguest rumours respecting him had been freely circulated.

The most preposterous wagers were laid respecting the probable issue. Redgrave had his backers; but public opinion, in a general way, went very much against him.

A great many were most anxious that he should be acquitted, but it cannot be said that anybody sympathized or cared any more for him than men do for the racehorse they bet upon.

The crowd now grew weary of waiting for the business of the day to commence, and took to a little savage practical joking to pass the time away, and then to cheering and hooting the judges and police.

The struggling mob fought desperately round the doors of the court; as is usual in such cases, women, who had perseveringly forced their way into the thick, were heard loudly complaining.

There was the usual amount of screaming and fainting, the usual amount of wrangling; here and there was a little quiet pocket-picking.

The court itself was, of course, densely crowded, and intensely hot. Every place where any one could or could not sit, was occupied, except the prisoners' dock and the judges' seat.

There were a great many ladies; for the case, as we have said, was very interesting, and much more entertaining than a theatre.

A wonderful collection of wigs and gowns occupied the space allotted to the legal profession. The reporters were there, cutting their pencils and getting their note-books in readiness. The strangers' gallery was full to overflowing.

The lobbies and corridors were all crammed; the ushers were hoarse with calling silence, and purple with indignation at the little attention which was paid to their commands.

Still more and more people kept arriving; the crowd grew more and more dense; the mob struggled, and fought and stormed for admission—admission into a hall already crowded to suffocation. Some fainted in the passages and on the staircases: others, after hours of struggling, at last forced their way into the hall.

At last there was a great bustle, and a cry of " Silence !"

The judges were coming into court.

The spectators all rose as they entered. Then some ordinary formalities were gone through, during which there was a long murmur of expectation; then followed a deep silence; then a movement in the crowd, behind the prisoners' dock; then the prisoners came slowly forward, and stood silently before their judges. Every eye was turned upon them; but the one who excited the most attention was the youngest of the two—Owen Redgrave.

Very pale, but with a firm step and flashing eye, and a hand which trembled not in the least as it grasped the woodwork of the dock, the young man stood forth. All around him was a sea of upturned faces.

A thousand eyes were fixed upon his, but he flinched not in the least. Boldly he faced them—coldly he looked round upon his audience, deliberately and without any sign of fear.

There was a faint murmur of sympathy for this handsome young prisoner, and of distrust and disapprobation for Jonas Drake, who, skulking by the other's side, glared evilly forth beneath his beetling brows.

When the murmur was hushed, the trial commenced, and then came an ominous and awful silence, broken only by the low voices of the officers of the court going through the usual routine of their duties, and by the faint rustle of papers as the barristers fluttered their briefs.

Then the prisoners were called upon, in the usual way, to plead.

" Not guilty !" replied Drake, with a frown and a glare of defiance at the court.

" Not guilty," he said; but it was not likely that any one should believe him; for when taken, as the reader will remember, with the plunder about his person, he had confessed his crime, and accused Redgrave of being an accomplice.

With Owen it was different. From the very first he had vehemently declared his innocence; now, when called upon to plead, he spoke but two words, which the greater part of his hearers, in spite of the accumulation of circumstantial evidence brought against him, fully believed to be true.

His voice, though he spoke but in a low tone, was yet distinct and firm.

A murmur of sympathy then passed round the court, as he said, with his eyes fixed upon the judges, " Not guilty !"

More bustle, and rustling of papers, and whispering ensued; and then the counsel for the prosecution began his opening address. He was a celebrated barrister, and he spoke well, and to the point.

Before he had said fifty words, the spectators began to swerve in their alliance, and to think that, after all, Redgrave's chance of escape was a very feeble one. As each sentence passed the speaker's lips, his auditors saw that the prisoner's case grew blacker and blacker; and when he had concluded, there appeared not to be the smallest loophole for him to creep through. The witnesses were now called.

The impression upon the minds of the auditors grew more and more unfavourable to Owen Redgrave. Those who at first had looked upon him with sympathy now began to look upon him as a fearful miscreant. Soon every chance of his innocence being proved was gone.

One man only in the court was undaunted by what he heard. Still Redgrave stood boldly forth—still his hand was firm—still his regard unflinching. He was not afraid, for he knew in his heart he was innocent. When first he was taken into custody, it was supposed that he would have been tried for burglary and murder, but the latter charge was withdrawn when it was found, upon medical examination, that the cause of his mother's death had been the bursting of a blood-vessel.

The charge of burglary still remained, and the prisoner had nothing but his bare word to urge against it. When called upon for his defence, he made a statement, which, however, no one believed.

He said that upon the night of the robbery he had been unable to sleep, and that he had sat reading in his bedroom until almost daylight. Then, disturbed by a noise in the lower part of the house, he had discovered Drake in the act of making his escape. He had been unable to seize him on the spot, but had followed, keeping him in sight, had at last overtaken him, and demanded the restitution of the stolen property. This being refused, a struggle had ensued, the police had come up, and upon the combatants being separated, Drake had confessed his own guilt, and in revenge declared Owen Redgrave to be an accomplice.

This statement of course led to explanations.

What connection was there between him and this man, Drake? How was it that he had been in communication with him upon the previous evening, when Drake was evidently spying about the house with felonious intent? How was it that so long a time elapsed after the robbery and flight of Drake, and the struggle of which the police were spectators?

Redgrave explained that he had been endeavouring to obtain the property from the robber without resorting to violence, and he also confessed to a compromise.

Was he, then, in this man's power?

He was.

With hesitating speech, downcast looks, and a flushed face, in which shame and confusion struggled painfully, Owen Redgrave told the story of his connexion with the other man. During the career of profligacy which he had led in London, he had in a rash moment, and with Drake's assistance, obtained a small sum of money upon a forged bill of exchange.

A very few days after it had passed through his hands, he obtained the money to take it up; but upon going to the bill discounter, with whom he had left it, he was informed that it had been paid away, and that when due it would be presented to the person whose forged acceptance it bore.

In the meantime Drake had obtained possession of it, and he held it then, and ever afterwards, as an instrument of terror over his companion's head. It was through this forged bill that the villain had intended to extort money from old Mrs. Redgrave, and it was upon

No. 2.—THE BUCCANEERS.

this subject that he had held a conversation with Drake n the garden, when interrupted by Mr. Hardstaff.

The fact of his being in this man's power of course accounted for all that was strange in his conduct with respect to the robbery and the pursuit of Drake; and having told his story, he now threw himself, with a passionate appeal, upon the mercy of his judges.

But Drake, when called upon for his defence, loudly denied the story of the bill; and suggested that, if it were true, and he had the bill in his possession as Redgrave had stated, it must most certainly have been found on his person when he was searched at the police-office, and no such document had been discovered.

The judge summed up unfavourably to the younger prisoner; as far as the other was concerned, there was no question about his guilt.

The judge said, if the jury liked to believe Redgrave's statement, it might influence them in their decision; but he owned that, on his part, he did not believe a word of it.

The twelve persons, who had been listening with more or less attention to the facts of the case, arriving at a fresh conclusion at the end of every speech, retired out of court, and, waiting to get home to their dinners, settled the matter among themselves to their own satisfaction by leaving it altogether to the foreman, who went back to say that they were unanimous in their verdict of "Guilty!"

A loud murmur ran through the court. A piercing shriek burst from the lips of a veiled woman in the gallery, who was carried out in a fainting state.

The younger prisoner grasped the woodwork before him convulsively for a moment.

Then, pale as death, turned and left the dock.

Drake gave a grim smile, and, shrugging his shoulders, slouched out after him. He exhibited no emotion, for he felt no surprise.

He had, from the first, anticipated no other result.

The trial was over.

Next day the prisoners were brought up again to receive sentence.

Transportation for fourteen years!

****

And thus ended Owen Redgrave's dream of happiness!

In a week from that time the prisoners under sentence of transportation, who were intended for penal settlements, were removed from the prison at Carlingford, and taken on to Woolwich, from whence they were to sail for Norfolk Island.

The day and hour of their departure, as is customary, had been kept secret by the authorities; but, as usual, some of the friends of the prisoners had obtained the necessary information, and were at the gates, ready to meet the sad *cortége* as it passed out from beneath the gloomy walls.

Among the few there assembled was the same veiled woman who had shrieked and fainted in the court-house.

Scarcely had Owen Redgrave passed out from beneath the shadow of the portal, when Grace sprang towards him, and threw herself weeping into his arms.

"Owen, dearest Owen," she cried, in a voice choked by sobs, "do not believe that all think you guilty. Bear up against this awful misfortune that has befallen us—bear up for a short time, for my sake! Your innocence must be—shall be proved!"

"Nay, Grace," Owen replied, with a sigh, "there is little hope of that. If I have any luck, I may receive a felon's privilege, and return before my sentence is worked out; but I shall return with a brand of crime and infamy which can never be effaced. Heaven knows whether I shall live till that time comes!"

"Oh! yes, yes, you will come back! We shall be happy yet. If all the world frown upon you, you know that I shall ever remain unchanged; that my love will endure, spite of the scorn and calumnies of those who know you not."

She lay there sobbing in his arms, her tearful cheek laid on his breast, her trusting eyes turned upwards towards his face.

Only for a few brief moments thus; and the wardens, who had hitherto—being only human men, with soft hearts of their own—refrained from interference, now felt it to be their duty to separate these two loving, grief-torn hearts.

The girl was carried away, the convict driven on.

The sun was shining gloriously in the heavens; the air was filled with the songs of birds and the joyous laughter of children; and yet all the world was dead to these two, whose dream of happiness, in spite of the feeble consolation which the brave girl had striven to impart to her affianced husband—dead—dead for evermore.

That night, alone, the heartsick girl lay sobbing in her chamber, praying to God to take away her life or to restore her lost love.

Down in the crowded hold of a convict ship, disguised in the hideous felon's dress, a young man, the ghost only of the light-hearted Owen, whom we saw building his foolish day-dreams that summer's evening in the garden of his mother's house, sat moodily dreaming; but dreaming now a dream of violence and crime—of mad attempts to be made at escape.

A dream which, in the end, would perhaps come true, when, goaded to desperation by the hardships and miseries of his daily life, and brutalized by the hideous companionship forced upon him, Owen Redgrave's nature changed, and he became like unto one of the rest —more devil than man.

CHAPTER V.

THE CONVICTS MAKE AN ATTEMPT AT ESCAPE.

RICH in natural beauty—with a climate almost unrivalled—its green hills and deep ravines abounding in graceful pines and shady fern-trees, wild jasmine climbing the stems—bright flowers of exquisite form and colour spread upon the dark green mossy turf;— this luxuriant land, formed by nature, it would seem, to be one of the loveliest of earthly paradises, is Norfolk Island, a receptacle for the ulcers of civilization—a convict settlement.

It was to this place that Jonas Drake and Owen Redgrave had been carried.

It was here that they dragged through two weary years. It was here that they fretted away their lives, longing for the hour of release—one sentiment overruling all others in their minds—a wild longing for restoration to liberty; eagerly lying in wait to seize upon the first opportunity which might offer of attempting to make their escape, let the consequences of that attempt, should it prove unsuccessful, be what they might.

Hitherto chance had thrown the two men apart.

They slept at no great distance from each other, but they worked in different gangs. They had never yet had occasion to speak since they had been together on the island. They had never yet been brought face to face.

Their eyes had never met. They, however, instinctively seemed to be aware of each other's approach when their gangs passed upon the road to or from work, and their glances were invariably turned in another direction.

They never spoke to one another, or of one another,

and yet they perfectly well knew that there existed between them an unpaid debt of hate and vengeance—an account which some day must be settled—by blood!

At last, towards the close of the second year, they were brought together, with what fatal consequences the sequel will show.

On the northern side of Norfolk Island the cliffs rise high and are crowned by woods. A slight indenture of the land affords a somewhat sheltered anchorage-ground, and an opening in the cliffs has supplied a way to the beach by a winding road at the foot of the dividing hills. A stream of water, collected from the many ravines, finds its way by a similar opening to a ledge of rock in the neighbourhood; and falling over in feathery spray, has given the name of Cascade to this part of the island.

Off the bay, one night in July, a Government vessel was lying at anchor, having on board stores for the use of the penal establishment; and a sentinel—placed at the foot of the cliff, and leaning against one of the huge fragments of rock, which having, some time or other, fallen from above, lie scattered here in quaint and curious shapes—was watching the moon-beams playing upon the rippling waters, and tinging with silver the spars and rigging of the ship.

While thus engaged, he was occupied, perchance, by a sweet reverie of his far distant home across the seas, when the measured plash of oars suddenly roused him.

"Who goes there?" he cried in a clear, sharp voice. As he spoke, there shot out from the deep shade of the cliff an eight-oared boat, rowed by convicts, whose faces and leaden-coloured forms, as for a moment they suspended their labours, and the boat glided noiselessly past, looked as though they had been chiselled out of stone.

An officer in command of the boat replied to the sentinel's challenge, and the convict crew pulled on in the direction of the brig. They were bound thither with ballast, and were to return presently with stores.

The sentinel looked after them dreamily, resuming his lounging attitude with a sigh.

"She starts to-morrow by daybreak," said he. "I wish I was on board of her. I wish I'd never set eyes upon this hateful spot. It's ever so much worse than purgatory; I wish I may be shot if it isn't. I think, of the two, I'd rather be a convict than a soldier, if I must be here at all."

He was a discontented spirit, this, and would probably have been discontented in any foreign station—or home station, for that matter—and he found time to hang very heavily upon his hands.

He found the time to hang very heavily indeed upon this particular evening when he was on duty.

He had just been left at his post, and his watch was to be a long one.

He, therefore, began to yawn in anticipation, and because he knew that under no circumstances whatever should he dream of closing his eyes; it was as much as he could do to keep them open at all.

The surface of the sea was agitated but by the tiniest ripples. Everything was calm and peaceful. The brig lay there at anchor, gently swaying to and fro, with a movement scarcely discernible.

The waters washed the shingle at the foot of the cliff with a low, hushing sound, having in it a kind of soft, lulling music, which had a most soporific influence upon the heavy-headed soldier listening to it, as he leant upon his musket.

Thus passed the time for an hour or more; and the sentinel was just upon the point of dozing off to sleep, when the distant sound of a gun aroused him.

With a sudden tingling of blood through all his veins, the soldier sprang into an upright posture.

Could he believe his ears, or had he been dreaming? He listened intently.

Again the sound was repeated, and this time he distinctly saw smoke curling from the vessel's side.

With terror and amazement, he stood gazing out to seawards. What could have happened? Was he to blame?

He listened, holding his breath; but all was still now, except that the brig was moving—was standing in steadily towards the shore.

Nearer and nearer she approached, until the sentinel, now convinced that something very wrong had happened, shouted loudly, and fired off his musket, to give the alarm to the little garrison upon the cliff above.

By the time that assistance had arrived, however, the ship had wore, and was standing off from the land; and while the soldiers, who had come running down by the winding pathway, stood in a throng, anxiously peering over the dark blue waters, there burst out on board a rapid succession of shots, with which was mingled human cries, the clash of swords, and the hurrying of feet.

It was evident that a deadly fray was going on.

But while the soldiers remained in anxious speculation as to the cause of all this, the brig was every moment increasing the distance between them and it.

Meanwhile, leaving them to form what conclusion they may, we will follow the convicts on board the brig, where a scene of horror and carnage was taking place.

They had rowed in silence to the ship's side, and had as silently clambered up upon the deck. Here they were standing in a group, in the charge of a sentinel, whilst their officer descended below, to consult with the officer in charge of the vessel respecting the business which had brought him thither.

Like so many statues, the men stood in almost exactly the same position as he had left them, apparently as sullen and stupid as might have been a herd of jaded oxen.

But had you watched them narrowly, you might have perceived from time to time that they exchanged stealthy glances, full of secret meaning. The sentinel, shouldering his gun, plodded to and fro, at a few yards distance. When he was furthest away from them, a faint, scarcely audible whisper—totally inaudible to the Marine—ran through the little group.

Only a few words at a time. Then silence again, and the same sullen, stupefied look resumed by the faces which, a moment ago, were full of sinister meaning.

"There are only thirteen men on board." This from an old, grey-headed man who stood close behind Jonas Drake.

"Five of the crew, five Marines,—four below, one here, two officers, one of ours."

The sentinel coming up now, the whisper suddenly ceased, and the men looked as dull and indifferent to all around them as they had done before.

When the sentinel had again reached the limit of his walk, the whispering began again.

"You're certain of what you say?" said Drake.

"I was on board only an hour ago. I've counted every one who has left in the boats for shore."

"Now is the time, then, while they're all below!"

"Are you all agreed? Shall we try it?"

A low murmur ran through the group. They were all prepared to risk their lives in the attempt. The frenzied thirst for liberty, never slaked, possessed them—maddened them!

"When?"

"Now!"

It was Drake who spoke last, and spoke aloud.

As he did so, the sentinel, who was close to him at the moment, turned round with a start.

He had not time, however, to utter a sound, for Drake, with a tiger's spring, had grasped him by the throat.

Two others of the convicts seized him from behind, whilst others again wrested from him his arms.

He was easily overcome, for so many had set upon him so suddenly that he had no time to struggle.

"No noise!" said Drake, in a hoarse whisper. "Over the side with him!"

They had forced a gag into his mouth, so that it was impossible for him to cry out. His arms were as rapidly tied down to his sides.

He had no means of defence; no hope for his life. A look of frenzied terror was upon his face—a wild appeal for mercy in his eyes. They bore him to the side, and threw him overboard.

There was a sullen splash, but no cry, and the dark waters closed over their victim.

A few moments afterwards, those looking out on to the sea saw his white face rise up into the pale moonlight, and again disappear.

He was seen no more.

"Quick—quick! fasten down the hatches!" cried Drake, fearful lest the noise, slight as it had been, might have reached the ears of those below.

He was right in the supposition, for as he approached the companion-ladder, the officer who had come with them in the boat came running up the steps.

Drake met him, and with a violent blow with the butt-end of a pistol which he had taken from the sentinel, struck him down senseless at his feet.

Raising his body, they carried him, as they had done the other man, to the side, and hurled him into the water.

Everything which the convicts could lay their hands on was now piled upon the hatches to render them secure; and while one among them was placed at the wheel, and four others left in guard over the hatches, the remainder set about the necessary preparations for getting the vessel off.

But the movement of the ship, and the scuffling of feet upon the deck, had by this time thoroughly aroused such of the crew and Marines who were below, and a general rush was made to ascertain what was the cause of the disturbance.

The convicts were almost entirely without arms. The musket taken from the sentinel was charged, but they had no other ammunition.

The pistols which they had taken from him were unloaded. How could they hope to contend against the crew and the Marines below?

A brief consultation was held. Drake was in favour of a wholesale massacre. Suddenly, Redgrave, who had been wandering alone over the deck, discovered three or four hatchets, which were rapidly distributed.

A sudden rush, it was proposed, should be made down below; but Drake was in favour of allowing the Marines and crew to come up only one at a time, and to fall upon them as they reached the deck.

The consultation, however, was suddenly broken up by the sharp report of a musket, followed by another and another. The Marines below had forced their way into the captain's cabin, and were firing upon them through the grating.

The first shot was fatal; two of the convicts fell dead. The head of one was blown to atoms; the other, horribly mutilated, lay upon his face, a pool of blood quickly staining the deck beneath his lacerated breast.

The other men rushed behind such shelter as they could find, and for a short time remained panic-stricken by the horrible fate of their comrades.

At this moment, had the Marines been able to force their way out, they might, by a sudden rush, have regained possession of the vessel. As it was, however,

they did not attempt to do so, being unacquainted with the small number of convicts with whom they had to contend; and they did not know that even these were without arms.

The convicts on their side easily perceived that their only chance lay in a hand-to-hand fight; for, except at close quarters, they could not hope to contend against the guns.

For a moment they whispered together; then, creeping upon their hands and knees, and grasping the knives and hatchets which they possessed, they stole towards the companion-ladder.

Noiselessly removing such things as they had piled up against the door by way of barricade, they collected themselves together, and made a sudden rush below.

A volley from the Marines' muskets met them as they came; and the shrieks of the wounded blended, next moment, with the savage howl of the combatants, as they met together in the deadly fray.

There was no light burning; all was pitchy darkness. It was scarcely possible to discern friend from foe; and a scene of bloodshed and horror ensued which it would be impossible to describe.

An hour passed, and the ship, standing out to sea, had left far behind her the rocky shore and wooded heights.

The convicts had triumphed; they were in possession of the vessel. Not a man of the thirteen whom they had found on board lived to tell the tale of that night's doings.

A death-like silence now reigned in the vessel, broken only at rare intervals by the low, murmured conversation of the convicts. Several hours had elapsed since the termination of the conflict. Some of the men had broken into the spirit stores, and half stupefied themselves with drink.

The man at the wheel was scarcely sober enough to know what he was about; the rest were almost helpless from the effects of their wounds, and from the quantity of liquor they had imprudently taken. The vessel was sailing fast away from the island they had left; but no one on board had any distinct idea of the direction in which they were going; and none, except Drake and Redgrave, and the man who had been placed at the wheel, knew anything of sailor's craft.

It was at this still time that Redgrave, who was lying upon the deck, trying to snatch a few moments' repose which the tortures of a flesh-wound in his arm almost forbade, was suddenly aroused by a hoarse shout from one of the men below.

The awful cry of "Fire!" resounded through the ship.

Owen started to his feet, and, rushing from the lower deck, perceived, for the first time, that a dense smoke was issuing from the fore hatchway over the hold—a dense volume of smoke, which almost choked him.

He added his cries to those which had already been raised, and in another moment all was terror and confusion.

Buckets were searched for, but none could be found. An attempt was made to rig and man a pump, but the convicts summoned to the work were too drunk to be of any use.

The suffocating smoke grew denser and denser. Cries of despair rent the air on every side.

Drake, Redgrave, and the other sailor did all in their power to save the vessel, but they soon found that it was impossible.

The other convicts, at length sobered by terror, proposed that a boat should be lowered, and that they should make for the shore; and, in their selfishness, would have revenged themselves by Drake murder, deeming him the cause of all their misfortune.

There was nothing left for them at last but to lower the boat, and desert the ship, which was too hot to hold them.

Scarcely had they effected their escape, when the flames burst forth from her hold. They first appeared out of the cabin windows, curling upwards towards the taffrail.

The moon had sunk; the night was pitchy dark, but the bright light from the burning vessel cast a ruddy glow around, and topped the far-surrounding waves with a bright tinge of crimson hue.

Now the whole poop was on fire, and the triumphant flames encircled the mizenmast. The vessel having veered round, lying head to windward, the progress of the flames was but yet slow forward. The mizenmast fell first; then, with a terrific crash, the mainmast followed.

Next the foremast. Then the entire hull was one roaring mass of red-tipped flame.

The doomed vessel seemed, as she floated away, like a beacon blazing fiercely in mid-ocean.

Those in the boat, straining their eyes to watch her to the last, saw the flames dwindle down; and then, at length, she was lost in the surrounding darkness, as her charred fragments sank beneath the dark blue waters of the ocean.

They had escaped. But they were out in the open sea without a compass—far from land.

Five only of the eight men who had made this rash attempt to regain their liberty were left alive.

Yet was the number doomed to dwindle less, until Owen Redgrave and the man betwixt whom and himself existed such deadly hate should be left to face the dangers awaiting them.

CHAPTER VI.

THE SUFFERINGS IN THE BOATS.

THE burning ship having sunk beneath the waves, left not the faintest glimmer of light to indicate the spot where the ocean had engulphed it.

The five men whose lives had been saved rested from their exertions and looked back wistfully into the pitchy darkness; then with something not unlike a sigh, returned to their oars.

Whilst the ship had been blazing, and the wild exciting scene still passing before their eyes, all thoughts of their ultimate destruction had been banished, but now it was necessary to think and to act.

They were five in all.

Owen Redgrave, Jonas Drake, an Irishman, Paul Maloney, a Spaniard, and a negro. These three last worked in the same gang with Redgrave, and during the term of his imprisonment upon the island, by his generous conduct and manly daring, he had won the hearts—as far as such wretches could be supposed to possess hearts—of his fellow-convicts; and now, in the hour of their danger, they seemed to be inclined to elect him leader.

Either he or Drake must take the lead, and the latter was comparatively unknown to them. None of the others knew anything of navigation, or the management of a boat. It was, therefore, necessary that some one should direct, and it became apparent at the very outset that the jealousy which existed between them would not be long before it found an outlet, and that a struggle would ensue in which the best man would be master.

Strange to say, neither at the commencement endeavoured to usurp the place of leader, but they darkly glowered at each other, neither volunteering a suggestion—keeping as far apart as the narrow limits of the boat would permit—exchanging neither word nor look

In the consultation that took place, it appeared that the boat's crew had embarked in such haste, that they were totally unprovided with those articles they were most likely to stand in need of upon a voyage which promised to be a long one.

They had fire-arms, but no ammunition!

They had no compass!

No water!

At the moment of starting, every one had told somebody else to provide such and such things. Several distinctly remembered impressing it upon the rest, that two small kegs of water should be put into the boat, but nobody had taken an active part himself; and the consequence was, that a small keg only had been taken away from the ship, the end of which had been partly staved in, and was found to contain barely one gallon of water.

One gallon of water among five men—and for how long?

Even now, more than one among them felt the pangs of thirst, and they had only just started upon the voyage.

So pitchy dark was the night, so trackless the ocean, that—ignorant as they were of their whereabouts, and totally without means of guiding themselves in any desired direction—there was nothing left for them but to wait until the dawn of day.

Although the water had been forgotten, there was an abundant supply of spirits in the boat, and very soon their effects began to show themselves. Drake, from the first, had been drinking furiously, and seemed half stupefied when he got into the boat; but alone, of all the party, Redgrave had touched nothing.

He sat apart and silent, whilst the others drank, and mumbled, and quarrelled together, respecting their future prospects.

The wild delight of their newly acquired freedom had not yet subsided, and, from time to time, they burst into wild screams of laughter, or yelled out snatches of bacchanalian ditties.

To while away the time, the negro produced a pack of greasy cards, and the Irishman, finding an end of candle and a match, they began to play, and very soon to quarrel.

From quarrelling to fighting was so easy and rapid a transition, that it was difficult to tell how the dispute arose, and who hit the first blow.

But there was a struggle. The Spaniard had drawn his knife. The Irishman fell bleeding at the bottom of the boat. The boat rocked furiously to and fro as the rest rushed upon, and strove to separate, the combatants.

Throughout the remainder of the night the devil's playthings were abjured, and drinking set steadily in, varied only at intervals by hoarsely shrieked choruses, and short but savage brawls, threatening again and again to terminate in murder.

If ever in his life Redgrave had hated and despised the brutalized miscreants with whom fate had linked him, he did so now, when he saw what they could be without restraint being imposed upon them; and what they would be presently, when fresh opportunities for a fresh display of their savagery occurred.

He lay at the end of the boat, well-nigh worn to death with fatigue, yet afraid to sleep, lest he might become a victim to their violence.

The darkness still continued. The long black night seemed spun out to almost endless length; and he strove in vain to occupy himself with his thoughts in such a manner that he might chase away some of the tedious wearisomeness of the slowly passing hours.

At length, with unspeakable joy, he saw the first faint gleam of daylight.

A dull leaden hue crept up from the distant horizon, and spread slowly over the dark waters. It cast a grim and ghastly light upon the sodden, smoke-besmeared visages of the convicts, who lay about in various uncouth shapes, sleeping heavily.

All around as far as the eye could stretch lay nought but one vast, monotonous sheet of water.

Not a sign of life—not a sign of land.

They were drifting slowly with the tide, heaven knew whither.

Perhaps they were drifting out into the open sea—perhaps they were slowly but surely returning to the island from which so lately they had at such risk effected their escape.

What course was open for them? What else could they do but journey slowly onward.

Perhaps from the first it had been a mad scheme. It is very certain that Owen Redgrave had not suggested it—indeed, had striven to persuade the rest to abandon their desperate project. But how could he hope to turn them from their wild venture? As well might he have tried to drive back the angry waves rushing up upon a rocky shore. Had not he himself been carried away by the all-powerful thirst for liberty which none but those who have suffered bondage can comprehend? Had he not joined with the rest in the deadly fray, considering not the sacrifice of human life and shedding of innocent blood?

The men woke up one by one, and stretched themselves, glaring evilly at one another from their bloodshot eyes, and beneath the over-hanging masses of their matted hair.

Presently the food for the day was allotted out to each man, accompanied by such small quantity of water as it was deemed desirable to distribute. The supply of each was, as may be supposed, extremely scanty. It was all of very inferior quality.

In the confusion, they had brought away only some junk of the very hardest and saltest; but they had no biscuits, no bread, nothing with which they could allay their hunger without promoting thirst.

As things looked at present, it was quite likely that they might be several days out at sea. If so, what was to become of them?

They would be perishing with hunger—they would be driven frantic by the tortures of a gnawing thirst which it would be impossible to allay.

It was not very easy, however, to induce such reckless, desperate men to act with caution, or to provide for the future. They, therefore, fell upon and ravenously devoured their share of food, and even proposed that they should eat up the rest; but Owen, drawing a cutlass, stood guard over the scanty stock of provisions, and kept the hungry men at bay.

They drifted on for the greater part of the day, sometimes taking a spell with the oars.

They drank up all that remained of the spirits. They played cards, and quarrelled and fought as before.

Then night came on, and they floated onwards in the pitchy darkness, knowing not how near the coming day might find them to their preservation.

The next day passed almost in the same fashion as that which had preceded it, except that they took a larger share of water, suffering more intensely from thirst.

They finished all the food.

Again night—again day. The night once more closing in without hope of release.

Still a trackless sea—still no sign of land.

Food and water alike exhausted.

The men, gaunt, hungry, savage and hollow-eyed, scowled at each other like wild beasts.

Then a faint murmur, which had been gathering for some time past, broke out into a savage yell.

It was a cry for blood!

It was a demand for one of the five lives to be sacrificed.

"What are we to do for food?" one had asked.

"We must eat one another!" some one had replied. And a horrible, wolfish glare in the men's eyes showed that proposition was one which met with the majority's consent.

Redgrave, however, was one who strove to oppose it.

"Let us wait until to-morrow?"

"No, no, no!"

"Let us wait to see what this day will bring forth?"

"No, no, no!"

"At least, let us wait until sundown?"

Again a murmur of dissent.

"Until this afternoon?"

"No, no, no!"

"Until noon?"

It was agreed that this should be the case. The time passed slowly. Redgrave looked eagerly out to sea, searching in vain for the land which appeared never likely to be reached.

At length, unable to delay the fatal moment any longer, he reluctantly yielded his assent to that of the others.

"How shall we decide?"

"Let us draw lots!"

It was soon arranged how it should be, and the lots were drawn. It was an awful moment, as each shudderingly took his turn.

There was something terrible in the half-suppressed cry of the miserable creature who had lost his chance of life.

It was the negro!

Something like an expression of disgust passed over the features of the other men, ravenous though they were; and Maloney was the first to propose that, although the lot having been cast, the black should be the first to die when the time came, they should delay the fatal moment as long as possible.

Until the next day, then, they waited, the poor wretch, as may be supposed, looking out eagerly for land, the sight alone of which could save him.

Next day, however, all hope of reaching any place where they might procure other food being gone, they bade the victim prepare for death.

I will not, however, disgust and horrify the reader by a description of a scene too revolting for a romancist's pen—a scene, however, which has been enacted heaven knows how many times, under like circumstances by starving men.

Those who had assisted at the dreadful repast now suffered other and worse tortures.

The agony of their thirst became utterly unbearable.

The Irishman madly began to gulp down sea-water, and, after suffering unspeakable tortures, went raving mad, and flung himself headlong into the sea.

Unwarned by his companion's fate, the Spaniard followed the same mad course of conduct, and met with the same terrible death.

At last, upon the fifth day, Redgrave and Drake—having suffered indescribable miseries, being reduced almost to skeletons, and so weak and helpless that they could scarcely sit upright—were the only two left alive!

These two bitter enemies were left to face together the new and terrible danger in store for them.

CHAPTER VII.

THE DEATH STRUGGLE.

UPON the fifth day there was a heavy fall of rain, and they placed everything they had with them capable of containing water to catch it.

Oh! how delightful did it taste as it passed through their parched mouths and moistened their cracked lips and burning throats!

The welcome liquid seemed to revive and strengthen them. They felt now as though they could hold out much longer—as though they could bear the pangs of hunger with greater ease. Their strength appeared slowly to return.

They felt themselves equal to renew the struggle with death.

Their strength, alas! was needed, though in a way which they little anticipated.

They had been lying silently at different ends of the boat, scarcely noting the progress of time, scarcely heeding aught that was passing around them, and the shades of night were quickly gathering around then, when Redgrave all of a sudden became conscious of a strange agitation of the waters around them.

He raised himself with a kind of languid curiosity, and looked over the boat-side at the troubled ocean.

What was it which agitated the water?

It was growing dark, but yet he fancied that he could plainly descry at a short distance from him some huge dusky form.

Was it a rock?

No. Another look at it, and he was satisfied of the dreadful fact!

It was a shark!

Yes—there was the hideous monster, so close to him that had he stretched out his hand he could almost have laid it upon its back!

He raised his voice to its loudest pitch, and at the same time waving his arms in the air, shouted with all his might.

The monster started back, alarmed by the cry, and instantly dived deep into the water, a thousand bubbles indicating the spot where it had gone down.

Redgrave, for the moment, congratulated himself upon having frightened away his enemy, but his self-congratulation was very short-lived, for casting his eyes upon the other side of the boat, he saw that his enemy had reappeared there.

And yet, no—that could not be; for at the spot where the shark had dived, there he was again. There were two.

There were others behind him.

They were surrounded by the same huge, dusky forms; savage monsters, waiting to devour them!

They were in a sea of glistening teeth.

What could be done? Redgrave sank down into his place, unable to think of any plan by which they could escape their awful impending fate.

Their danger was imminent. The boat, although large and strong, was not heavily weighted, and might easily have been capsized.

Then nothing could save them.

Night was now rapidly closing in.

Heaving and rolling with a long sickly motion, they floated onwards, helpless and almost hopeless.

A fitful breeze, which had blown all day, had now subsided, and scarcely a breath of air stirred the heavy torpid atmosphere which brooded over the dark waters.

But a storm was brewing. Both knew that this was the calm preceding the hurricane.

"Pray heaven it may!" thought Redgrave. "It is our only chance of getting rid of our ugly travelling companions."

There was no other chance, for they possessed no means of defending themselves. If it had been daylight, that faint hope of coming to land, or of being picked up by some vessel, might yet have cheered them.

But there was nothing to hope for now that night had set in. There was nothing but a horrible death awaiting them—death in the jaws of the sharks!

Every moment, the rocking of the boat grew more and more violent. The hungry monsters jostled each other in their eagerness to be near their future victims. Their horrible gambols flung so much water in upon the terrified men, that swamping seemed almost momentarily to be expected.

With all gleaming teeth—on every side gleaming teeth!

But the storm was coming. As Redgrave gazed anxiously out upon the dull, leaden sea, he saw the horizon grow bright and ruddy in one long, narrow streak, from which white streaks glanced out over the dark waters.

The wind was fast rising!

Above, all was black and starless; only as each sea curled and burst, the foam sparkled for a moment a gleaming white, and then subsiding again, left all black, dead level.

The gale blew with steadily increasing strength. Anon, the roaring, rushing wind came thick and heavy with the driving brine.

The little craft tossed, and leaped, and tore over the sea; every now and then shipping so much water that she threatened to go down at once.

Plunging heavily on and on—tilting with every wave, the boat pursued her course, drifting at the mercy of the elements.

But the sharks had not yet deserted them—still were following in their trail, with their greedy mouths agape.

So weak was he through want of rest and want of food, that Redgrave could not, even in this hour of awful peril and danger, refrain from wearily closing his eyes, in the hope of snatching a few moments' feverish sleep.

When he had closed his eyes, it was not long, however, before slumber overcame him, and he laid perfectly unconscious of the terrors around.

Such, however, was not the case with his companion. He had been sleeping a good deal during the day, and was now so thoroughly aroused by the besetting dangers of his situation, that slumber was the last thought likely to occur to him.

No; his mind at this moment, when it seemed doubtful whether he should live to see another day, was evilly brooding upon a diabolical vengeance!

It was the first time, almost, since their escape from the ship, that Jonas Drake had found an opportunity of getting the better of his enemy.

The others, who would have taken Redgrave's part, were removed by death.

He lay asleep and helpless.

Why not murder him now?

Around them still swarmed the savage monsters. If his body was flung over, it might cause them to relinquish the pursuit of the boat.

Never again, perhaps, might such an opportunity occur! Perhaps that night might be his last. How could he hope to fight such fearful odds as were presented by the tempest and the sharks pursuing him?

But he would die easier, he thought, if he had had his revenge.

The wind roared fearfully. The boat rocked to and fro at the mercy of the foaming waves. From time to time the heavens were rent by vivid flashes of lightning, followed by peals of deafening thunder, which struggled with the din of the heaving, surging, crashing ocean?

Drake rose from his seat, and cautiously crawled along the boat, clinging to the side from time to time, to keep his balance.

When he got close to his companion, he paused, and peered at him eagerly, for the darkness was so intense that he could not readily perceive in what attitude he lay.

But presently, a livid glare of lightning illuminating the vast expanse of sky, revealed the white face of his enemy half covered by his arm, thrown carelessly across it to guard it from the drenching showers of brine cast by the angry waves into the boat.

The position was one favourable for attack, and Drake prepared himself to rush upon him.

He drew from his breast his dagger-knife, and unsheathed the murderous blade.

Then he crouched as a tiger would, making ready for a spring.

But at that moment a deafening burst of thunder aroused his sleeping companion.

He opened his eyes, to find death staring him in the face.

But his danger lent him strength.

He sprang up and caught the treacherous arm, which, in another instant, would have carried the assassin's knife into his breast.

He clutched the assassin by the throat, and held him back, grinding his teeth with fury.

Then, in another moment, they were locked in each other's arms, in a deadly struggle—in a struggle which, should Drake gain the mastery, could end only in a brutal murder.

They were well matched, and for a long time it would have been difficult to have said which of the two was likely to have been the victor. They rolled and tumbled at the bottom of the boat, each striving his hardest to keep uppermost.

Drake, with the glistening knife naked in his hand, was yet unable to use it, as Redgrave grasped his wrist. But at the same time he contrived to maintain so firm a hold on its handle that his antagonist found it impossible to wrest it from his tightly-clutched fingers.

With grinding teeth, and bloodshot eyes, with panting breast, short-coming breath, and quivering frames, the two men struggled savagely, desperately for the victory.

It was an awful sight to see those two men, their faces dark with passion, striving for each other's life, while above and around them the elements appeared lashed into a fearful fury, which threatened instant annihilation to both.

But a blow of Drake's wrist against one of the seats of the boat happily dashed the knife out of his grasp; and while he was struggling to regain possession of it, Redgrave made good use of the brief opportunity afforded him, pinned the miscreant down, and planted his knee on his breast.

Then drawing forth his own dagger, which hitherto in the struggle he had been unable to make use of, he twisted one hand in his antagonist's neckcloth, whilst with his teeth he dragged open the largest blade.

The baffled miscreant, thinking his last moment come, looked the picture of abject terror, and, in a faint voice, begged for mercy.

But Redgrave, without loosening his hold upon Drake's throat, slightly shifted his knee, so as to take a better and deadlier aim, and brandished the knife high in the air, whilst the glare of the lightning revealed for a moment to the eyes of the quaking wretch his face awful with concentrated hate.

But once again, at the most critical moment, was the conflict doomed to be suspended.

A sudden shock vibrated through the boat.

A grinding, crunching noise—a trembling and rocking, succeeded by a momentary stillness.

Then a great splash of water, and a toss high in the air! Then a grinding crash again!

Then perfect stillness!

Redgrave cast up his eyes. Before them was a black, frowning mass, standing out against the fainter darkness of the sky.

They were aground! They had been dashed in among rocks!

Redgrave still, however, maintained his grasp upon his foe, uncertain whether or not he should have his just revenge upon his would-be assassin.

But soon a better feeling took the place of hate and vengeance in his heart. Perhaps here was land close at hand—here was safety—here was hope!

He had got a chance for his own life. Should he not afford one also to him whom, in another moment, he would have slain?

Yes; the world was surely wide enough for them to live in it apart. He had been spared himself by heaven's mercy, and he would spare the villain who had so wronged him.

But, at the same time, he must take measures to guard against such an attack for the future.

The first step was to deprive him of any offensive weapons; and Redgrave immediately picked up and put into his pocket the dagger-knife with which Drake, a short time since, had endeavoured to murder him.

Then he bade him rise.

"I will give you your life this time," he said; "but take care we do not have another struggle, for you may not again get off so easily."

The convict, rising slowly to his feet, skulked away to some short distance, and rolled himself up in a corner, scowling ferociously, but very wisely refraining from any taunt or threat.

Redgrave, without paying much more heed to his companion's movements, now occupied himself by taking a survey of their position.

The boat was fast jammed in between two rocks, and it had been thrown into such a place, that it was, to a great extent, sheltered from the violence of the waves, yet raging furiously around them.

As each succeeding billow surged and splashed in their close vicinity, they expected that they would be swept out of their hiding-place and dragged back to a watery grave.

But such was not to be. The night passed monotonously, full of a weary, heart-sickening terror—ever revived, never totally subsiding.

But at length, when day broke, the violence of the storm had abated. The first streaks of early dawn revealed to their anxious eyes the dark frowning masses of rock overhanging them, and, in the distance, they obtained a glimpse of a flat country stretching far away, and seen indistinctly through an opening in the rugged fortifications which nature had formed to guard it from the inroads of the sea.

But, as yet, it was impossible for them to hope to effect a landing. They must wait until the angry waves had toned down—until the receding tide lessened the distance betwixt them and the nearest spot on the shore they could hope to swim to.

As the day advanced, and the sun rose in the heavens, the waves slowly retreated, and they thought that the time had come when the attempt might be made.

Redgrave was the first to lead the way. He disencumbered himself of the rough jacket which he wore, made it into a small bundle, and fastened it with his braces on to his back; then he took one vigorous bound, and sprang into the foaming sea.

The waters closed over his head with a surging crash. That moment he rose to the surface. The shore was further off than he had supposed. He was weak and unfit for the struggle.

But the hope of escaping from the horrible boat in which he had suffered so much, urged him onwards, and he cleft the water with desperate strokes. Could he last out for a short time longer? Must he die with land so near to him?

No. 3.—THE BUCCANEERS.

His strength was rapidly failing.   He could struggle no longer.

Ah! thank heaven, something was here to help him for a moment.

He clutched at the slippery surface of a rock standing out from the water.

He clung to it frantically, and contrived to gain a position upon it which would rest him for a short time.

But he feared to remain long, lest cramp might overtake him, for he shivered violently, and an icy chill seemed creeping upwards towards his heart.

Again he sprang boldly back into the sea!

The water surged and boiled around.   The thunder of the chafing sea echoed loudly in his ears.

He struggled on and on!

He reached the shore at last.   He crept, more dead than alive, over the rugged rocks and sharp shingle.

Panting for breath, he flung himself upon the welcome herbage, and then his senses left him, and he lay in a death-like swoon.

CHAPTER VIII.

THE HORRORS OF THE ISLAND.

How long Redgrave thus remained in a state of unconsciousness he had no means of judging.

When he recovered his senses, however, the day seemed to be very far advanced.

He felt cold and cramped. His bones were all aching painfully, and it was with the greatest difficulty he contrived to struggle into an upright posture.

He was giddy, and faint, and sick, and his head spun round when he tried to stand, so that, losing his balance, he fell again heavily to the ground. After a time, though, he crawled to a rock at a few yards distance, and steadying himself by its aid, stood up and looked out to sea.

He looked for the boat which he had just left.

It was there as he had left it, but it was empty!

His eyes were weak and dim, and his vision bleared; but he could see well enough to be sure that he was right.

What, then, had become of Drake?

Had he swum ashore? or had his strength failed him by the way?

Was he drowned?

Redgrave looked about him, fancying that he might discover some trace of his missing enemy.

Helping himself onward by the aid of the rock which now supported him, he crawled round to a point where he could obtain a better view of the country.

It was clear, from the stunted appearance of the herbage, that at times this point, although high above the sea, was invaded by the angry waves.

He had proceeded only a few yards, when something lying on the ground before him caused him to start and stop.

Was it Drake? No!

The body of a man lay there, the face turned from him.

Redgrave stooped down to make a close inspection of the stranger.

He was dead.

The convict, with a shudder, crept away, and peered about in search of some more cheering sight.

The man had evidently been washed on shore from some wreck.   At a short distance from the spot where he lay, Redgrave found a portion of a splintered mast, to which some tangled cordage and a fragment of canvass still adhered.

But further on he came to a spectacle more horrible yet than that which before had met his eyes.

Two corpses, cold, and stiff, and black, and swollen, lay half-naked side by side, and as Redgrave approached, a bird of prey, engaged in tearing the flesh from the dead men's breasts, rose, and flew screeching from its hideous feast.

Owen stood gazing in horror upon the bodies before him, and then his weary eyes turned slowly round upon the bleak and dreary prospect which the flat table-land presented to his view, with a scanty crop of stunted herbage, studded over at intervals with scattered masses of rock, bare and black.

As he wandered on despairingly, resting every now and then, when his fast-waning strength compelled him to sit down for awhile before resuming his pilgrimage, he looked high and low in search of some place where he might hope to creep out of the reach of the elements.

The fragments of wrecks were strewn upon every side, and he soon conceived the notion of changing his drenched apparel, which had only partly dried upon his body while he lay in the sun, for certain articles which he presently came across. He found a sailor's trunk, which had been dashed in among the rocks, and the sides of which were staved in, although the contents had for the most part escaped from the water, unhurt.

Here he found a rough great-coat, and some warm trousers, and a dry shirt, for which he was truly thankful; and still more so for a small bag of soft biscuits, which he detected with greedy eyes, and ravenously clutched at.

But the first mouthful was more than enough for him.

He had gone without food for so long, he could not eat it.

He swallowed only a few crumbs, and was taken with such a violent fit of sickness that he was obliged to lie down, more dead than alive, and clutch his aching head with his hands.

When he had recovered sufficiently to move on again, he took his biscuits with him, and pursued his voyage of discovery, trusting that he should soon find a spring of fresh water.

Heaven was merciful to him in his sufferings, and at length he came upon a tiny rivulet, by the brink of which he lay down, and applied his dry, cracked lips to the cool and refreshing water.   Then he soaked a small piece of biscuit, and cautiously ate of it; and, feeling stronger, and bolder, and more hopeful for the future, pursued his ramble.

He came, in time, to a small cavern, the mouth of which he accidentally discovered hidden away by an overhanging rock, and into this he crept, peering somewhat fearfully around, lest some wild beast might be crouching in its dark corners lying in wait, and ready to spring out upon him,

He thought that he would endeavour, if possible, to rest here for the night, and he crawled back, first to the grass land, to gather as much of the sun-dried hay as would make him a bed.

Returning with a large armfull, he spread it in a corner upon the ground, and lay down to sleep.

The shades of evening had by this time stolen upon the rocky shore, hiding out the now tranquil surface of the sea beyond.

He lay there now upon his back, dreamily watching the twinkling stars, of which he could obtain a view through the opening of the cavern's mouth.

Although he was so weary, he could not go to sleep, for an undefined dread of approaching evil agitated him in spite of his efforts by reason.

Why should he fear an unarmed man? How could Drake hurt him?

It was scarcely probable either that he could be alive, for Redgrave recollected to have heard Drake own to being a very indifferent swimmer; and he him self, who was a good one, had had a very narrow escape and struggling with the waves to shore.

Surely there was nothing to dread; and yet the certainty respecting his enemy's fate was the real cause of Redgrave's fears.

If he had only known that Drake was alive, and at large, he would have been more satisfied; but now, in this lonely spot, at this still hour, he was half fearful les' his dead enemy's spirit should appear to him.

He worked himself up into such a nervous state, by brooding over those groundless and unreasonable fears, that it became, at length, impossible for him to rest where he was.

He rose, therefore, and went out into the open air.

The night was very still, and the moon shone down upon the black and rugged rocks stretched far away on either side.

He listened eagerly to the sound of the waves breaking upon the shingle beneath, and to the screech of the night-birds—the vultures, at the unholy feast among the unburied dead.

He turned and gazed long and earnestly towards the shore, fancying, sometimes, that he saw something like the reflection of a distant fire.

But no, it appeared to be an uninhabited island upon which he had taken shelter.

Unless it was his deadly enemy, no other living soul was there with him to share the dreary solitude.

At length, wearied and worn out, he crept back to the cave, and lay down upon his bed of dried grass, and very soon he was fast asleep.

But he awoke again in less than an hour, aroused by some slight movement near him.

He had the presence of mind not to start, or stir, or make any noise.

But lay perfectly still and motionless, listening.

The cave was pitch-dark, except at its mouth, through the opening in which the moon-beams penetrated.

He turned his eyes slowly round in search of the object whose movement had disturbed him; but he could see nothing.

He could hear a creeping sound, though, still. For a moment it paused, then again resumed.

It drew nearer to him.

Something cold and clammy crossed his face.

He held his breath, and his heart grew sick with terror.

There was no mistaking the character of the intruder.

The revolting truth forced itself upon his horrified mind.

It was some creeping reptile.

Some hideous monster had crept into the cavern through the opening at its mouth, and now was crawling over his body—perhaps debating in its mind at which end of him it should commence its meal.

Slowly its scaly body scraped over the road, crawling round and round. Then it crossed his legs, almost crushing them with its weight; but in spite of the pain it caused him, he contrived to remain perfectly still in one position, for he well knew that the slightest movement might cost him his life.

Round and round, and over and over, the horrible monster slowly dragged its huge carcase, creeping up nearer and nearer to his face.

At last, it reached his breast, and lay, coiled up, a huge, heavy mass that nearly stifled him, and a strong moonbeam at the moment penetrating to the spot, his blood curdled with horror in his veins when his eyes lighted on the curving neck, and small, vicious-looking head, of a python snake, which seemed to be preparing itself to dart upon and plunge its poisonous fangs into his flesh.

He had a wild idea at first of springing to his feet and rushing wildly out from the cave.

He half thought that he might be able to fling its weight from off his breast, and clear the door-way before the snake could reach him.

But then, if he should chance to slip his foot, his death would be certain. There would be no hope for him.

Even if no impediment lay in his way, though, how could he hope to escape from so lithe and agile a reptile, which could double and twist with lightning speed, and wind itself round its wretched victim ere he could double and escape?

No, there was no help for him. He must lie perfectly still, and allow the monster to crawl to and fro to its heart's content.

Several times its cold, slimy body glided across his face, and his flesh crept with loathing, but he dare make no movement to rid himself of the awful object of his disgust.

Who can say what misery he suffered during the time that the snake continued to hover round him?

His sufferings seemed to have endured for a lifetime when he had remained in this terrible position for some ten or twenty minutes. But that was not an end to his agony.

For many hours he lay thus, until the cramping of his limbs caused him intolerable pain. And still the serpent lay upon him, and still crawled to and fro, he daring not to move hand or foot for fear of exciting its wrath.

And thus did the weary night pass on—a night of such intense anguish as could never have been forgotten had he lived to double the age ordinarily allotted to mortal man.

The dreadful reptile, at last, hovering about his mouth, made him fear to breathe, and he half suffocated himself in his efforts to retain his breath.

But the terror of the situation was too much, at last, for human strength to endure; and fright, combined with the weakness caused by long fasting, threw him into a fainting fit, which lasted for several hours.

When he recovered his senses, the snake had left his body.

He started into an upright posture, and gazed around in silent terror.

For a few moments he could not recollect where he was, or call to mind the circumstances connected with his present place of refuge.

But when the remembrance of the awful reptile occurred to him, he felt sick with fear lest his sudden movement might have disturbed it, and at that instant, unseen by him in the pitchy darkness, was preparing for a spring.

But he could not any longer endure the suspense—he could not bear to wait for the horrible fate which he felt certain was in store for him.

Springing to his feet, he made one wild bound towards the mouth of the cavern, and, in another moment, stood in the open air.

All was awfully dark without. The moon had disappeared, hidden by clouds of the deepest black.

A darkness reigned around so intense that it appeared to entomb him, and to shut out from his sight all earthly objects, even the white surf glistening upon the summit of the waves.

But were there any waves? He listened in vain for the murmur of the sea washing the pebbly beach, but could hear nothing of it.

A death-like silence it was—a silence so dread, so terribly oppressive, choking, stifling, that it seemed to press upon him like a veil.

And while he stood gazing upwards at the black canopy over his head, the lightning streamed forth and lit up the heavens with a blinding glare.

Then, again, succeeded pitchy darkness, and the crashing, roaring reverberations of the thunder, which seemed to shake the very earth beneath his feet.

A horrible night this, in which the thick, palpable darkness alternated with livid flames, and the deafening thunder with a grave-like silence.

And then, amidst the other noises of the storm, and the fierce lashing of the waves, which now raged as madly as before they had glided so noiselessly, Owen heard the awful smashing and falling of the rocks around him.

Then the fear of being crushed to death by some huge mass of stone rolling down from the heights above, urged him to seek some other place of shelter.

But he could not see which way to go; the pitchy darkness hid from his sight the path by which he had approached the cavern.

He was obliged to wait for the vivid lightning's flashes to guide him in his perilous ascent; and even then he was so weak and giddy he could not keep his footing.

He reeled, and staggered, and fell, cutting and bruising himself cruelly.

He lay in the spot where he had fallen for a long while; the faintness which had already overtaken him several times, again taking prisoner his wandering senses.

He raved wildly, and was delirious at intervals, and again subsided into a state of lethargy resembling death.

Wild and terrible dreams haunted his brain.

He lived again through the horrors of Norfolk Island, with its ruffian companionship and heart-crushing toil.

Then his vagrant fancy carried him back to the dear home he had left far away in England. He thought he was returning once more, toil-stained and weary, to fling himself at his mother's feet.

He thought that she had forgiven him once more, and pressed him to her loving heart.

And then came back to his mind the scenes of the trial—the hot and stifling court—the sea of eyes—the sentence—the gloomy prison.

But the worst misery of all, his parting with that brave, true-hearted girl, who had sworn to join him again—to be his wife in spite of all the world.

But could her promise possibly come true now?

He could never show his face again in England after what had happened.

He must end his days now a wretched, skulking outcast. Naught was open to him but a career of crime.

Where was his love at this moment? Was she thinking of him?

Suddenly casting up his eyes, he fancied he saw a woman struggling in a man's grasp upon the edge of a huge crag over head.

The lightning revealed their forms and faces as plainly as though it were noon-day.

He recognised the ruffian to be his bitter enemy, Jonas Drake; the woman, Grace, his lost love.

She seemed to be clinging to the ruffian's arm with one hand, and with the other, striving to ward off a deadly blow, which Drake, with his brawny fist, was aiming at her pale and supplicating face.

But he heeded not her prayers and sobs, and, regardless of her struggles, dragged her to the extreme edge, and forced her over the precipice.

Then pointing downwards to where Owen lay, he shrieked out, "Die with him!" and struck her down.

Then Owen sprang to his feet with a wild shriek, which the thunder drowned in its deafening crash.

Was it reality that he had seen, or a horrible dream?

He could not be convinced that the whole scene was a freak of his imagination until he had wandered for some time wildly about the rocks, groping in the pitchy darkness for the mangled remains of his darling Grace.

But assured at last that there was no truth in this new terror, he began to scramble up the rocks, determined to leave a place so horrible to him.

CHAPTER IX.

THE SAVAGES.

BUT Owen again, to his no small alarm and consternation, found a drowsiness stealing over him; and in spite of all his endeavours to shake it off, he felt that it was increasing every minute.

His late exertions were beginning to tell upon him seriously; and he felt that he must inevitably succumb to the fatigue if he were not able to take some immediate and vigorous measures against it.

What was to be done? As a primary step, he must climb to the higher land, where, freshened by the sharper atmosphere, he hoped he could succeed in passing the night amongst the rocks without sleeping.

At the worst, however, he could only fall asleep there; and he felt that the high land would offer him a much greater security than where he was, even in sleep.

This thought no sooner crossed his mind, than he proceeded to put it into execution.

It was no easy task to mount up this steep acclivity without any assistance but the slight and painful hold which the sharp projections of rock offered.

The danger attending the ascent, too, was considerable, some portion being nearly perpendicular.

At these Owen Redgrave was obliged to grasp the fragments of rock more firmly, and they cut deeply into his flesh, lacerating his hands in a terrible manner.

But dread of passing the night where he was lent an impetus to his efforts; and in spite of the painful smarting of his hands, he persevered manfully.

At length his courage was rewarded by a capital break in the ascent in the form of a kind of flat shelf of rock projecting out from the solid about two feet.

He paused here to rest awhile, and drew a long breath.

And now he was only a few feet from the summit.

He observed this with exultation; and gathering up his energies for a final effort, in an instant had completed the long and dangerous ascent.

Proud of the feat he had achieved—of the appalling steep he had ascended, the difficulties he had conquered—he drew himself up to his full height, and looked down upon the cave with something of the expression of the victor to the vanquished.

The storm was over. The moon had come forth once more, and all objects before him were plainly visible in her soft, silvery light.

Then he turned, and surveyed the country around.

It was another land, another scene—infinite in its variety, and full of life; not the life of man—for, as our hero took in the objects around with a rapid glance, he could see nothing to indicate the presence of the human species in that beautiful and fertile spot.

Most curiously intermingled with the rich vegetation was a quantity of rough and rugged rocks, giving the scene an appearance of former life to which it had no claim.

These rocks were mostly overgrown with a kind of moss, tipped with a small blue flower, and not at all unlike the heather of the northern districts of our own island.

Owen Redgrave noticed this, and his thoughts turned instinctively towards home. He thought of his former friends—of the devoted and broken-hearted girl, Grace Atherton, who was to have been his wife, and a big, scalding tear rolled down his cheek.

The bitterness he ordinarily felt on this subject was in a great measure assuaged by the softening influence of the tranquil scenery around, and gradually gave place altogether to a feeling of sadness.

This was greatly enhanced by the extreme quietude of the glorious scene; and this feeling, in its turn, by an easy transition, gradually gave place to a gloomy despair.

A deep sob of anguish burst from his breast, and its dismal echo rolling along the rocky coast smote on his saddened heart, and brought his dread solitude before him in all its terrors.

Alone, unloved, no single friend to mourn his loss, what hope had he in life?

No single friend? Yes, there was one—his own dear Grace.

Then came the agonizing thought—*Was* she his own? Had she preserved her troth through all the trials and temptations by which she was doubtless surrounded?

Long ere this she was perhaps another's. Could he indeed expect her, however great her love for him, to remain faithful to his memory—he, a convicted felon, and transported?

This thought was unbearable, and he sought oblivion in violent exercise. He walked sharply on, surveying with mingled emotion the surrounding country—his thoughts, in spite of himself, lingering on the heartrending subject of home, and on the probable falsehood of Grace Atherton.

By degrees, however, the beauty of the country attracted his attention, and the more unpleasant thoughts gradually faded from his mind.

He walked on in a dreamy kind of mood, and mounted a gentle rise in the ground, scarcely noticing whither he was going, when he was somewhat surprised, on reaching the top of the hill, to see spread out beneath him a beautifully clear stream of running water.

A row of graceful willows upon the opposite bank threw their quivering shadows over the river with most pleasing effect.

Enticed by the extreme beauty of the scene, he seated himself upon the bank, and silently watched the large bronze flies—a species of the dragon-fly abounding in that part of the country—pursuing their fantastic gambols upon the face of the water.

The bright moonlight imparted a silvery tint to the water, which was reflected with striking effect upon the spangled coats of the dragon-flies, and rendered them visible for miles along the river bank with the clearness of the fatal will-o'-the-wisp.

After watching for a time the antics of the silver-winged insects, he perceived that there was one old fellow who led the van, that appeared to be in authority in the little tribe.

Round and round he flew, followed by the whole herd, and describing as true a circle as a horse in a hippodrome—to which circle they kept with wonderful exactness.

Suddenly, his kingship, seeming to tire of this monotonous rotation, struck out of the course and flew about close to the water—so close as almost to skim it with his lustrous wings.

Barely had it commenced its gyrations in the new track, when a large fish, springing half out of the water, enclosed it within its voracious jaws.

Owen Redgrave, being in a contemplative mood, could not help comparing this winged monarch's sudden fall with his own sad lot, and again and again he asked himself whether he was really fortunate in having preserved his life from his late peril with the snake.

And once more his thoughts turned to the more gloomy view of his present solitary, sad life. Once more his great despair having reached a climax, he gazed into the clear, blue stream before him, and meditated self-destruction.

There was an awful calmness about the scene—a monotony in the gentle ripple of the water, which seemed to invite him to end his earthly struggles by one desperate plunge and a fearful crime.

A crime! This was the awful consideration that stayed his fearful purpose, and, with a shudder, he gave up the idea, and boldly endeavoured to change the current of his thoughts.

He now began to experience a faintness from want of food—yet scarcely hunger. And this led him to consider what means he must adopt to satisfy his immediate wants.

The night was yet young, and he had no hope of snaring any game before daylight. And yet he felt that he must either eat or sleep.

The latter he dare not even think of. His late encounter had quite unsettled him for rest, and he experienced a nameless terror in the thought of slumbering unprotected in that wild and dangerous district.

But how to obtain food? In the midst of his musings, the annihilation of a second fly by a monstrous fish caught his attention, and he muttered half aloud, "If I only had you, my friend!"

Scarcely had the words escaped him, when it struck him that, with some trifling ingenuity, he might succeed in landing the finny marauder. He remembered that he had about his person some stout hooks, all ready prepared for fastening on to the line.

But here a serious difficulty presented itself. The line was an absolute necessity, and he had none.

He was about to give up in despair all thoughts of his angling experiment, when he caught sight of his dilapidated old boots, which were fastened, and, indeed, almost tied together with strings.

This he speedily converted into a line, on to which he fastened the stoutest of his hooks. Then he looked about him for a rod.

This was an easy part of the business, for the country was plentifully wooded. He picked out a thin and pliant sapling, and having stripped it of its leaves and branches, fastened on his line, and looked about him for bait.

This was the simplest task of all. His friends, the flies, naturally suggested themselves first, as it was their immolation which had given him the idea of seeking for food in their destroyers.

He quickly secured one, and fastening it on the hook with the expertness of a practised angler—that is, in such a way that it might drag on a life of torture for a considerable time—cast it into the stream.

The death-throes of the doomed fly were stopped as it touched the stream by our old friend, the fish, who opened his voracious jaws wider than ever, and greedily swallowed bait, hook, and some two or three inches of the thick string which Owen used as an apology for a line.

The landing of the spoil was a matter of some little difficulty; but this arising, as the angler knew, from its being a weighty fish, the difficulty was rather a pleasurable one than otherwise.

When, however, he succeeded in drawing it on shore, he was agreeably surprised to find that it was even larger than he had anticipated.

He administered the *coup-de-grace* to the struggling fish with his knife; and then, flushed with success, rebaited his hook, and again cast the line into the limpid stream.

The effect, as before, was instantaneous, and Owen drew in a fish so closely resembling his first spoil, that he mentally settled that they must have been twin brothers.

Again and again he threw his line, and again and again with the same success.

At length, having secured sufficient spoil to last him for a week, provided it did not turn bad, he began to think of cooking his meal, and proceeded to light a fire.

This was not such a very difficult matter, for a small water-tight tin box, which he had carried in his pocket, had preserved a few matches from the sea water that had saturated his clothes, and there were plenty of dry sticks and dead twigs and leaves lying under the shelter of a rock close at hand, which the rain had not reached.

Having, for the present, no further use for his fishing-rod, he fashioned two or three stakes out of the thin end of it, on which he contrived to fix the fish before the fire.

The wood crackled and blazed, and the fish, as it gradually cooked, emitted such a savoury odour, that Owen Redgrave fell to, and did justice to the rude repast.

He fancied that he had never before so enjoyed a meal. His sensations were almost bordering on the cheerful as he surveyed the bright blaze of his wood fire, and he piled on the fuel until the flames reached a height of eight or ten feet, and illumined the whole of the country for miles around.

The generous blaze made his face and hands glow, and its welcome warmth seemed to communicate itself to his heart. He felt that he was no longer *alone*. This was the whole secret of his satisfaction.

Once more, as he sat poring into the flames, his thoughts reverted to England; but now the bitterness he had before felt was gone—melted by the fire, as it were—and his musings bore a healthier tone.

He continued to pile on the wood, and the flames roared higher and higher; and now there was one bright jet of flame that towered up above the others, that must have been twenty feet high.

But now this immense blaze, which had given him so much pleasure before, as a thought crossed him, seemed to be rather a source of alarm to him.

What had become of Jonas Drake all this while? Where had he so mysteriously disappeared from the boat? Was he upon the island—if, indeed, it was an island? And, if so, would he not be attracted by Owen Redgrave's beacon fire, and make for that part of the coast?

This latter consideration was, at least, alarming; for Owen could never more feel any security with the treacherous ruffian.

He knew too well the reckoning of deadly hate there was between them; and was also assured that Jonas Drake would pause at nothing to secure his vengeance.

Had he not already attempted his life? And Owen shuddered as his thoughts turned upon their mortal struggle in the boat, which had nearly proved so fatal to himself.

Now, more than ever, he was determined to pass the night in vigil. But, even as he made the resolution, he yawned. His eyes felt heavy, and he longed for rest; and desperate now became his struggle with exhausted nature.

Nature, however, it was evident, must finally get the mastery. His supper, and the bright fire which had so nourished and cheered him, had, at the same time, the disagreeable effect of promoting sleep.

Once or twice he dozed, and as his head jerked forward on his breast, he awoke, and roused himself with a start; and, jumping up, walked briskly up and down, and amused himself by replenishing the fire.

His legs ached with his late exertions, and he was glad shortly to resume his seat. Now, however, the effort to keep his eyes open was painful to a degree.

They smarted, and the flames seemed to affect them so seriously, that he was glad to close them in self-defence.

From this, as may be readily foreseen, he gradually sank into a sound slumber; and there he sat, facing the fire, with his head bowed upon his chest.

Singular that he should have so wished to avoid sleeping. It would almost seem that he had some fearfully strong presentiment against it—some instinctive idea that there was danger lurking near.

We shall see if his presentiments had any foundation in truth.

He had not slept long, when a low noise caused him to start from his slumbers and listen intently, while his distended eyes endeavoured to pierce the gloom in every direction.

Rising on to one knee, he looked cautiously around, but could perceive nothing. The sky by this time had become somewhat overcast, and partially obscured the moon.

On the further bank of the river, this darkness, favoured by the shadow of the willows, was intense. In this direction he fancied the noise had come, and he strained his vision to the utmost.

After gazing for some minutes thus, the gloom became clearer to him: that is, his eyes became accustomed to it, and he was enabled to discern, although faintly, the objects upon the opposite bank.

The long dank grass which lined the bank quivered, of a sudden, as if some enormous snake were making passage through it; and Owen began to meditate shifting his camp. The difficulty was that he could not very well shift the fire, and this he was extremely loth to leave.

His eyes were still fixed upon the oppposite bank, but the grass was motionless, and so it remained for full five minutes, in which time he became somewhat reassured.

Perhaps it was merely his fancy; or if the grass really had moved, it might have been the wind. But no—not a breath of air was stirring—not a leaf shook with the faintest motion.

Again the grass shivered for an instant, which was followed by the faint sound of an invisible body falling into the water. It was a very slight splash, such as an expert diver would make.

Owen's quick ear caught the sound, and he peered into the water in the direction it had come.

A slight ripple, and the expanding circles which follow a splash in the water, were all the evidence of the deep, solemn calm of the stream having been disturbed.

He was suddenly startled from his fixed scrutiny of the water by a hoarse screech some little distance in his rear, which was immediately followed by the sharp whizzing of a missile in the air, and a long spear, or assagai, descended close at his side, burying itself in the ground, and quivering like a freshly-planted sapling.

To turn, pluck up the spear, and throw himself into a posture of defence, was the work of an instant.

But if he had been startled by the falling spear, what were his sensations at the sight now before him?

With a wild yell, rose up from the ground some dozen tall and frightful savages, bedaubed with grease and ochre.

With another yell, more hideous than the first, they rushed towards the white man.

Before the affrighted Owen could even calculate the chances of such a terrible encounter, he felt himself seized from behind by a cold, wet hand, and borne to the ground.

In an instant the whole of the savages were upon him, and he felt his time had come.

CHAPTER X.

IN THE TOILS.

OWEN REDGRAVE fully expected that his last moment had come, and summoning what fortitude he could to his aid, prepared to meet his fate.

But at the critical moment when he lay at the mercy of the furious savage, and the glittering blade of the scalping-knife flashed through the air above his head, a loud shout arose in the close vicinity, and he turned his eyes in the direction from which the sound came, with a faint, despairing hope of help being at hand.

But, alas! the sight which met his gaze was not calculated to reassure him.

Half a dozen dark, swarthy forms were visible emerging from the bushes, their eyes gleaming, their naked bodies horrible with their war-paint.

In a body they rushed to the spot, and surrounded the prostrate victim.

But when he expected that next moment he would have been hacked to pieces by their knives, he was astonished to find, instead, that they had fallen upon the savage who was, at the moment of their arrival, intent upon his death; and, surrounding him, so that escape was impossible, they felled him to the ground, and beat his life out with their clubs.

Then while yet he writhed in his death agony, one of the chiefs, kneeling upon his breast, possessed himself of the savage's scalp, and hung the reeking trophy to his belt.

Owen Redgrave lay still, expecting that his death would soon follow; and, sure enough, when the savages had completed the deed of blood upon which they were engaged, they turned with shrill screeches and encircled him.

But now, for the first time, did the foremost of the savages perceive that they had to deal with a white man, and, letting fall the arm which held upraised the terrible instrument of death, he retreated several steps, waving off his comrades with rapidly uttered words unintelligible to the wounded man.

Their effect, however, upon the rest was perfectly magical.

They clustered round, and gabbled eagerly among themselves.

They pointed to Owen's prostrate form, and then in the direction of the sea-coast.

There appeared to be some consultation going on between them respecting the course of conduct proper to be pursued, but poor Owen could not comfort himself with the notion that any act of mercy was intended, but rather that some fate far worse than would have been immediate death, awaited him.

No; what were evidently horrible menaces, accompanied by derisive and threatening gestures, were every now and then directed at him by one or other of the gang, and a furious dispute arose, in which it was very evident that some were for killing him at once, while others were for taking him away—probably to their village, where he would be mercilessly tortured.

Half a dozen hands were at length laid upon him, and he was torn and dragged in different directions, while every moment the naked blade of a knife was passed so close to his throat as almost to graze the skin, and hatchets brandished above his head, threatening to crush in his skull.

Then his arms were bound, and reeling in the gripe of his brutal assailants, with clothes torn and bloody, his face pale as death, yet calm and unshaken, Owen Redgrave was dragged through the bushes by his captors at so rapid a pace that in his weak state he was scarce capable of keeping on his feet.

When they had walked thus rather better than a mile, and the unfortunate prisoner was well-nigh fainting from fatigue, they came to a spot where, concealed among a clump of trees and bushes, was a roughly-constructed waggon, into which they threw him, still securely bound, and, after a brief delay of a few minutes to harness their horse, they resumed their journey.

They set off at a brisk pace after this short halt, being evidently pressed for time, and travelled on and on, hour after hour—Owen, who was dying with thirst, vainly hoping that there would soon occur some rest or stoppage where he might beg for something to drink.

The cords with which he was secured cut cruelly into his flesh, and the jolting of the rough cart caused him excruciating pain; but there appeared, as yet, to be but little hope of relief—as for hope of rescue, that he had none.

They were out now in a wild, open country, where there existed not the faintest trace of civilization.

Onward they journeyed across vast tracks of wild moorland, where naught but a few blades of rank, weedy grass could flourish.

Across a vast, barren country, sterile and blighted, trackless, too, as it seemed to the prisoner, though his captors evidently were not wandering vaguely, but guiding themselves by certain well-known landmarks, or by the trail which was left by those who had crossed the vast wilderness before them in the same direction.

Then reaching the desert's limits, they plunged into a great forest, where the huge trunks of the trees grew so closely together, and the entwined branches hung down so near to the ground, that it was no easy matter for the savages to find a path wide enough to allow the waggon to continue on its way.

But they still journeyed onwards without pausing for rest or refreshment, twisting and turning in a tortuous course not unlike the progress of a snake.

The unhappy prisoner the while suffering a martyrdom with the agonies of thirst and cramp.

But as the shades of night began to gather about them, and he had grown half delirious from the effects of his long drawn out sufferings, they at length came to a halt.

In the darkest and densest part of the forest, by the side of a small creek of fresh water.

Here a tent was pitched, and the waggon drawn close up to it, while the horse was picketed upon a small patch of open ground close to the spot, and several yards of rope attached to it, allowing it a certain amount of liberty and choice of pasture.

Two of the savages then came to the cart where the prisoner was yet lying securely bound, and half lifted, half dragged him out.

They made him lie down upon the ground at the door of the tent, and secured him with a care which showed that they set no small value upon his safe keeping; yet, at the same time, with such elaborate cruelty were these preparations made, and with such a total disregard for the pain inflicted, that it was easy for Owen Redgrave to guess at the awful fate in store for him when he reached the journey's end.

They cut out a stout stake from one of the trees, and laying it across the prisoner's breast, firmly bound his arms to it at the elbow and wrist.

Another stake was then laid crosswise, and to this, with notches cut in it to prevent the cords from slipping, his neck and ankles were fastened.

He could move neither hand or foot.

Having thus secured their prisoner for the present, they set about the preparations for a meal, and a fire was soon lighted, at which some food was cooked in a rough fashion—the savages scarcely warming the flesh of the animal they ate, but when one side of it was scorched by the red-hot ashes upon which they laid it, tearing it asunder, and scrambling and snarling over the ragged morsels, like a company of ravenous dogs.

Their meal concluded, they came to have a look at their unhappy prisoner; but though he endeavoured by signs to make them understand that he was half-dead with thirst, they either could not, or would not, understand his meaning.

They jeered at him, and showed their teeth, and jabbered for awhile, then left him again.

After a time, however, it appeared to be agreed among the savages that they should rest for the night.

Two therefore lay down, one on either side of Owen Redgrave, each having a cord attached to their waists, the other end of which was fastened to the captive's wrists.

Thus they could tell when the prisoner made the slightest movement.

All soon were at rest, and the foot-fall of a sentry, who paced to and fro upon the other side of the fire, was the only sound that broke the deep silence reigning in the gloomy depths of the forest.

The moon was sailing peacefully in the heavens above, but the thickly interlaced branches of the trees hid its light from the encampment.

Redgrave lay thus listening to the heavy breathing of the savages, he himself being unable to close his eyes, so great were the torments that he suffered.

With such a brutal disregard to his feelings had the cords been tied.

So intensely painful had his thirst become.

A hot, devouring, parching thirst, which almost drove him crazy.

He lay there, from time to time passing his hot, swollen tongue over his cracked, parched lips.

At times his senses deserted him for a few moments, and he dreamt mad dreams of cool, refreshing fountains, the sparkling waters of which splashed musically within his reach—of deep, peaceful lakes—of silvery brooks, and sparkling waterfalls.

Only, alas! to awake, after a few brief moments' unconsciousness, to the horrible reality, of all-devouring, maddening thirst.

Not the faintest hope of escape had he, either, to support him through this awful night's misery.

He well knew that the torments which he now suffered would be far surpassed by those which the fiendish ingenuity of the savages would prepare for him when at length they reached the journey's end.

He had often enough heard tell of the enormities practised upon the prisoners of war captured by savage tribes.

In spite of the pain that he now endured, the thought of what was to come made him shudder, and his blood to curdle in his veins.

Soon, as he lay there, a fresh source of misery arose.

Some of the horrible flies that infested the country where he had had the ill luck to make a landing-place—for surely death at the teeth of a shark would have been far preferable to the fate now in store for him—attracted by the fire and the smell of the food, came to the spot, and began to buzz about the sleepers.

Small and almost imperceptible gnats, the igoogouia, came first, in large numbers, determined blood-suckers, very sly in their approaches, but leaving behind them a bite which itched terribly for a long while afterwards.

Then, another, the ibolai, an insect twice as large as our common house-fly, with a sharp whistle, and a sting long and strong enough to pierce the thickest clothes, and as sharp as the thrust of a needle.

Then, the nchouna, making no noise to warn its victim of its approach, but inserting its bill so gently that it got its fill before the bite was perceived, though the awful itching which followed, varied at intervals by sudden, sharp stabs of pain, seemed like a scorpion's bite.

Then the iboco, the size of a hornet, which punctured even the coarse, hard hide of the sleeping savages, so that the blood trickled down from the wounds as though a leech had been feasting on their bodies.

Some of these dreadful creatures, stinging one of Redgrave's guards, he rolled over, with a muttered exclamation of rage, tightening the strain upon Owen's wrist to such an extent that he groaned aloud with agony.

Another sting, and another roll, tightening the ligatures already cutting into Redgrave's flesh

The miserable prisoner asked himself despairingly what he was to do?

Whether there was any chance of escape?

If he could but break his bonds and seek his way through the gloomy forest and the dreary desert beyond?

He would, in all probability, perish by the way, but there would be a chance of escape—oh, how faint a chance!—yet would he willingly have embraced the opportunity had it offered.

At times he vainly struggled, thinking that he might be able to burst his bonds.

But they defied all his efforts.

Again and again did he make the attempt, not satisfied by the failure of once or twice.

Alas! each struggle but caused him fresh pangs, as the cords cut deeper into his wrists.

His thirst, meanwhile, increased.

He thought, at last, that he must go raving mad, and shriek aloud, so awful was his torment.

The pale moon's rays struggled with the massive foliage. It would have been a great boon to the unhappy prisoner could he but have seen the face of the placid luminary; but to lie in a pitchy darkness was intolerable.

The livelong night passed wearily away in this fashion.

The prisoner's fevered pulse beat time to the fleeting moments, every one of which, however, appeared to him to be stretched out to an unnatural, unsupportable, unendurable length.

At last the first faint gleam of day crept slowly up the sky, although the heart of the forest yet remained in impenetrable gloom.

The last dying embers of the fire were mouldering away.

Now and then there was a scarcely perceptible crackling and rustling among the leaves of the trees, or among the underwood round their stems, occasioned, perhaps, by the stealthy progress of a snake winding its slippery course through the long grass.

The savages were fast asleep, and the sentinel, even, worn out by his long march, was nodding.

"Oh, if I only had my hands free now!" thought Owen, with a bitter sigh.

But he was as securely bound as ever, and the cords cut deeply as he madly struggled for his freedom.

No. 4.—THE BUCCANEERS.

CHAPTER XI.

THE INDIAN MAIDEN.

At this period of repose—repose for all but the unhappy prisoner, from whom the pangs of thirst and the cruel chafing of his bonds excluded all hopes of rest—a slight crackling of the branches afar off indicated the approach of some one, friend or foe.

Owen, whose sense of hearing was painfully acute, was one of the first to catch the sound, and wild as the idea was, he could not help fancying that there was some faint hope of release arriving.

But when the noise had continued for a short time, it suddenly ceased, and with it Owen's brief exultation.

All was then, for a long time, perfectly quiet; but suddenly, not many yards off, as it appeared, a sharp cry was heard, such as might have come from the throat of one of the numerous wild birds peopling the woods.

The sentinel, who was evidently dozing at the time, suddenly started upright at the sound, and listened eagerly.

Again was the cry repeated.

Then, placing his hand to the side of his mouth, he answered the signal, for such it was, in the same peculiar fashion.

As he did so, the sleepers, one and all, began to toss and roll, and open their eyes.

When the cry again rent the air, they were all wide awake, and sitting up in various attitudes all indicative of surprise and alarm. All, then, scrambled to their feet, and in another moment all had vanished into the wood.

Owen, lying firmly secured, rolled his eyes around, wondering what new torture was in store for him, and waiting, with what patience he could, for the arrival of his new enemies.

He had not to wait long.

In a few moments the savages returned, bringing with them some eight or ten others, all attirred as though for the war trail, and hideous in the glaring paint with which their faces and bodies were adorned in streaks and patches.

There was nothing in the appearance of these new arrivals to give him any hope. They all seemed as savage and bloodthirsty as those who had taken him prisoner, and they evidently belonged to the same tribe.

But there was among them one person upon whom he could not refrain from gazing with intense interest.

An Indian woman.

She did not in any respect resemble the squaws of Indians he had heard described.

There was nothing poor, or mean, or debased in her appearance. There was no trace visible in her face or form of moral or physical degradation, such as is so common among the wives of savages, whose lot, poor creatures, is very little better than that of a packhorse, or beast of burden.

She, however, was tall and faultlessly graceful in her bearing and movements, whilst the Indian dress was at the same time costly and elegant in the extreme.

Her almond-shaped eyes wore, at times, a half-wild expression, something like those of a timid fawn; but oftener they were full of a bold, defiant scorn, and there was something almost fierce in her demeanour, which, in one less beautiful, might have excited dislike, yet, in her case, but challenged love.

She was very beautiful.

Her skin a fair olive tint, her lips as red as a cherry, and her teeth, when for a moment they glittered in a sunny smile, were as dazzlingly white as pearls

The fantastic beauty of the strange, wild garb she wore would baffle description; but it was richly ornamented, and upon her delicately-shaped fingers, her slender wrists, and polished throat glittered ornaments of so chaste a design, and such evident value, that it was puzzling to think how she could have become possessed of them; although, upon reflection, this riddle was far less difficult of solution than of how she came to wear them with such evident care and grace, to be alone acquired, one would have thought, in the haunts of civilization.

She walked among the warriors with a stately step, and they evidently paid her great respect, and only addressed her with a kind of cautious deference, very unlike that with which savages treat the women of their tribe.

And yet it would have appeared that she was not altogether free to do what she thought fit, or to go where she willed, and every movement she made was watched with jealous care by her numerous attendants.

"Was she a captive among them?" Owen asked himself. Such would appear to be the case, for two of the savages never went very far from her side; and although affecting a certain indifference to her conduct, were, it was easy enough to see, by the restless rolling of their eyes, keenly alive to every look and motion of the girl's beautiful and expressive face, the deep blue eyes of which, at times, wandered restlessly to and fro, taking in all the surrounding objects with a comprehensive glance, that lost not a single detail, however trifling and apparently insignificant.

It was much more upon this dark beauty's account, than because he felt any anxiety respecting his own fate, that Owen Redgrave now most ardently longed to know what was the subject of the muttered conversation passing around him.

He was perfectly ignorant of the language in which it was spoken; for although long ago, among his wild wanderings during his sailor life, he had upon several occasions been brought in contact with the natives of the barbarous countries he had visited, the tribe into whose hands he had now had the ill-luck to fall spoke a different tongue to any he remembered having heard before.

It was most conjecture, therefore respecting what was said, and what was the subject discussed; but he could not help fancying that the beautiful Indian girl was more than once mentioned, as from time to time the talking savages cast eager glances full of curiosity, not unmixed with respectful admiration, towards her.

The dark beauty made no remark, however, and standing in an attitude so full of grace that a sculptor would eagerly have sought to transfer it to his marble, she gazed pensively into the expiring embers of the fire, which cast a ruddy glow upon her symmetrical form, and sparkled brightly upon the glittering jewels that she wore twined among the tresses of her soft, raven hair.

But presently the general interest was diverted into another channel, and Owen Redgrave himself became the subject of conversation.

The newly-arrived savages came in a body, and stood near the spot where he lay; and while one addressed him in what were evidently terms of reproach, another appeared to jibe and taunt him, while a third contemptuously spurned the prostrate man with his foot.

But while they were thus treating him, and when the excitement of some of the savages appeared to have reached such a pitch that it wa, more than probable his life would be sacrificed, the Indian girl, who hitherto stood at some distance, and apparently an uninterested spectator of the scene, stepped suddenly forward, and with an angry wave of her hand motioned to a number of the savages to stand on one side, and, allow her to have a better view of the prisoner.

She stood there as she stood looking into the fire, silently and sternly regarding his pale face, upon which the intense suffering through which he had passed had left very evident traces in his sunken eyes and pinched cheeks.

He was still, however, strikingly handsome; and there was a something of breeding in his air that his rags and misery could not very easily disguise.

The Indian girl watched him with deep interest for some time without saying a word.

Then she spoke—and greatly to Owen Redgrave's surprise—in perfectly good English, which had but the faintest foreign accent—a fact which lent to it a certain piquancy, instead of being any defect.

"Who are you?" she asked, in a haughty tone. "You wear the dress of a thief!"

"I am no thief!" replied Owen, with a slight flush of anger colouring his wan face; for there was something so insulting in the way that the Indian maiden spoke, that he felt both shame and anger struggling fiercely in his breast, and contending for the mastery.

"How is it you are so attired?"

"I have made my escape from Norfolk Island!"

"Norfolk Island? So far!—and how?"

Owen, in a few words, described what the reader already knows.

The girl listened attentively, and a slight smile of scorn played upon her lips.

"A wonderful story!" she said.

"But it is true!"

"I do not wish to question it. Pray, how came you into the hands of your captors?"

Again Redgrave gave an explanation.

"It would have been better had you been killed by the savage you were contending with, than have fallen into the hands of these!"

"I think so, too!"

"Do you know what they mean to do with you?"

"I have no means of knowing; but from their treatment of me hitherto, I can imagine that no enviable fate is in store for me!"

"You are right! It would have been better that you had never been born, than that you should suffer the torments their cruel ingenuity will inflict upon you!"

"I can readily believe what you say!"

"And you expect no mercy?"

"Mercy from them? It is a virtue they do not understand!"

"You speak truly!"

There was a silence of some moments, during which the savages—who stood round, an attentive audience, though they understood not one word that was uttered—murmured among themselves, and appealed to the girl to know what it was all about.

She afforded them no information, however.

But she waved them off with the same scornful gesture as before.

Presently she resumed her questions.

"If I put the means of escape in your hands, will you accept them?"

"Need you ask?"

"Yes—it is necessary."

"I do not understand!"

"I mean that if I enable you to kill yourself——"

"Kill myself?"

"And by an easy death escape the tortures in store for you——"

"Well?"

"Would you avail yourself of the chance?"

"Not I!"

"You would enjoy a few more hours' life, and the misery which you are suffering, and not think it dear at the price you are paying for it?"

Owen was silent for a moment or two, then said, "I do not think I have any right to take my own life; for it is not mine, but God's! I think it would be a coward's action to shirk the misery in store for me, if

such exist, by any such paltry artifice! No! I will wait the issue!"

"You are prepared to meet your fate?"

"I will endeavour to do so like a man!"

The girl laughed a low, mocking laugh.

"Ah," she said, "you can talk boldly now; but wait until the fire is lit, and the pincers heated, then you will tell a different tale!"

Owen could not help shuddering, brave as he was, at this dreadful glimpse of what was in store for him. But he did not show the white feather.

"I am as weak as a child, maiden," he said, somewhat reproachfully, "and sorely reduced by what I have suffered the last few days! I may scream out, or faint, if the agony is more than I can bear; but rest assured that I shall not ask for mercy!"

She looked at him silently; and had the darkness not thrown a deep shadow upon her face, it might have been possible for the captive to have seen something not unlike a look of deep admiration flit for a brief moment across those lovely features.

"You will not accept my offer, then?" she said.

The prisoner shook his head mournfully.

"No—I will wait and put my trust in heaven."

"You think that you may escape with your life; but I pray you do not cherish such a mad hope."

"While there is life, hope never dies," Owen answered, with a faint smile. "But I allow my chance of escape, except in death, is a very poor one."

"Yes," said the girl, with emphasis; "it is."

And she turned upon her heel. But before she had gone half a dozen yards, she returned, and said, in a tone which was softened, gentle, and curiously unlike that in which hitherto she had conducted the conversation, "Can I do anything for you? Are you hungry or thirsty?"

"Bless you, maiden!" said the captive, the tears unbidden rising to his eyes; "I am well-nigh dying of thirst. My throat is parched, and my tongue swollen."

She walked away, and fetched a pitcher of water standing at some short distance from the spot.

Then stooping down, very gently raised his head, whilst she allowed a few drops of the cool liquid to run between his hot lips.

Oh, how delicious was the draught!—never was nectar more delightful.

He greedily opened his mouth for more, and would have swallowed the whole contents of the pitcher, if his benefactress would have permitted him to do so.

But she only gave him a small quantity, knowing that it would be imprudent for him to drink more. Then she bathed his hot face and his feverish hands, and left him.

The savages appeared to be somewhat irate at this kind treatment of their victim, and remonstrated with the Indian girl; but she did not heed their remarks; and, indeed, retorted in a way which was probably bitterly sarcastic, if Owen could judge by the sheepish fashion in which they withdrew their opposition.

Not very long after the good office which the Indian girl had performed, Owen Redgrave fell into a gentle sleep, the duration of which he had no means of judging except that it must have been somewhat lengthy; for, when he opened his eyes, day was breaking through the trees.

He awoke to find a figure stooping over him, and saw to his astonishment that it was the Indian girl.

In his first surprise, he naturally made an effort to rise, and great was his wonder at finding that his hands were free.

He was about to spring to his feet, when she, however, stopped him.

"Hush, for your life!" she whispered. "Do you think that you will be strong enough to walk?"

"Yes, yes; I am certain."

"Rise, then, but carefully."

In spite of her caution, however, he half rose to his feet, and fell again to the ground, for his limbs had been so cruelly cramped by his bonds, that there was scarcely any use remaining in them.

The sound of the movement alarmed the sentry, and he called out to know what was the matter.

The Indian girl lay flat upon the ground, and remained perfectly still, Owen following her example; and after a few moments, the sentry, apparently assured that all was safe, dozed off again.

Then the Indian girl whispered, "Come."

Owen rose upon his hands and knees, and the two crawled together to the bushes.

Once in their shadow, they rose to their feet, and stole stealthily onwards.

"Be careful," the girl whispered; "there is a scout out in the wood. We are lost if we fall across him."

CHAPTER XII.

THE ATTEMPTED ESCAPE.

THEY stopped suddenly just as they were about to issue from the shadow of the overhanging foliage.

A slight noise upon one side of them caused them to pause and hesitate.

They strained their eyes to pierce the surrounding gloom.

Then drew back with a shudder as their eyes fell upon a savage face leering at them from round the trunk of a sturdy tree.

Owen, grinding his teeth in desperate rage, grasped the handle of the pistol he had obtained from the Indian girl, whilst at the same time he kept his eyes fixed unflinchingly upon those of the wily savage creeping towards him.

It was only for a moment that they thus stood facing one another.

Then the savage, crouching like a tiger, gathered himself up, ready for a spring.

Redgrave was ready for him, and as he came, presented the pistol at his breast.

But it missed fire!

There was no time to load again. The savage was upon him with a cry that sounded more like the howl of a wild beast, than aught coming from human throat.

Next moment, locked in a deadly embrace, the two rolled upon the ground.

The struggle was desperate.

Redgrave was of slighter proportion, though exceeding the savage in stature by several inches. But this superiority availed him little.

It was, if possible, rather a disadvantage in the conflict that ensued.

The gripe fastened upon the savage's throat was like that of a vice. But Owen might as well have grappled the throat of a bull as that of his stalwart and muscular antagonist.

Defending himself by kicking furiously and struggling vehemently, the savage contrived at length to extricate himself from the other's throttling grasp.

Then he suddenly closed with his foe, and they were locked together in a death-like grip.

Straining, tugging, and practising every sleight and stratagem coming within the scope of feet, knees, and thighs.

Now tugging—now jerking!

Now advancing—now retreating!

The conflict raged furiously!

But with doubtful result!

Owen rolled and plunged in the grasp of his enemy, till at length, by some accident, his leg got doubled under him.

The intense pain that he suffered caused him to relinquish his hold upon his antagonist.

The other was not slow to take advantage of this.

In another instant, Owen was dashed to the earth.

The savage sprang upon his breast with crushing violence.

Sprang, and twisted at his neckerchief!

The hot blood gushed upwards to Owen's brain.

He gasped for breath.

His eyes lolled horribly from their sockets, and his tongue protruded.

In his ears there was a hoarse, murmuring sound, such as one hears inside a seashell—a sound like the rushing in of the tide.

But just as he was about to lose all sense and strength, and while the savage, with set teeth and gleaming eyes, was searching for his murderous knife, the Indian maiden came to the rescue.

She had not, at the commencement of the struggle, shrieked and fainted, as a young lady heroine would be supposed to do. On the contrary, she had been eagerly watching the progress of the fight, trusting in the strength of the young Englishman, and watching for some opportunity to occur where she might render him some service.

The time had now arrived.

Just as Owen was sinking, overpowered by his antagonist's superior strength, her eyes fell upon the pistol, which lay on the grass useless.

She stooped and picked it up.

It had missed fire; but the cap seemed to be unimpaired.

It was worth another trial; and, quick as thought, she sprang forward, placed the muzzle against the savage's head, and drew the trigger.

With a hollow groan he fell forward upon his late antagonist.

Hastily disengaging himself from the savage's embrace, Owen rose to his feet.

"Thanks!—thanks, my generous preserver!" he cried. "How many lives do I not owe you? How can I ever hope to repay you?"

The girl looked earnestly into his face, but for a moment made no reply.

Far behind them at that instant, though, a low murmur as of human voices warned them that they had no time to spare.

Their pursuers were on their track.

They must fly from the spot.

At this critical juncture, though, when the time had arrived for them to exert themselves to the utmost, if they must get away at all, the brave girl's strength began to flag, and placing her hand upon her head, she seemed as though she would have fallen to the earth, had not Owen eagerly stretched out both his arms to save her.

"Speak—speak! what ails you?" he asked, anxiously.

But for a moment she made no answer. Then, turning to him with a faint smile, said, "It is nothing—a slight wound!"

"A wound?"

"Yes, yes!—but do not heed me!"

"But you seem to be in great pain!"

"I have hurt my foot—cut it in coming through the brushwood. But never mind me! Do not delay longer—escape while there is yet time!"

"What, and desert you?"

"Yes! I shall only be a clog on you! You will be

able to make good your escape, if you go without me!"

" And you really suppose that I should be such a cur?"

She made no answer. The weakness which before had overcome her, seemed to return again, and render her entirely helpless.

Owen, still holding her in his arms, looked eagerly in search of the wound of which she had spoken.

He was not long before he discovered the place in her foot where a sharp thorn had cruelly lacerated the tender flesh.

It was from loss of blood that this faintness had resulted.

Owen, next moment, was upon his knees by her side; and whilst she supported herself partly upon his shoulder, and partly by the aid of the tree, under the shadow of which they stood, her companion tore off his neckerchief, and contrived, with great dexterity and rapidity, though with as much gentle tenderness as any loving mother could have shown to an ailing child, to bind up the wound.

Even now, though, flight seemed to be an impossibility, for she could not walk six yards without excruciating pain.

There was only one way.

He must carry her.

With the wild desperation of a drowning man clutching at a straw, he made his mind up to the alternative, although he feared that if it came to a trial of speed between him and his enemies, it would not be very long before he should be obliged to succumb.

He caught the almost insensible girl in his arms, and, thrusting upon one side the twigs and brambles which barred the passage, forced his way out from the thicket.

But hardly had he left the shadow of the trees, than he again heard the sound of his pursuers close at hand.

It would never do to go forward, or he would be discovered before he had proceeded twenty yards.

No; as his pursuers were coming out of the wood, he surely would be safest if he remained within.

He turned again, then, quick as thought.

But a very unexpected obstacle appeared in his path. It was the wounded savage.

He had struggled up upon his hands and knees, and, striving to gain an upright posture, clung to Owen's legs, and held him back.

He was weak, though, and easily shaken off.

The only fear was that his cries should bring the rest to the spot; and Owing, foreseeing this danger, stopped him in time.

The savage, flung violently back upon the ground, was writhing like a crushed snake in his efforts to regain an upright position.

With a violent struggle he did so, and would, next moment, have raised the echoes of the forest with his shrill war cry, when Redgrave, rushing upon him, felled him to the earth with a terrific blow in the face from his clenched fist.

The savage fell back with a hollow groan, and lay still among the brushwood and long weedy grass.

Then Owen, bearing his fair burden in his arms, rushed onwards with all the speed of which he was capable.

Happily for him the foliage was so dense, and the savages themselves made so much noise in their progress through the bushes which impeded their progress, that they could neither see nor hear anything of the fugitives.

They were not at that moment more than half a dozen yards from each other, and it was absolutely a miracle that they did not perceive the body of the insensible savage lying stunned and bleeding among the bushes almost within their reach.

The slightest movement—the faintest cry upon his part—must inevitably have called their attention to the spot where he lay only half-concealed, and then to find the trail of the fugitives from the spot would have been a matter of no great difficulty.

Owen Redgrave, meanwhile, had no time to think about his danger. He must put a long distance between himself and his pursuers before he could feel at all at his ease.

He rushed wildly on, never caring how much the brambles and briars, through which lay his difficult path, scratched his hands and face, though he carefully warded them off from his fair charge.

Crushing and trampling through the brushwood, he ran, or rather staggered, forward; for his strength had been cruelly taxed, and he could endure little more of this violent exertion without rest.

Sometimes he thought that he had reached the limits of his powers of endurance, and that nothing was left for him but to lie down and await his death-blow.

On one occasion he thought he heard the steps of his pursuers close behind him, and he turned to face them, determined to sell his life dearly—not to be taken alive.

But it was a false alarm, and he struggled on again.

He got very nearly three-quarters of a mile in this way—not in a straight line, for he twisted to the right and to the left, and once almost doubled upon his steps, for the brushwood was in many places so thick as to altogether bar his passage, and oblige him to go out of his way, and wind round by a circuitous path.

Not that he had any particular notion of the direction which he should pursue, for every way was alike to him—all fraught with danger.

He came to a sudden stand-still, at last, upon the bank of a broad but shallow stream, which ran through the densest part of the forest.

It was probably the stream upon the banks of which, further away into the forest, the savages had encamped over night.

Owen paused here to rest himself for a few minutes, and he strained his ears to the utmost, lying upon the ground as he did so, to catch the sound of his pursuers.

But all was silent. For the present, they were safe.

It was madness, though, to think that they could long remain here with any degree of security. He listened again and again, but although he could still hear nothing of his pursuers, he was by no means sure that they might not be close at hand, for it was only probable that they were now proceeding in a stealthy and noiseless fashion, such as savages adopt when in pursuit of a foe.

Or had they lost the trail?

If they lost it once they might not again find it, and Owen saw a way by which escape seemed feasible.

It was an old trick that he had heard of scores of times, but still it was a good one, for all that.

Carrying the young girl in his arms, he plunged into the stream, which was above his knees, and waded onwards.

Before he had gone any great distance, the girl, with a gentle sigh, opened her eyes, and looked round her, for for some moments past she had appeared to be in a swooning state.

" Where are we?" she asked.

" Safe—safe!" he replied. " We shall soon leave our enemies behind."

" In what direction are we going?"

" Ah! that puzzles me. If we are unlucky enough to come upon the encampment, we are lost."

" You cannot bear the fatigue of carrying me. Why do you not leave me to my fate?"

" I will never do that."

" But it is madness to refuse me, for alone you would have a chance of escape, while together——"

"Together we will meet death, if it must be so; but I shall never desert you!"

The girl silently pressed his hand, and her deep blue eyes filled with tears of gratitude.

How very beautiful she was, he could not help thinking even at this moment of danger; but the recollection of a pale, loving face which he had left in England rushing upon his mind, made him lower his eyes with a blush of shame and contrition.

They pursued their way for some time in silence; but suddenly the Indian girl pointed to a clump of bushes by the waterside.

"See there!" she said.

Owen turned his eyes in alarm in the direction indicated, expecting no less than that his eyes would light upon the grim, war-painted visage of a savage, glaring out at him in vengeful hate.

But he saw instead a cavity in a rock overhanging the water, which appeared to be the entrance of a cavern.

"We might hide there," she said.

"Would it be safe?" he asked. "Would not they be certain to look there directly?"

"If they follow us up the stream."

"They will be sure to do that when they find the trail."

"Yes—yes; and they will find it, that is very certain."

"What do you say, then?"

"My experience of wild life teaches me that there is a way by which we might hope to escape detection."

"How is that?"

"To cover up the mouth of the cave with branches."

"Is that possible?"

"Yes; I will show you how. I am stronger now. Put me down, and we will set to work, for there can be no time to lose."

"No, there can be no time to lose."

He carried her to the cave, and set her gently down inside its mouth. Then, with her directions, began the work of concealment which she had suggested.

A large willow grew in the bank, and overhung the water, half hiding the entrance to the cavern. Another willow grew at a few yards' distance, sloping in the same direction, but affording no covering to the hiding-place.

From this latter tree Owen cut several branches, which he stuck into the clayey soil at the entrance of the hiding-place, and slanted them in such an artful fashion, that they appeared to grow from the other willow.

He then got a thick bush from the middle of the stream, where it was growing, cutting through the trunk low down in the water, and conveying this behind the barricade of willow branches, effectually blocked up the opening.

Before closing it, however, Owen stole out and took a long and careful observation of the exterior.

"I don't think they will find us out there," he thought to himself. "Nobody but a savage would ever dream that that could be a hiding-place."

He came back to the spot where he had left his fair companion, who asked anxiously whether he thought the screen would conceal them?

"We are safe, I fancy," replied Owen; "nothing but desperate bad luck can ruin us."

"The water is not muddy outside, is it?"

"No, not now. The stream runs so rapidly, that the water by this time is as clear as crystal."

"Let us block up the entrance now, and wait to see what happens."

"We will wait till they pass, for I feel pretty certain they will come this way."

They lost no more time in idle talk, but arranging the bush before the cavity, which was just large enough to admit of their standing in it in an upright position, waited silently for arrival of their enemies.

Scarce had they concealed themselves, however, when they heard a faint noise without, a few yards from the spot.

Their pursuers had come.

They were in the water, consulting together in excited tones.

Something must have caught their eyes which had excited their suspicions.

The fugitives held their breath, and waited with fast-beating hearts for the savages' approach.

CHAPTER XIII.

THE HIDING-PLACE.

OWEN REDGRAVE and his fair companion, crouching behind the thin screen which, with the aid of the green boughs, they had constructed, remained listening eagerly to every sound without, and palpitating with fear whenever they that fancied the sounds had approached a few steps nearer.

For some time neither of the fugitives moved or spoke, so fearful were they lest they might place themselves in some position in which those upon the outside could perceive the outline of their forms.

They need not, however, have stood in much fear of such a catastrophe; for although, by applying their faces close to the leaves, they could easy enough find crevices sufficiently large to serve them for loopholes, yet was the interior of the cave so dark, owing to the screen in front, that, from without, it was impossible to detect any outlines, even from a short distance.

The fugitives stood there, and, with what patience they could call to their aid at this awful juncture, waited for what might happen.

But the suspense at length became perfectly unendurable.

They must peep out.

They could no longer remain inactive or in suspense.

Then Owen cautiously crept to the opening of the cave, and placed his face close to the leaves.

He was almost startled into uttering an exclamation of alarm, so near did he find the pursuers.

They were, indeed, wading knee-deep in the water, not a dozen yards from the spot where he and his fair companion were concealed.

He had only just time to grasp the girl by the wrist, and point in the direction where they stood.

In another moment, she would have betrayed herself by speaking out loud.

"See!" he whispered. "They are there!"

"I cannot see them; but tell me——"

"Tell you what?"

"How many there are."

"There are four in the water," said Owen, after a pause; "but—but——"

"Well?"

"I think there must be others on the shore, for they seem to be talking together."

"Can you hear what they say?"

"I cannot understand, but I can hear plainly. If you could creep forward——Hush!"

As she moved, he kept his eyes fixed upon the dusky forms of the savages, and watched them jealously.

The slightest plash of her feet in the water, the faintest rustle of her garment, the tiniest jingle of the beads and trinkets which adorned her dress, might prove fatal.

But he need not have feared upon her account; for every movement of her lithe and graceful form was as glidingly noiseless as the motion of a snake.

Without he himself being aware of her approach, she was by his side, and her hand gently resting on his shoulder.

Then, together, with bated breath, they gazed forth between the tangled boughs of the shrubs that screened them, and took a long and cautious observation of the enemy.

The Indian girl listened, and was presently able to report the substance of the conversation which she had overheard to her companion.

They were looking for the trail, and had lost it.

They were also confused by there being only the marks of Owen's footsteps.

Some of the savages suggested that the girl must have fled in some other direction.

They were uncertain which way, therefore, they should bend their steps.

They were consulting together somewhat noisily—angrily, it seemed, and every one pointed in opposite directions.

It was evident that the pursuers were all abroad.

"They are going," whispered the girl, as, after a long consultation, the savages moved a short distance up the stream.

But this hope was not doomed to have very long endurance, for scarcely had the words passed her lips, when, as though they had heard her, they turned in a body, and drew towards the fugitives' hiding-place.

It was an awful moment.

Owen Redgrave held his breath, and his fingers closed vengefully round the handle of his knife.

In the hand of the beautiful Indian girl, too, a bright poniard glittered murderously.

But what would the efforts of these two avail them against the superior numbers of the enemy?

Breathlessly they watched and waited.

They thought that they were waiting for death; but the hour of fear had passed, and their nerves were wound up to the highest pitch of tension.

They were prepared for the worst that could befall them, but were determined only to sell their lives after a severe and bitter struggle.

Meanwhile, they must do nothing to hurry this catastrophe, which there was still a slight chance might be avoided by a due exercise of caution.

No—they must wait.

They must be silent and motionless, and abide the result.

Can you reader, picture to yourself the awful anxiety?

Thus did these two fugitives watch the coming of the savages, horrible in their war-paint, with bright, gleaming, vindictive eyes, and ready in their hands the murderous weapons with which to deal the death-blow.

They came on cautiously—one, who appeared to be in command of the party, taking the lead.

By the direction which he chose, it appeared certain to those hiding in the cave that he must come direct to the spot where they were hidden; and, indeed, he walked straight forward, looking in front of him, and having his eyes fixed, as Owen supposed, upon him.

But such, however, was not really the case; and though he was gazing hard in the direction of the fugitives, he in reality saw nothing of them; and now an incident occurred which, for the moment, seemed to be greatly in the fugitives' favour.

It was this.

The bottom of the stream, or, rather, small river—for its proportions at this place were almost sufficient to entitle it to that description—was very uncertain, and there were in some places deep holes suddenly approached, without any shelving to warn the person wading through the water that an unusual depth might be expected

Into one of these pit-falls did the savage who was leading the way now unexpectedly plunge, covering himself almost to the neck.

He very soon contrived to flounder out, but then pursued his way with very little luck, for next minute he had fallen again into another hole—this one still deeper than the first.

To see him spluttering and jabbering when he came to the surface would have been a comic spectacle under any other circumstances; but, as may be readily believed, Owen Redgrave did not at this moment feel very mirthfully inclined.

The savage, however, seemed determined not to have any more duckings, and ventured no farther in the same direction.

Had he but tried his luck once more, it is very probable that he would have hit upon a part of the stream where the water was shallow enough.

Owen, as we know, had been more fortunate in his selection, although it must be owned that this was merely chance. In the place where he had passed along, he had been only wading knee-deep.

The ill luck of the savage, as it turned out, proved a very fortunate circumstance to the fugitives; for could he only have continued his course in the direction he originally intended, there is no doubt but that he would have come straight towards Owen's hiding-place, and pushing against the bushes, with which the mouth of the cave had been so artfully hidden, most probably have disarranged them by accident, and so exposed the persons concealed behind them.

But as it was, the savage stated it as his opinion that the waters at this particular point could not be forded; and his followers, bowing to his superior judgment, the band divided themselves into two parties, and one followed the course of the stream upon either bank.

Meanwhile, two more savages came panting up, and another eager discussion took place.

Although Owen could not comprehend the language that they used, it was not difficult to discern from their furious gestures that his fate would be an awful one were he to fall into their clutches.

"What do they say?" he asked his companion, in a low tone, scarcely above his breath.

He turned as he spoke, and saw a strange smile lighting up the beautiful features of the Indian girl.

"They would have served you very badly before," she said; "but they say your fate shall be worse now that you have stolen me. You see, I am very valuable!"

There was something in the tone in which these few words were uttered that jarred unpleasantly enough upon the listener's ear.

If she were caught, it seemed to say, her fate would not have been so very terrible; and what became of him, the humble instrument of her flight—the poor pack-horse, so to speak—did not very much signify!

And yet, again, her conduct during their escape did not exhibit any selfishness. Upon the contrary, she had several times begged of him to leave her to her fate, and make good his escape.

She was a very incomprehensible riddle, this beautiful savage—an enigma, that required more thought than Owen at that moment could bestow upon it, for he had something else to think of just then.

The men upon the opposite bank were now slowly progressing towards them, having swam across to the other side.

Behind the little cave in which they had secreted themselves the fugitives could distinctly hear the crackling of branches, which showed that another party of the savages were out in that direction.

No. 5.—THE BUCCANEERS.

They were indeed surrounded.

The fugitives held their breath, and moved not hand or foot, expecting that some breath of air stronger than the rest would disarrange the boughs, and so expose them to the view of their pursuers.

The tortures of suspense were almost more than they could bear. But as yet the worst had not come.

Almost directly opposite to the spot where the fugitives were concealed the party upon the other bank came to a stand-still, and began to examine some object which caught their attention.

Owen strained his eyes to the utmost to ascertain what it was; and he had not very long to remain in suspense, for one of the party raised it on high to show to those upon the other side of the bank, who now scrambled through the bushes growing upon the water's edge, close to the spot where Owen and his companion were hidden, and began to shout across the stream.

"What is it?" one demanded, in the Indian language.

"Look—a broken bough!"

It was a small branch Owen had intended to use as a part of the screen before the opening of the cave, which had probably slipped from the mud into which he had endeavoured to plant it, and had floated across the stream to the opposite side.

"Where has it come from?"

"From some tree higher up."

"They must have passed this way, then?"

"Yes—that is certain!"

"Are they hidden anywhere?"

"Where?"

Now came the most critical moment which had yet occurred.

The eyes of all the savages eagerly scanned the appearance of the bank on either side of the stream.

Every shrub and bush did they appear to notice and to scan critically.

Owen expected that the end had come, and grasped his knife.

They must be discovered now!

There seemed no hope for them!

One of the savages, indeed, upon their side of the water, who stood upon a spot which was not more than a yard distant from Redgrave, tossed a stick through the bushes, and struck Owen a sharp blow upon the breast.

Luckily for him he bore the shock without flinching.

Had he made any movement he must inevitably have fallen into the savages' hands.

But it was not to be. Presently the whole party seemed to be satisfied that the fugitives were not thereabouts concealed, and moved onwards.

They slowly progressed along the sides of the stream, examining the bushes as they went. Their footsteps grew fainter, and at last Redgrave could not refrain from a delighted chuckle at the idea that they were at last out of danger.

His joy, however, was somewhat premature.

Just when he was about to open his lips and give vent to some expression of pleasure, the twigs snapping close by his side caused him suddenly to pause and cast an anxious glance in the direction from which the sound proceeded.

One of the savages yet remained behind, or had come back—he could not make out which.

What his motive was, it was difficult at first to imagine.

But when he approached a little nearer, Owen fancied that he must be searching among the bushes for something he had dropped.

Owen peered anxiously in the same direction, and sure enough saw the blade of a knife glittering among the rushes at the water's edge. It had been unhooked from his girdle in some way by one of the overhanging boughs, and had fallen there.

He had perceived his loss shortly afterwards, and returned for it, and thus was his presence to be accounted for.

The savage crept nearer and nearer, not noticing the object of which he was in search, but parting the bushes carefully with his hand as he advanced.

It would be difficult to conceive a more provoking situation. Owen felt quite certain that it was the dagger the man wanted, and there it was at his feet, if he could only have seen it.

On the contrary, however, he was wandering from the spot, and getting closer and closer to the fugitives' hiding-place.

Step by step he came!

Owen clenched his teeth and waited.

The savage was close upon him.

He parted the boughs with his hands.

Another step forward, and they would be face to face!

Then the savage raised his eyes and met those of Owen, full of determination, fixed upon him!

CHAPTER XIV.

UNDER THE SPELL.

It was an awful moment.

A moment which in a lifetime would never have been forgotten.

The expression of the two men's faces, when they found themselves thus confronting one another, formed a picture that was terrible to look upon.

The same thought seemed to pass like a lightning's flash through the brain of both.

One of the two must die. There was no help for it.

Which was it to be? That was the only question to be decided. But that one should perish was an absolute necessity, if the other were to escape.

But Owen Redgrave had made up his mind, as he saw the other slowly creeping towards him—slowly creeping towards the up-lifted knife which waited for his coming.

This was not a moment for the exercise of charitable feelings. He knew enough of the savage character to know that the gift of life would not be accepted, did he felt inclined to offer it.

He knew that the only way to guard against opposition, on this man's part, to the dear prospect of escape, was to remove his enemy out of his path.

He had some advantage, too, over the other, for the savage had come upon the ambush unprepared.

Owen did not give him time for preparation.

Springing out like a tiger, he clutched the swarthy foe by the throat.

Dragged him through the bushes.

Plunged his knife into the savage's heart.

The man's struggles were few and feeble.

With a hollow groan, he rolled over on his face, and lay perfectly motionless—dead.

Owen then waited but a moment to make sure that he need have no more fear upon account of this one of his enemies.

He took his companion once more in his arms and plunged into the stream. He knew very well where were situated the deep holes into which he had seen the savage fall, and wisely avoided them upon his own journey.

Further on, he knew, from personal experience, that the water was shallow enough, and he waded boldly onwards.

The beautiful Indian reclined in his arms with, perhaps, rather less care for the inconvenience which her weight might cause him than could have been desired in a person whose interests ought to have been one with his.

But his strength was quite sufficient to carry her onwards as quickly, if not more so, than many other men, alone and unencumbered, would have got over the ground.

He pursued his course thus for more than a mile, every now and then casting his eyes backwards to see if anything was visible of his old enemies; but having got thus far without interruption, he concluded that he might consider himself to be tolerably safe, and might, therefore, venture upon dry land.

They came to a place where the bushes were less crowded, and they could, therefore, get on with considerable rapidity.

Owen was at first tempted to plunge into the forest, but a moment's reflection convinced him of the fallacy of such a proceeding, for, to a certainty, they would double upon themselves, and come back to the spot from which they had started, to fall into the hands of the savages.

No; the wisest course would certainly be to follow the direction of the stream, because, by so doing, they would be sure of travelling in something like a continuous course—not a straight line, because the river might wind and twist very much.

They were very certain of one thing, though, and that was, that it did not form a circle; consequently, as they were walking in a different direction to that taken by their pursuers, they must in the end escape from them, did not the enemy retrace their steps.

They made the most speed they could, and soon left the late place of their concealment far in the rear.

The trees in some places grew so thickly upon the banks, that they were obliged to diverge into the forest, and make considerable sweeps to follow the course of the stream.

Coming round a dense clump of foliage after one of the digressions from the straight path, Owen started back in alarm as his eye fell upon a dark object lying in the water.

He thought it was some huge amphibious monster when first he perceived it, but upon approaching nearer, he was very much astonished, and not a little pleased, to find that it was the bottom of an overturned canoe lying among the bulrushes.

Redgrave did not delay a moment ere he plunged into the water, and, having set the boat right, dragged it to the side, so that the Indian girl could get into it.

But he was beginning to think that even then they were in a fix, as they had no means of propelling the boat on its way. He had an idea of cutting down a long, slender ash, which he might use as a prop; and the bottom of the stream being so shallow, guide the canoe onwards without much difficulty.

He had opened his knife, and was looking about for a young tree, when the Indian girl, uttering an exclamation of pleasure, pointed to something lying upon the bank, half concealed by the long grass.

Owen eagerly approached the spot.

The two paddles were lying there, and a packet carefully wrapped up in a kind of mat manufactured from dry rushes.

Placing this parcel in the stern of the boat, Owen did not waste any time in examining its contents at this moment; but, taking his seat in the rower's place, went vigorously to work.

In the young sailor's hands the oars soon cut a way through the water, and the retreating banks glided rapidly past as they pursued their course.

Owen seemed not to require to pause for breath, now that he was set to a task congenial to his sailor's habits; and the Indian girl could not but look with admiration upon the handsome face glowing with excitement, and the strong muscular frame of the gallant fellow who had enlisted his brave heart and strong arm in her service.

He rowed on for some time without showing any sign of fatigue, nor paused until he had reached the limits of the forest, where the little river merged into a broad lake; and here, in a sheltered creek, hidden by high trees and thick bushes, in such a way that had any one been following in pursuit in another boat, nothing could have been more probable than that they should steer unconsciously past the spot where the fugitives were hidden, Owen proposed that they should wait and rest awhile.

He then stooped, and busied himself in unfastening the packet of which mention has already been made.

Owen drew out his ever-useful knife, and cut the thongs with which it was fastened.

"Aha!" he said; "I thought as much—at least, I hoped as much. I should have been very much disappointed if I had been mistaken."

As he spoke, undoing the wrappers in which it was enveloped, he disclosed to view a great hunch of pasty and some other eatables, together with a pint flask of what proved to be good cognac brandy.

"There is no guessing how these things come to be lying about waiting for an owner," said Redgrave, with a smile; "but they need not have waited so long if we had only known where to look for them."

As he spoke, he had been extemporising a table, with some broad green leaves for a table-cloth; and having set the provision before his fair companion, mixed a small quantity of brandy in about half a tumblerful of water, which he contrived to pour into an impromptu drinking cup, manufactured out of another broad leaf, rolled and doubled and tied round with a rush.

The beautiful girl was faint and weary, and heartily glad of this rude repast, which, nevertheless, Owen contrived to serve up with an amount of dexterity which showed that he could turn his hand to almost anything at an emergency, and play the part of host with a good grace, even out in the wilderness, with leaves for plates, and the wooden seat in a savage's canoe for a dining-room table.

He did not attempt to partake of any food himself until his fair charge had finished; but smiling, said that there was time enough for him, though it must be owned that, when his time did come, from the voracity with which he fell upon the food, the poor fellow evidently stood in need of it.

To tell truth, he had not had anything like such a good meal for many a long day, and had not he possessed a muscular frame, and a constitution of iron, he must long ago have succumbed beneath the weight of hardship and physical suffering he had been compelled to endure since he had made his escape from Norfolk Island.

But now, for a short time, there was a brief interval of peace and plenty, and Owen's light and buoyant nature soon asserted itself.

The danger for the time past, he had more time to study his companion, and to puzzle his head over the strange and incomprehensible incongruities of her character.

Who was she? he asked himself.

Did she belong to their tribe, or was she a captive?

All these were knotty points he was not clever enough to solve; and when, after a time, he had vainly racked his brain to find an answer to any one of them, he was compelled to come back to the spot from which he started.

He fancied that it was pretty sure she was a sort of prisoner of the savages, from whom she had escaped; and, probably, a prisoner on whom they set great store.

Yes, it was very certain that this beautiful Indian girl, into whose companionship fate had cast him, was some person of distinction; and for some reason of which he was doomed for the present to remain in ignorance, was tenderly taken care of, and was being conveyed somewhere for an unknown reason, though Owen could not help fancying that a heavy ransom must form a part of the savages' motive for wishing for her safe keeping.

For the present moment, though, his chief thought was how lovely was the Indian girl's face, and how matchlessly graceful her symmetrical form, clothed in the magnificent huntress's dress which she wore.

The scene around, too, was very beautiful, and formed a picturesque back-ground to the girl's figure, and that of the handsome young man by her side.

It was truly a lovely spot. The surface of the lake was as smooth as glass, and as limpid as pure air, reflecting the steep banks upon one side clothed in dark pines.

The tiny bays, too, here and there were seen glittering through an occasional arch formed by the thick clustering foliage overhead—a vault of bright broad leaves, lit up with scarlet flowers.

There was an air of deep repose lying upon the vast forests around and the smooth water before them, which seemed to lull their senses for a while into a blissful dream.

It might have been the dawn of a wild and passionate love which was to sway the destinies of the man who, idling there, little thought of the strange and stirring scenes through which, ere his life had ran its course, he was doomed to pass.

Had he been questioned upon the subject, it is very sure that he would indignantly have denied the existence within his breast of any other sentiment than that of passing admiration for the beauty, and curiosity respecting the history, of the fair being by his side; but it is nevertheless the truth that, even during this short time, she had obtained over him a strange influence and power, the extent of which he would not have admitted even to himself.

He still believed himself perfectly true and faithful to the loving girl whom he had left at home in England; and yet within his heart there had crept something.

But there is no end to the faithlessness of men and the faithfulness of women; and I should not like to expose the most devoted of living lovers to the influence of bright, piercing eyes and raven locks, and tiny glittering teeth, shining like a gleam of sunlight betwixt the opening roses of one of the most beautiful mouths in the world.

And this was in the heart of a wild wilderness; and who knows, there might not have been another woman within a circuit of a hundred miles, except the bright and glorious creature who now sat by his side, and smiled upon him sweet destruction.

"I trust you will pardon my question, if it is an impertinent one," said Owen, after some slight hesitation, for he felt that the subject was rather a difficult one to broach; "but do you belong—have you resided long with the tribe of Indians in whose company I found you?"

"You mean to say, do I belong to those savages?"

"I did not say that——"

"That I was a savage."

Owen blushed, and stammered out some somewhat lame apology.

"You need not be afraid of hurting my feelings," the girl retorted, with a scornful smile. "I am not a savage, although I wear this dress, with its jingling gewgaws, and cheap trumpery."

"But—but—you are, then——"

"I am an Englishwoman," she answered, turning proudly upon her companion.

Owen expressed the astonishment he felt.

"I thought that it was very extraordinary you should speak English so well, but I could not understand, and cannot still——"

"You cannot understand my story, I suppose," said the girl, with a quiet smile, "unless I relate it to you?"

Owen expressed by his looks how eager he was that she should do so.

But after he had waited for some time, his fair companion, turning her eyes full upon him, said, in the same low, deliberate tone of voice, "My story is a secret which must remain in my own keeping."

Again Owen blushed, and bit his lips with vexation.

"I would not, for the world, intrude upon your secrets," he said. "Pardon me for having asked so much. If I can be of any service to you, I shall be only too happy to lay down my life in your aid, for I shall always consider that I owe you my existence."

As he spoke, he rose to his feet, and loosened the boat from its moorings.

Suddenly the girl looked up, and called to him in a low tone of voice, which had in it something touchingly pleading.

"Owen Redgrave," she said, "do not be angry at my words, which were not meant to offend you. I will tell you all concerning myself that I dare tell you. I had made my escape from a certain place, and had taken shelter with a friendly tribe of Indians, who had agreed to escort me safely through the forest. The party into whose power you fell had been sent by those from whom I had escaped, to bring me back."

"And what was your intention if you had escaped? Whither were you bound?"

"For the sea-coast, where I would take ship for England."

There was something in the sound of that familiar word which conjured up a host of pleasant memories in the young man's breast, and for a time he was silent and thoughtful.

"Do you think it is possible that you could reach the destination that you propose without a guide?"

"If you are willing to brave the dangers of the woods and the wilderness," said his companion, "we might together accomplish the journey."

"I have already said," replied Owen, "that I will venture all to help you, if my assistance is worth the having."

"Without you," replied the beauty, with one of her most bewitching smiles, "I should be altogether powerless. Say, therefore, that you will not desert me."

In token of his good faith, Owen bent down and pressed his lips upon his fair companion's hand.

As he raised his eyes to her face, and encountered the glittering orbs which beamed down upon him, a thrill ran through his frame.

The chain was riveted.

CHAPTER XV.

HE WAS HER SLAVE.

Lost!

Just at this moment a peculiar sound, which might have been the scream of a bird, but which yet seemed to have something human in it, smote upon the young man's ear.

He sprang into an upright posture, and listened eagerly.

For some moments there was a deep silence, unbroken by the faintest sound.

Then, again, the cry was heard.

Owen turned slowly round, still listening, but uncertain from whence the cry had come.

When he turned again towards his companion, he saw, by the expression of her face, how great was her terror.

"I know the cry well," she whispered. "The savages are upon us."

"We could easily enough escape by aid of the canoe," said Redgrave. "But the difficulty is to ascertain from what direction the cry proceeds."

Again they listened.

"I think that it comes from the woods," he said; "but in the direction to which we were going."

"In that case," said the girl, "we had better remain hidden here."

"I am afraid that we shall not find this hiding-place as good a one as the last."

"Suppose you were to go out into the stream and reconnoitre."

"To do that I must desert you."

"Not for long, and I am not afraid."

"Are you sure of that?"

"Yes. I can remain here very well upon this mossy bank, under the shade of the trees, until you return."

"And if anything should happen to me?"

"Pray use the utmost caution, and let us both put our trust in Providence."

"But remember that alone you cannot hope to brave the dangers of your long journey. Say, shall I leave you?"

"Yes, yes! I would rather that you tried to ascertain where our enemy lies hidden."

"Be certain that I shall remain away no longer than I can help," said Owen, as he got into the canoe.

He was pushing noiselessly away from the bank, when a thought struck him, and he returned to her side.

"For heaven's sake let me entreat of you," he said, in a low and anxious tone, "to stop where you are, and on no account to stir until I return."

She gave him her assurance that she would do as he desired, and he left her.

The surface of the lake was still placid and glassy, and the scene as still as it had been hitherto.

The woods lay in the noon-day sun; a deep shadow beneath their spreading branches left the surrounding shrubs in a grim obscurity, which even Redgrave's piercing sight could not penetrate.

The forest gave up no sound, no song, no cry, not even a murmur; but looked down from the sloping hill-side on to the smooth water which they lined in solemn stillness.

Only the regular dipping of the paddles broke the silence, but with a sound so faint as scarcely to be audible at a few yards' distance.

Owen rowed on, peering anxiously about him, and listening eagerly for some sound that might show him whether or not the presence of savages was to be feared.

But he heard nothing, and after he had progressed some considerable distance in the lake, still keeping under the shadow of the trees, and finding all to be perfectly quiet, he came to the conclusion that they might safely continue their journey in that direction.

But just when he was thinking that he would turn round the canoe and go back to his fair companion, a noise in the woods startled him and filled his heart with dread.

Was it the same cry that he had heard just now? or something like a woman's stifled scream for help?

He listened, but the sound was not repeated, and fancying that it must have been the cry of some wild animal that had startled him, he rowed slowly back.

He had not gone very far, however, before he again heard the cry. Fainter it seemed, though, and more distant.

He pulled with all his might in the direction from which it came.

As he went along, he looked eagerly for the creek up which, awhile ago, the boat had been moored. But he must have come much further than he at first supposed, for he could not again discover the place.

He rowed on now, straining every nerve; for he felt certain that something had happened to his beautiful companion.

Yet he could see nothing of the creek.

On, on he rowed, but with the same result.

At last, some object, which as they had journeyed along had attracted his notice, again caught his eye.

This was before they had reached the creek. He, then, had passed it.

What was to be done? Only to turn and redouble his speed.

Again, by some ill-luck, he must have passed the entrance to the creek, for he presently found himself at the spot which he had rowed to when he was upon his voyage of discovery.

Mad with rage and disappointment, he turned again.

With a similar result he once more passed along the woody shore.

But he was not to be daunted, and pursuing his search, at length arrived at the hiding-place which nature had so elaborately concealed.

He pushed the boat up the creek. When once inside, he knew the place again at a glance.

But the girl was gone.

He cast his eyes eagerly around as he sprang upon the shore,

There were evident signs of a struggle having taken place.

The grass was trodden down; the tiny branches of the shrubs about, snapped and broken, showing that a way had been forced through them by more than one person.

Owen Redgrave was upon the point of raising his voice and calling loudly to her, when the thought that this would be the maddest act he could commit, froze the half-uttered cry upon his lips.

There could be no doubt that she had fallen into the hands of the savages, and if he must rescue her it could only be by resorting to the wily stratagem which the Indian adopts.

And that he would rescue her he was determined.

He looked about, and where the ground was softest, by the water-side, he could plainly detect the marks of the savages' feet.

He knew little, or absolutely nothing, of the way which men followed a trail.

It was a venturesome expedition, that upon which he now determined to embark, but he had made up his mind to it, and had ten times the danger stood in his path, he would have carried out his resolution.

Gently parting the bushes, he crept through, and followed in the track which the savages had left.

CHAPTER XVI.

THE TRAIL.

INEXPERIENCED as he was, Owen Redgrave found no great difficulty in the outset in following in the footsteps of those who had carried off the beautiful girl.

The bushes which they had broken down in their progress served admirably to guide his steps, and at first he pushed his way onwards with some amount of recklessness as to the noise he made, feeling pretty certain that by this time they must have got on a great distance ahead.

But who can describe his blank astonishment when, all at once, after many twistings and windings, he found himself again on the banks of the lake, to which the trail evidently led.

He looked about him eagerly, with some idea that the savages must have taken the wrong road, and when they had reached this spot had turned again and retraced their steps.

But upon carefully examining the soft soil round about, which readily took and retained the impression of every foot pressed upon it, he saw that the party, whoever they were, had departed by water.

Carrying his inspection to the extreme edge of the overhanging bank, he found, without much trouble, an indentation that the head of a canoe had made there, and some places where the oar of the rower, in pushing off, had uprooted the turf.

What was to be done now? Nothing but to return at once for his own canoe. He lost no time in so doing, for he was most eager to be upon the track of the savages, lest they should get so far ahead that they would altogether elude him.

If he could only manage to catch sight of them while they were yet upon the water, there might be some chance of his efforts proving successful. If, however, they, unseen by him, effected a landing, the chase was at an end.

He felt in no small flutter and perturbation as he took his place in his canoe. He knew that upon his efforts alone depended the rescue or continued captivity—death, perhaps, of the maiden. And he was very fearful of the result, for he was most inexperienced in the ways of the wily savages, with whom he was about to enter into a contest.

During the exciting adventures which had occupied him for some hours past, he had not been noticing the flight of time.

Twilight was beginning to creep over the woods, and it was with some difficulty that he could discern the surface of the lake at a few hundred yards distance.

At last, however, he fancied he could descry a dark object moving along far ahead.

The silence of this moment was unbroken, and he laid his head low in the boat to listen.

For some seconds he heard nothing, but his patience was at last rewarded by the faint plashing of paddles.

He had not been mistaken. It was the savages' boat.

Owen Redgrave followed as noiselessly as possible, for the utmost skill and precaution now became necessary in the management of his canoe.

His paddles must be lifted and returned to the water with the greatest tenderness, and ever and again he strained his eyes to pierce the fast gathering gloom, and ascertain whether the others were listening to his movements, as he had awhile ago listened to theirs.

Onward he travelled, and the darkness by this time entirely obscured the object of his pursuit, obliging him, even at the risk of detection, to hurry his movements.

Suddenly he paused and lay upon his oars, for he heard the bows of the other boat grating upon the ground, and knew that they must be effecting a landing.

With as little noise as possible he glided towards the shore, at a distance from the spot from which the sound proceeded.

The clouds had broken a little, and the moon shone forth, glittering through the topmost branches of the trees, and it was most fortunate for him that he had crept into the shadow, for in another moment he must have been detected.

He listened intently to the movements of the enemy, and heard them muttering in low voices as they landed, and heard the crackling of the bushes and the splashing of the water.

The tide was running towards the spot, and when these sounds were no longer audible, he allowed himself gently to drift in the same direction, taking care, however, with an occasional motion of one of the paddles, still to keep within the shadow of the trees.

But as he went he eagerly strained his eyes to pierce the darkness, for he dreaded coming suddenly upon one of the savages, who might have been left in charge of the canoe.

He was, however, greatly delighted to find that the boat had been dragged up high and dry upon the beach, and was lying there unguarded.

He moored his own among the rushes, and finding that he could move the other boat without much difficulty or noise, dragged it down again from the place where the savages had left it, and pushed it into the water, where the tide soon carried it away.

" There's no knowing how soon I may have to make a run of it," he thought. " It will be as well if I make pursuit as difficult as possible."

When he landed, the voices of the savages were entirely inaudible, and there were no rustling of bushes, or breaking of twigs, or sound of footsteps to guide him. But when he had clambered up a steep bank, which rose at a few yards' distance from the water's edge, he was at no loss for a guide as to the road they must have taken.

He started suddenly, for he could plainly perceive that there was a fire burning not far off within the woods, by the way in which the upper branches of the trees were illuminated. And as he slowly crept onwards towards it, he could every now and then hear the sound of voices—the low and melodious laughter of Indian women, and the cackling and crowing of childish voices.

As he approached nearer still he fancied he heard on all sides of him the sounds of footsteps among the trees, and every now and then he started round, fancying that some one was behind him.

The most practised and guarded foot might have stirred a bunch of leaves or snapped a dried stick in the dark; and how could he hope, unaccustomed as he was to such a scene, to escape detection?

All at once, and without a moment's notice, he came out from behind a thick mass of bushes into an open space, where the firelight shone brightly.

He sprang back again, fearful lest his want of caution might have led to his discovery. But, after a brief pause, finding that he was safe, he peeped cautiously round the bushes, and obtained a clear view of the camp.

A large fire had been made to answer the purposes of light and cookery, and the burning brush was blazing high and bright, casting a lurid glare around.

The evening meal was almost concluded, with the exception of two or three hungry savages, who were still gorging themselves with half-cooked meat, and gnawing at the bones, like under-fed curs. But the hour of rest and relaxation had arrived, and most of the company were stretched out easily and lazily, in the most comfortable attitudes they could assume.

Eight or ten warriors reclined upon the ground, the firelight flickering upon their naked limbs. Their firearms lay near to them, so that they might be snatched up at a moment's notice.

A little distance off, the females belonging to the

camp were collected together, and the children played around, or hung about their mothers' skirts.

Most of them appeared to be cheerful and light-hearted enough, but one old hag was seated apart at the opening of a tent, with a fierce and watchful expression, as though she was keeping guard over some one within.

Owen gazed anxiously around, in the hope of finding the mysterious and beautiful girl whom the savages had taken away. She was, however, nowhere to be seen, though the fire blazed so brightly, that every portion of the camp was illuminated. Once or twice he fancied that he heard the sound of her voice, but listening again, he found that, alas! he had been mistaken.

Presently, while he was watching and wondering, the old woman rose to her feet, speaking angrily, as though answering some one within the tent, and having made way for them to pass, an old savage walked forth with a slow and stately step, and pausing a few feet from the entrance, beckoned to somebody to follow.

And then, with a proud and disdainful smile upon her face, came out the woman of whom Owen was in search.

She affected an indifference to the watchful regards of those around her. Yet Owen fancied that he could trace some slight uneasiness in her wandering eyes, as they eagerly scanned the outlines of the dark forest enclosing the camp.

She walked in the same slow and stately fashion towards the fire, and took her seat by the women, who fell back a few paces, eyeing her mistrustfully, and murmuring among themselves.

It was very evident that they were not pleased by the advent among them of the handsome stranger, whom they perhaps dreaded as a dangerous rival.

She sat there motionless and as though lost in thought, the firelight playing upon her beautiful face and the faultless symmetry of her form.

Presently, the Indian women, finding that she took no notice of them, began to draw nearer and nearer, and to press upon her. But suddenly she rose angrily to her feet, and waved them back, while one of the chiefs, with a threatening gesture, warned them to abstain from further annoyance.

At this moment, and while their attention was directed to him, Owen whistled softly, in imitation of one of the cries of the many wild birds peopling the forest. He had heard the cry often enough during the last few days, and, for a first attempt, the imitation was most successful.

However, he failed in his object, for the person whose attention he was desirous of attracting took no notice of him.

What was he to do? In the silence which succeeded, he dare not again venture upon this signal of his presence. His only chance, then, was to wait until she looked in his direction, and then to suddenly show himself, and withdraw again into the gloom which was sheltering him.

For a long while, however, he waited without being able to seize the desired opportunity. But at last she raised her eyes.

In a moment he thrust his face out beyond the bushes.

He could see that she had caught sight of him, for she sat motionless, looking fixedly in his direction.

He dared not remain more than a second before he again withdrew himself; but finding that she still continued to look towards him, he once more appeared, and waved his hand.

By a bright gleam of intelligence which shot across her face, he knew, then, that he had satisfied her as to his identity.

She dropped her eyes, however, and appeared again to be buried in thought.

Owen once more asked himself how he was to proceed. If it was intended that she should pass the night in the tent, at the entrance of which the old woman kept guard, all hope of escape was gone.

But what could he do while the camp yet remained awake and active?

Presently the old woman approached the girl, and beckoned to her to follow.

Owen watched them eagerly. The old woman held the captive tightly by the wrist, and moved towards the entrance of the tent, while Owen crept noiselessly round, so that he reached, at last, a spot where he was sheltered, although within a few inches only of the canvass.

Whilst he was thus noiselessly progressing, the old Indian hag and her captive passed by the entrance to the tent, which it appeared the former had no intention of entering. She had evidently been placed in charge over the girl, and did not choose her to quit her sight. Now she was bound for a spring of fresh water, at some fifty yards' distance from the spot where the tent stood, and carried with her a gourd to fill, which she took down from the branch of a tree.

But when they had come out from the light of the fire, and reached a spot plunged in the deepest darkness, and while the old woman yet held her captive tight by the wrist, Owen sprang upon her.

He suddenly clutched at her throat, and held her so tightly that she could make no other sound than a sort of gurgling, suffocating noise.

" Quick! quick!" he whispered to the maiden, whom the old hag had now released. " You will find the boat down there among the rushes. Cut it loose—keep close to the brink—go with the tide—I will be with you directly, when I have silenced the old woman !"

These words were uttered with great rapidity, and in a low tone of voice; but his fair companion easily understood them, and flew in the direction indicated.

Meanwhile, Owen might have made good his escape, had he not been, perhaps, too considerate of the old Indian, with whom he had to deal.

He did not, therefore, pinch her very hard, but contented himself by making threatening gestures, which he thought would scare her into silence.

In this, however, he was mistaken, for no sooner had he relinquished his hold upon her, and risen to his feet, than she uttered a piercing shriek.

The camp was instantly aroused.

The trampling of the savages' feet struck ominously upon Owen's ear.

A huge, half-naked figure appeared against the background of ruddy light, waving aloft his tomahawk.

Owen turned to fly, but too late!

————

CHAPTER XVII.

THE TORTURE.

THE most fearful yells and unearthly cries rent the air on all sides.

Owen did not hesitate a moment, but plunged into the bushes that lined the shore.

To reach the spot where he had left the canoe required but a few seconds of time.

As yet his fair companion had not loosened it from its moorings.

She was anxiously awaiting his arrival.

He stooped to give the canoe a vigorous push away from the bank, and was in the very act of doing so, when one of the savages forced his way through the bushes behind.

With a fierce cry he bounded forward, and sprang like a panther upon Owen's back.

There was not a moment to lose, and if the girl did not get away now there could be but little hope of her escape.

Even if he were sacrificed himself, he was determined that she should be free, and he gallantly pushed away the canoe before he made any effort to free himself from his enemy.

Then, as the boat passed from beneath his fingers, he fell forward into the water, the savage still clinging to him.

The river was not more than three feet deep at the spot where they fell, but yet it was deep enough to have drowned Redgrave had the other succeeded in holding him down.

But the savage also had been ducked beneath the surface, and was compelled to relinquish his hold so that he might get his own head above water.

For a few brief seconds there was a furious struggle, as though two monsters of the deep were locked in a deadly embrace.

Then they sprang up erect, still clinging to each other, and both alike watchful of the murderous knife.

But at this moment, when the result of the contest seemed very doubtful, the dark forms of half a dozen savages came leaping through the bushes, accompanied by wild, ear-splitting war cries, and fell pell mell upon the unfortunate Owen.

They seized him, and led—or rather dragged him from the water, and through the bushes, towards the camp-fire.

So eager were they, however, to recover the captive, that they heeded not the canoe containing the beautiful fugitive, of whose escape, by the way, they were as yet in ignorance.

Still it lay concealed by the bushes close at hand, and it was not until the savages had dragged Owen away that the mysterious woman struck out boldly into the stream.

When the savage who had sprang upon Owen's back was brought to the fire-side and had recovered his breath and his recollection, for he was more than half strangled and suffocated, he described how he had seen the maiden in the canoe.

But then pursuit was hopeless.

Meanwhile, the savages who had hold of Redgrave, conducted him to the fire, where they were able to scrutinize his appearance.

Very soon some of the party recognised him as the man whom they had taken prisoner upon the previous day.

At this discovery a loud yell was raised, and half a dozen menacing knives brandished round his face.

But Redgrave kept his countenance in spite of these demonstrations of anger upon the Indians' part; and though he had then but very little hope of escaping with his life, yet he put on a bold front, determined not to disgrace his colour by any show of cowardice.

The men who had taken him prisoner the previous day, formed, as I have intimated, a part of this tribe. They were a shooting party sent out to forage in the forest for the rest, at the same time as they were, if possible, to recapture the mysterious lady disguised as an Indian girl in the manner which she had described to Owen.

These chiefs had already described the way in which Owen had escaped, and his fame preceding him, he was treated as a hero by his new captors.

Unfortunately, however, he had to expect a hero's fate now that he had fallen into the savages' hands.

He knew well enough that he would be horribly tortured before he died, and so very vague appeared his chance of escape, that he was more than half inclined, had the means laid within his reach, to terminate his existence.

Yet, though there was a faint glimmering hope to buoy him up, he might still get away perhaps. He would wait.

They did not, as they had done before, strange to say, fasten him so securely.

His hands were tied together, but they allowed him to take a seat upon a log by the fireside, and warm himself.

Presently one of the chiefs pushed some food over within his reach, which, however, in his fettered condition, he with great difficulty managed to partake of.

The women of the tribe came round and watched him wistfully, and some pointed out to others peculiarities in dress and features.

It was evident, too, that some of them looked upon him admiringly, though when he turned his eyes towards them, they withdrew theirs hastily and in confusion.

By this time it was growing late, and the greater part of the chiefs had retired to their tents.

Some five or six who had gone in pursuit of the fugitive, returned with a report of their want of success.

Then the preparations were made for turning in for the night, and it became necessary to make the prisoner secure during the hours of sleep.

They were going to let him live until the morning, it would seem, and then what would be his fate?

They did not fasten him any more than he was already fastened. But they left him sitting on a log, with his back to a tree, guarded by a sentinel who walked continuously to and fro within a few feet distance of the spot, or sat in front of him—a rifle in his hand pointed at the prisoner's breast.

There was very little chance of escape under these circumstances; and for the present, at least, Owen Redgrave saw that he must give up the idea of getting away.

Still, somehow, he felt certain that he should be able to effect his purpose; and even when things looked at the worst, he was most hopeful.

The savages had now almost all gone to roost, and from the various tents the prisoner could hear their heavy breathing, and their uneasy movements, as they rolled to and fro, disturbed by dreams.

The time passed slowly enough to poor Owen, and he anxiously listened to the faintest sounds in the woods, hoping that they might indicate the approach of some friendly ally.

No such chance was there, though, in his favour. Now and then, the voice of some wild bird—among others, the one he had imitated—rent the air with its discordant note; but he could hear nothing which, at his most sanguine moments, he could construe into a signal.

"No," he said, bitterly to himself; "I am to be left here to perish now that I have been made use of."

He was thinking of the mysterious Englishwoman when he thus spoke.

But when he turned the matter over in his mind, he saw how unjust was this thought; because, in the first instance, it was she who had freed him from his bonds.

Again, she had not loosened the boat and made good her escape, as she could have done when she left him with the old woman.

No, it was clear that she did not intend to desert him.

Perhaps she could not help him. He had found it difficult enough to help her, and had done it at what risk we already know of.

But he could not be just.

"She won't leave me yet, perhaps," he said, "because, as yet, she has not gained her end. No, she will

No. 6.—THE BUCCANEERS.

help me this time; and it will not be until I am no further use that she will leave me for good. It's to be hoped that I shall not be among the savages when that happens."

His hands had only been tied, but the fastenings on these were so tight, and hurt him so much, that all thought of sleep was necessarily banished.

He counted the weary hours as they slowly dragged their course, wondering whether ever again he was to run free, and leave these hateful woods behind.

"Shall I ever see Grace any more?" he asked himself. "Poor Grace, I wonder where she is?"

He was not altogether without some remorseful thoughts upon this subject, for the recollection of Grace had troubled him but very little when in the company of the mock Indian.

He was pondering upon his own fickleness, and had half closed his eyes in a sort of drowsy, restless state, which could not exactly be called slumber, when a slight noise close to him caused him to look up with a start.

A woman's figure stood before him.

Its back was to the light. It was tall and dark.

Owen half rose to his feet, with a low but joyful exclamation.

"Ha!" he said. "You have come, then?"

As he uttered these words, he brought his face within a foot of that of the female figure standing before him. His eyes opened wide with astonishment.

He had been mistaken. It was not the person he supposed.

Instead of the Indian maiden he expected to see, it was the old hag whom, awhile ago, he had half strangled.

She saw the surprise depicted in his face, and grinned maliciously.

She clenched her skinny fist, and shook it fiercely at him, and made as though she would have clawed out his eyes.

Owen drew back in some alarm, for he was not prepared for this sort of warfare.

She spoke in a low, savage tone, and in broken English.

"Dog of a pale face," she said, "why have you come among us, when you got away once with a whole skin? But you shall suffer for this to-morrow at the torture. You shall pay for the insult you have offered to Minatowa."

And as she spoke, the old woman's every limb trembled with suppressed passion.

"Yes," she cried, raising her voice suddenly to a screech; "your flesh shall be torn from your bones, and your bones shall be picked white by the birds of the wilderness. Say, where have you taken the pale-faced beauty? What has become of her?"

"I know nothing of her," replied Owen, "except that, if possible, I believe she will manage to contrive my escape."

"Never! never! never!" screeched the old hag. "You will never leave the tribe again with your life. Ha, ha! sleep while you can, for to-morrow you will surely die."

"I can only die once!" replied Owen, defiantly; "and I hope to be able to show you that an Englishman can suffer, and yet be silent. There, leave me!"

But the old hag, on the contrary, brandished her bony fist in the air within an inch of his face, and several times smote him spitefully upon the cheek.

Owen Redgrave bore this treatment with as much fortitude as he could muster, though with a gathering rage at his heart.

Had he had it in his power but then, he would have exterminated all savage tribes, and swept them for ever from the earth.

The old hag would have proceeded to greater extre-mities than these very probably, had not the chief who was left in charge of him chosen to interfere.

"Leave him alone, Minatowa!" he said. "Wait, if you can, with patience until to-morrow."

The hag's eyes gleamed brightly at these words, and she waved on high her fist.

"Till to-morrow!—till to-morrow!" she cried, and disappeared in the surrounding gloom, which hid her from his sight, like some spirit of evil.

Left to himself, he tried in vain to go to sleep, and dozing and waking again at intervals, contrived somehow or other to pass away the time until daybreak.

Very early the camp was stirring; and it was with no enviable feelings that Owen perceived preparations were being made for his torture.

When the savages had had their meal, he was brought out and fastened to a stake in the middle of an open space, round which the whole tribe collected, ready to enjoy the sight prepared for them.

The elaborate agony which the captive was to suffer would afford great enjoyment, Owen well knew, to these wretches. But he was determined that the most fearful torments should not wring from him any acknowledgment of his own weakness.

They fastened him to the post in such a way that his head only had the power of moving. The first ceremony to be performed was for the young chiefs to fling their knives in such a way that they should enter the post not more than an inch from his head, but still not cut him.

The reason his head was left at liberty was that the savages might have the pleasure of seeing their prisoner wildly endeavour to dodge the coming blow, and laugh at his feeble efforts to avoid the death that threatened him.

When this was done the tomahawks were thrown, and after that rifle practice commenced, his head being the point to be avoided, but the surrounding woodwork, a hair's breadth from it, the part to be hit.

Owen, through this trying scene, bore all bravely, and though every moment he expected would be his last, he flinched not the least to avoid the deadly steel, the murderous axe, the death-dealing lead.

But this stoicism upon his part rendered the savages more vindictive.

They were determined that he should suffer, and that the real tortures should no longer be delayed.

They brought piles of brushwood, therefore, and placed them round the post where he was fastened helpless.

They arranged them at such a distance that they would roast him slowly, and so prolong his misery.

Then diabolical contrivances were thought of, such as sharp-pointed chips of pine wood to be thrust into his flesh, and lighted.

The savages gathered around, and gave way to hideous shriekings, and gibings, and jeerings—the women particularly being loudest and most cruel in this horrible pastime.

His last moment was fast approaching!

There was no help for him now.

The woman whom he had saved had deserted him.

He must die!

He cast his eyes despairingly around, not hoping for any help; yet, somehow, fancying that he could not thus miserably terminate his career.

The savages piled up the brushwood, and one of them brought forth the torch which was to ignite his funereal pile.

One of the chiefs advanced with a piece of the sharp-pointed pine before alluded to.

In another moment his martyrdom would commence.

The fire had been applied to some portion of the brushwood, which blazed up fiercely

Death—grim and horrible death stared him in the face! Death by fire!

CHAPTER XVIII.

THE ATTACK.

IT was a fearful moment. The flickering flames, if possible, enhanced the ferocity which distorted the features of the savages as they rent the air with one universal yell of fiendish delight at the anticipation of their victim's coming sufferings.

Owen's captors were maddened and intoxicated, as it were, by their evil passions, and naught but the most fearful cruelties committed upon their unhappy captive would content them.

But Providence did not intend that he should thus, in the depth of the gloomy forest, and at the hands of these human wild beasts, miserably pant out his last gasp of life.

No; greater things were expected of him—a wild and adventurous career lay before him.

His time had not yet come.

No; for at the moment that the fire was being applied to what was intended to be his funereal pile—at the moment that the savage who was to be the prime instrument of his torture was approaching Owen, with one of those sharp splinters of pine wood in his hand to which allusion has already been made,—as, indeed, he was bending over the victim, a gleam of cruel malignity in his face—he started back with a shrill cry, and placing his hand upon his breast, fell over on his back.

Owen started in astonishment at this strange event, but a moment afterwards the truth flashed upon him.

The fierce yells of the savages had drowned the sound of the rifle which had laid their comrade low.

But this one shot was followed next moment by the report of at least a score.

A sharp and deadly fire had opened upon the camp from the trees.

A loud hurrah then rent the air, and at the same time a body of troopers came galloping down the hill, mercilessly cutting down all who stood in their way.

The aspect of affairs was instantly changed.

The wildest confusion, terror, and dismay possessed the savages, who ran frantically to and fro, endeavouring to escape, though in vain.

Deafening shouts rent the air, interspersed by shrieks and groans.

On all sides was heard the sharp cracking of the rifles, and now and again the clashing of steel, when the Indians and their exterminators came to a hand-to-hand conflict.

The ordinarily wily and cautious savages had, upon this occasion, been taken completely by surprise, so devoted were they to their dreadful occupation.

Now they yelled in dismay, and struggled desperately, but impotently, to avoid the doom which threatened them.

The scene was a fearful one!

The horsemen galloped furiously to and fro, slaying all they could, without pity.

Women vainly begged for mercy, and children screamed and fled before their ruthless destroyers.

When the horsemen had expended their fire, they fell furiously upon the savages with the butt-ends of their rifles, which they wielded clubwise.

Others fell upon the Indians with their knives, and mowed them down like grass, for they were all so panic-stricken that they were capable of offering no resistance.

Frantically did they run to and fro among the trees, endeavouring to escape, but upon every side did the troopers surround them and cut off retreat.

Some backed into corners, and prepared to sell their lives as dearly as possible, fighting madly to the last.

But these, in time, fell beneath the deadly weapons of their assailants.

At length the last of the dogged and hounded savages was destroyed, with the exception of a few of the most beautiful of the Indian maidens, whom their captors took away with them as their slaves.

Then were the tents ransacked, and the valuables found there appropriated, and then a raging fire consumed to ashes all that remained of the Indian encampment in the forest.

The ruins smouldered. The dying embers drifted mournfully in the wind, and wreaths of faint blue smoke curled slowly upward from the black and charred remains of the smouldering ruins.

So the day wore slowly on after the troopers had departed, and darkness fell like a cloak upon the dreary scene of death and desolation.

* * * * *

And Owen Redgrave, all this time, what had been his fate?

He had received, at the commencement of the affray, a severe wound, which had rendered him senseless.

What else had befallen him, he knew not, for he had lain in this state for many hours—for how long, he had no means of judging.

When consciousness returned, he found that he had been freed from the thongs which had bound him to what had so nearly proved his death-stake.

He was lying upon his back on the grass, and a heavy weight lay across his breast.

He slowly and painfully raised his head to look at it, and saw, with a shuddering horror impossible to describe, that it was the corpse of one of the massacred savages.

With a violent effort he freed himself from this incubus, and crept into an upright posture.

He leant against a tree and pressed his hands to his throbbing temples, wondering, for a time, where he was, and what had happened.

Gradually, however, the remembrance of past events came back to his mind.

He listened intently, but the silence of the grave reigned around him.

Here and there, among the trampled, bloodstained grass, the pale moon's rays fell upon the bodies of the dead Indians.

Owen felt that he was the only living creature there, and an awful dread falling upon him, caused his limbs to tremble as though with the ague, and his teeth to chatter in his head.

He must leave this place, he thought.

If he had strength enough to drag himself away—to crawl to some distant spot, and die, he would do so.

He could not remain here.

But he was miserably weak and sickly, and he had barely gone fifty yards from the scene of terror before he sank down again exhausted upon the ground.

He felt miserably ill—well-nigh sick unto death.

"Oh, home! oh, Grace!" he murmured faintly, in his suffering; "shall I ever see you more!"

CHAPTER XIX.

A PERPLEXING DISCOVERY.

IT would be wearisome to give a detailed account of the events of the next three or four days of Owen Redgrave's life.

The monotonous misery and suffering which he endured.

The hours of almost intolerable pain, the pangs of thirst, the unendurable fatigue of travel in the wretched state in which he was, very nearly crushed him.

On, on—still wandering through the trackless forest, feeding, when he took any food at all, upon wild berries and birds' eggs.

He had not neglected to bring away with him from the field of battle one of the savage's rifles and some ammunition, but it was more for the purposes of defence than offence that he carried these, for he could not have eaten the flesh of any animal in his weakly state, had he shot one.

Creeping slowly and laboriously onward, chance brought him at length to the boundaries of the forest.

And then he came upon an awful swamp.

He struggled through the narrow openings between the trees, with difficulty forcing a passage through the dense undergrowth.

He forced his way between the narrow openings which the closely growing pollards afforded.

Ever and anon, he was compelled to crawl beneath tangled and matted masses of vines and interwoven boughs.

Then he reached a swampy opening, where tall straggling grass grew among the trees, and where the bottom felt soft and treacherous beneath his feet.

It was night when this happened, and there was a thick fog.

Ere he had advanced many steps, his feet sank into the mud.

Sank deeper and deeper as he advanced.

He turned and tried a new course, but with the same result.

Creeping onward cautiously and in terror, for every moment he expected to sink up to his neck in the bog, he found himself at last upon the margin of a dark and silent stream.

He was upon the bank of a wide and gloomy bayou, the still, murky waters of which extended far beyond the reach of his vision.

On all sides grew tangled wild wood up to the water's edge.

Suddenly he was startled by a movement in the water close to his feet.

He gazed down earnestly.

A dark, shadowy form rose slowly towards him.

A huge, black head parted the water.

The head of some horrible reptile.

It was an alligator.

He uttered involuntarily a loud cry of alarm, and shrunk away from the spot.

He pushed his way through the bushes, turning every now and then with a shudder when some rustling made him think that one of the horrible brutes was pursuing him.

But he was so exhausted with his day's journey, that he was compelled at any risk to rest himself.

He found a sitting-place upon a dry knoll, where grew a large willow, and here, nursing his rifle, he determined to pass the night.

All around was dark as pitch; the air was damp and bitterly cold.

The savage howl of wild beasts smote upon his ear.

The discordant screeching of the birds of night, and the shrill jabberings of the monkeys.

The hoarse croaking of frogs, and the rustling and hissing of venomous snakes.

It was a night of horror—an endless night of weary watching, alarm, and terror.

When morning came, he thanked heaven for his safe deliverance, and again resumed his perilous journey.

But daylight dissipated much of the horror of the situation.

He was able now, with some degree of certainty, to pick his way across the swamp.

There was nothing in the faintest degree resembling a pathway across this trackless waste, but by proceeding very cautiously he could form a pretty shrewd guess respecting the nature of the ground over which he had to pass.

He had no idea in what direction he should go; he had no means of telling whither his steps were leading him.

But he held on his way with a brave heart, hoping that his journey would soon come to an end.

Nor was he disappointed, for the end was very near at hand.

He came out soon upon a very wide, barren spot, where only the most stunted grass grew in patches here and there; and crossing this, he entered again upon what seemed to him to be an interminable forest.

But he had not proceeded very far in this direction before a sight which met his view brought him to a sudden standstill.

Could he believe his own eyes? Yes—it was indeed a human habitation.

A small wooden hut, it appeared to be; and as there was no smoke rising from its one solitary chimney—or, rather, from the hole in the roof which served in this primitive dwelling in a chimney's place—Owen supposed that it was uninhabited.

But he dare not approach it too recklessly.

The greatest caution was necessary in this wild country, where, on every side, enemies abounded.

How could he tell but that some savage might here reside, or a nest of savages, into whose hands he would fall again, and perish miserably?

He was resolved, however, that he would brave whatever danger might exist.

At the same time, he was determined not to be taken altogether unawares, and he carefully examined the priming of his rifle before he approached.

He parted the underwood which blocked the pathway, and walked cautiously.

So noiseless, indeed, were his movements, that he might very easily have neared the hut, and taken an observation of its inmates through a narrow slit in the wall, which served for a window, without much fear of detection, even though the persons in the inside were on the alert, and anticipating his arrival.

But nothing of the sort was now the case.

Within the hut all was perfectly silent—as silent as the tomb.

The door stood wide open, and Owen peered cautiously into the interior.

The hut consisted only of one room, and it was very roughly furnished; and yet there was a strange collection of articles, which it was difficult to account for having been gathered together at that wild spot.

Who could have brought them? Owen wondered. Had they been given to the owner of the hut?

Did they belong to him, or had he stolen them?

Owen stepped across the threshold cautiously, and looked about him.

He could see no sign of life, and a death-like silence reigned around.

The furniture of the apartment consisted of a rough wooden table, and two clumsy chairs, a curiously carved oak cupboard, and two oil paintings, in heavy frames, of a somewhat elaborate design.

Two or three guns were ranged upon the walls, and a spear, and a sword, and a scabbard of curious workmanship. Several vases and vessels of china, with painted flowers upon their sides, which proved their worth to be considerable, stood upon a roughly-hewn plank, which served as a mantelpiece, over the place where the fire was lighted upon a groundwork of stones, jammed tightly together, and knocked into some sort of shape, to serve the purpose of a grate.

There were, also, two large trunks, of quaint workmanship, and evidently very old, secured by ponderous locks.

"But where's the bed, I wonder?" thought Owen. "Does the owner sleep upon the floor?"

He saw a large rusty key, hanging upon a nail against the wall, and could not help thinking that it must fit one of the boxes; but, although he felt not a little curious to know what might be their contents, he did not feel himself justified in looking.

"There must be an owner," he said to himself, "and I suppose he will presently be here."

He thought the best thing to do, then, was to take a seat, and wait with what patience he could muster.

It was late in the afternoon—evening was fast approaching.

The owner of the hut would surely return from the chase which Owen supposed was occupying him.

He waited a very long while, though; and the twilight began to thicken into darkness, and yet no sign was there of the absentee.

After a while, Owen, more for occupation than aught else, began to make an inspection of the room, and to look more closely at the things which it contained.

The two big boxes again attracted his attention, and he inspected them attentively.

To his surprise, he found that the lid of one of them had been burst open.

He raised the lid, and found that the contents of the box were of a very trumpery character—a collection of worthless odds and ends.

The other box in like fashion he tried, and was again astonished to find that this also had been broken into, and the contents thrown into a state of confusion.

This set him thinking; and, upon finding that the lock had been prised off the cupboard, he could not help supposing that a felonious motive had prompted these acts.

When he looked round, he fancied that the floor of the hut showed signs of a struggle having taken place there—a desperate struggle, he thought, for there were marks of heels upon the clay floor.

And when he came, to scrutinize the ground, he was to his horror, that there were several drops of blood.

What did it mean? Had the owner of the hut been robbed and murdered?

Was that why he did not return?

As well as Owen could judge, he must now have passed more than three hours awaiting the return of the unknown.

He turned the question well over in his mind, and decided that he would wait no longer.

No, he thought if the owner had ever intended to return, he would not have left the door of the hut unfastened.

Still, it was late; and the terrors and dangers of the swamp, which he had so recently surmounted, were not to be again lightly encountered. After a short deliberation he determined to remain in the hut, at all events, for the night, and not attempt to recross the dreary tract of land until he had rested and recovered himself from his exertions.

Then there were plans for the future to be made.

What should he do?

Whither should he bend his step

Those should be deliberations for the next morning.

Acting upon his idea of passing the night in the deserted hut, he gathered together what dry sticks and leaves he could find in the neighbourhood, and endeavoured to light a fire; but the morass, in the centre of which this strange dwelling was situated, afforded him but little burning material, and the shades of night were falling before he could obtain the least heat from the damp wood which crackled and spluttered on the floor of the hut.

The pangs of hunger, too, were becoming acute.

In what direction should he turn for food?

He left the hut with his gun, in the hope some bird might fall to his weapon, but he saw none.

He dared not venture far in the rapidly-increasing darkness, through fear of losing the track and being engulfed in the treacherous swamp.

When Owen returned to the hut hungry and weary, the sense of extreme desolation came upon him.

Miles and miles away from any human habitation, friendless, and a stranger to the country, how could he hope to survive?

Would he have strength to retrace his steps?

Supposing himself capable of doing so, what dangers were there not awaiting him?

Were he again to fall into the hands of the Indians, he could not expect to escape a second time.

Thus gloomily reflecting, he cowered over the embers of the apology for a fire, which gave forth much smoke, but little warmth.

As a last resource, he determined to ransack the hut, in the hope of finding some morsel wherewith to assuage his hunger.

A few old bottles, a pickaxe and spade, an old flint gun, long since disabled; and last of all, in an old battered tin case, some four or five ship biscuits, green and mildewed in parts, but yet fit to eat.

Words cannot describe the joy with which he seized the hard biscuits.

Eagerly and ravenously he applied one to his mouth, but hungry as he was, his teeth were unable to obtain the mastery over them.

Filling an old tin drinking cup with water, he sopped the biscuits, and thus made a meal which, to any one less hungry, would have been most repulsive; but he was too nearly famished to note the taste, and the rotten biscuit and swamp water afforded him a meal, which was all he required.

Raking the embers of the fire together, securing the door to the best of his ability, and placing his gun within easy reach of his hand, Owen Redgrave lay down, and shortly fell asleep.

A strange, disturbed slumber it was, in which the events of his life appeared prominently before him in vivid dreams.

Again he saw himself in the hands of the savages; again the lovely Indian girl was by his side, relating that strange, incomprehensible story of her life, so full of mystery and adventure.

Suddenly he awoke with a start.

His dreams were dispelled, as he raised himself upon his arm and looked around, unable for the moment to remember where he was.

A cold shudder passed through his frame as he felt he was no longer alone in the hut.

The fire had almost died out, and on every side of him was darkness.

He leant forward, and strove to peer through it, in vain.

He listened intently, but no sound fell upon his ear.

Yet he felt certain some one besides himself was in the hut.

Who could it be?

Had the rightful owner returned?

Was it some wanderer, some outcast like himself, who had come thither to rest for the night?

Owen felt carefully along the ground for his gun.

It was gone!

He could not be mistaken; he knew the exact spot in which he had placed it, and it was no longer there.

Weak with his wound and recent exertions, powerless and defenceless, what now would be his fate?

Into whose hands had he fallen?

In feeling for his gun, his hand had come in contact with a piece of paper.

With that he hoped to make a momentary blaze, by which to discover who was the other occupant of the hut.

The suspense was becoming intolerable, and he felt he must learn his fate.

Owen cast the paper upon the red glow of the wood-ash, and waited with beating heart the result.

The paper turned, scorched, and blackened on the embers, caught fire, and sent up for a moment a bright column of flame.

Then again all was dark.

Still, that one moment had been sufficient to show Owen what he wanted.

Stretched out upon the floor on the opposite side of the fire was the figure of a tall, muscular negro.

His black face was relieved by a quantity of white hair, and a short, grizzled beard covered his chin.

No more than this, and that his general appearance was repulsive, had Owen time to observe.

A cold dew stood upon his forehead, as in the darkness he still fancied he saw the ebony features of the negro, with two small, glittering eyes fixed upon him.

But in that he was mistaken, for the black was asleep.

Owen was no coward; but the dread of remaining for the rest of the night in the hut with the negro seized him.

He knew not what he feared; but yet a foreboding of something dreadful warned him to fly before it was too late.

But whither?

It would but be a different fate were he to wander helpless and unarmed through the dreary swamp, exposed to all the dangers of Indians and wild beasts.

He waited some little while longer; but the knowledge of the negro's presence gave him no rest, and he rose to his feet, and felt carefully along the wall of the hut for the door.

He reached it; and in another moment would have been in the open air, when a savage yell from the negro told him that his escape was discovered.

Before he had time to act, the black's fingers were at his throat.

In another moment Owen was hurled violently to the ground.

His assailant knelt upon his chest; and in the darkness Owen could only see the bright eyes of the negro twinkling like a cat's, as he tightened his clutch on his windpipe.

Owen was rapidly becoming insensible.

He was on the verge of strangulation.

The suddenness of the attack had deprived him of all power, and he could offer no resistance.

Suddenly the negro's hold relaxed.

The fingers clasped his throat with less and less power.

The clutch was taken from his throat.

The eyes no longer glared at him.

His chest was relieved from the weight; and the black, with a low moan of pain, relinquished his victim at the very moment of victory.

But Owen, though conscious of all this at the time, was too much exhausted to make any use of his freedom.

The assault had been so severe, and so nearly had he been brought face to face with death, that, although liberated, he was insensible, and lay so for some time.

When he recovered consciousness he was at a loss to understand what had happened, and would almost have treated the whole affair as a frightful fancy of the brain, or as a dreadful dream, had not the pain in his throat told him it was indeed a reality.

He could not in the least account for his miraculous escape.

Why should the negro have relinquished his hold, when in another second he would have accomplished his diabolical purpose?

Owen moved cautiously, dreading another onslaught; but only the sound of hard breathing, and occasional low moaning, met his ear.

What did it all mean?

Had he unconsciously wounded his assailant in the struggle?

Collecting together everything combustible, he heaped it into the smouldering ashes, and fanned the red glow steadily with his hat, till he saw the sparks communicate one with another, and at last burst forth into a ruddy blaze.

By the light thus obtained he saw stretched on the ground the body of the negro, his face distorted with pain.

He was quite insensible.

Only by painful, laboured breathing did he show that life yet remained in him.

The cause of his unconsciousness was soon apparent to Owen.

In some way he had received a terrific blow upon the side of his head, from which the blood was slowly oozing, matting his white hair with its crimson clots.

Owen's first impulse was with a blow to put him out of his misery; but when he approached him nearer, and perceived that he was a very old man, and that to all appearances the wound he had received was not mortal, he relented.

The black, in his enfeebled state, he argued, could do him no harm; therefore he determined to wait till morning, and then, if possible, unravel the mystery in which the whole affair was shrouded.

It was a long, weary watch.

Owen was fearful of sleeping, dreading another attack.

All the means at his disposal for obtaining light were at an end, and there was nothing for it but to wait with what patience he could for morning.

He welcomed with joy that may be easily imagined the first streak of light in the banks of grey clouds in the east; and as the sun rose and dispelled the noxious mists which arose from the dismal swamp, he hailed with delight the termination of what had appeared to him the longest night he had ever passed.

The negro still lay senseless on the ground.

The blood had ceased to flow from the wound, and he appeared to be in less pain than when by the firelight Owen had first seen the injury.

Owen did what little lay in his power to ease the black's sufferings.

He owed him nothing, certainly, but he could not bear to leave a fellow creature to struggle alone with death in that dreary hut.

He bathed the wound, and shortly had the satisfaction of discovering his patient was regaining consciousness.

"My treasure—my treasure!" groaned the wounded man. "He thought to have it, but I killed him; yes, killed the white-faced dog;" and the negro chuckled malevolently.

"What treasure?" asked Owen, interested.

The black raised himself upon his elbow, and glared evilly at Owen. Had he possessed the power, he would have felled him to the ground.

"Ha! ha!" he laughed. "You thought to get it—to steal it away—to rob me of it, but old Jack was too many for you;" and, with another fiendish chuckle, he fell back exhausted.

"What could it mean?" Owen asked himself.

Was he but listening to the ravings of a madman, or had this black, living alone in the wretched hut in the middle of the gloomy swamp, managed to amass treasure?

All questioning was in vain.

The negro would give no account of it.

At times he babbled freely, but in an incoherent manner, of sacks of gold and chests full of doubloons, and then Owen would ask him, " Where is all this gold of which you talk?"

" What gold?"

" The treasure you say you have hidden away."

" I? I am but a poor negro—an escaped slave. What could I have to do with gold?" he would ask, in a piteous, whining tone. Then suddenly changing, his eyes would glare fiercely, and he would cry, " Who says I have treasure hidden? He lies. I will kill him—kill him as I did the white-faced cur who thought to steal it from me while I slept."

Later in the day, while Owen still watched by the negro's side, he started up, and with an abject, imploring expression, cried, " I am an old man—a very old man, and have not long to live. Do not torture me, and I will confess all."

Owen drew close to him.

" What have you to confess?" he asked.

" Who are you? I do not know you! Get hence!" cried the black, raising his arm to strike him, but the exertion was too great, and he fell back upon the floor, senseless.

At first, Owen thought he was dead, but after a while he detected the faint pulsation of his heart.

He raised him gently, and applied such restoratives as were to be obtained.

When the black recovered consciousness he no longer raved of his treasure, but talked more calmly.

His senses had returned to him.

" Who are you?" he asked, suspiciously fixing his glittering eyes on Owen's face.

" An Englishman."

" What brought you here?"

" Chance."

" Where are you going?"

" I do not know."

Then, apparently for the first time noticing the care and attention Owen had bestowed upon him in bathing and binding up his wound, he asked, " Who has done this?" indicating the bandages round his head.

" I have."

" For what purpose?"

" To preserve your life."

" Why should you wish to do that?"

" Have you never heard of charity?"

" Charity! Ha! ha! Charity from a white to a black? Yes, in the shape of torture, scourgings, curses, and cruelty! Kindness, never!"

" Nevertheless, I had no other object."

" Tell me how you came here?"

Owen recounted all his adventures, to which the negro listened with great attention; more especially to the narrative of the abduction of the beautiful English girl by the Indians.

He made Owen give a most minute description of her appearance, and nodded his head repeatedly with apparent satisfaction.

" You wish to see her again?" he asked.

" Yes; how can you doubt it?"

The negro laughed.

" Do you know where she is?"

" Yes."

" Where?"

The black did not reply.

" Speak! Tell me, for heaven's sake!" cried Owen, eagerly.

" She is a prisoner."

" Among the Indians?"

" No."

" Who, then, dares to detain her? Do you know?"

" Yes; I know the man," said the negro, slowly,

and with so much concentrated bitterness and hatred that Owen stared at him, astonished.

" Wait with me till to-morrow," continued the black. " I will make it worth your while, and then you shall hear the story of my life."

Owen agreed to do so.

CHAPTER XX.

THE NEGRO'S STORY.

THOUGH Owen had agreed to wait till the following day to attend upon the black, he more than once reproached himself with folly in so doing; for though the prospect of discovering the place where the lovely girl was confined, and the probability of becoming a sharer in the hidden treasure of the negro, were great inducements, still he was almost led to believe that the black's words were but the senseless ravings of a lunatic, and that to remain in the hut alone with him would be exposing himself to another attack from the madman.

However, having given his word, he resolved to abide by it.

The negro directed him to a hollow tree close to the hut, which this eccentric individual was accustomed to use as a larder, and there Owen found abundance of food, in the shape of such birds as frequented the swamp.

That day Owen fared sumptuously. The hard biscuit was thrown on one side for better fare; and, altogether, he had no reason to be dissatisfied with his new quarters, though it must be confessed that, as night came on, he felt somewhat doubtful about sleeping, dreading another attack from the black.

However, the night passed quietly; and when, the next morning, Owen resumed his duties as nurse, he could not fail to notice the alteration in the demeanour of the negro.

Kindness had done much to civilize him.

On the previous day his expression had been that of a tiger wounded and incapable of mischief, but still thirsting for blood.

Now it was quite changed.

He accepted Owen's little attentions with gratitude; and when he reminded him of his promise to relate his story, he at once proffered his readiness to begin.

" It matters little," commenced the negro, " either when or where I was born. My early history would neither interest nor benefit you in any way. Suffice it, while I was yet young, I was sold as a slave into one of the West Indian colonies, where, for years, I led a life of toiling, merry-making, cursing, and pilfering.

" I got tired of hard work and harder blows, and ran away.

" I was caught, taken back, and flogged till the flesh hung in stripes upon my back.

" Then it was I joined with others as discontented and as badly-used as myself. They were ready for rebellion, but could not lay their plans. I became their leader, and under me they prospered."

" In what way?" asked Owen.

" One dark night, the owner's house, which was built partly of bamboo and other inflammable material, caught fire. There was a high wind, and in ten minutes it was one mass of flame."

" And that was your work?"

" It was."

" And the owner—what became of him?"

" No one who was in the house escaped."

" Horrible!"

" Not so. It was but the law of retaliation," said the negro, coldly.

"Well, well! Go on!"

"My four comrades and myself escaped in the bustle and confusion, and hid away in caves and swamps till the search for us was at an end."

"How did you subsist during that time?"

"Perhaps you had better not ask," replied the black, gloomily. "When fruit and berries failed us, and one of our companions died, we——"

"Hush!" cried Owen. "It is too horrible!"

"After a while, a band of five blacks became the terror of the whole country. Nothing was safe from them. Houses were broken into, goods extracted, and, in some instances, lives were sacrificed. No one dared venture alone into the country roads. This band of black marauders earned for themselves a terrible name. Not a woman but shuddered when she heard it ; not a man but looked to his weapons when it was mentioned."

"And you were one of them ?" asked Owen.

"I was their leader."

Owen could not repress a shudder when he found the character of the man whose wounds he had dressed—whose life he had preserved—and with whom he now was face to face.

"Continue," said he.

"After a while, our deeds became too daring, a price was set upon my head by Government, and a body of soldiers sent to capture us. I alone escaped."

"How did you manage that?"

"I had spies, who warned me of my danger in time. I made my way to the nearest seaport, with all the booty I could collect together at so short a notice, and, twelve hours before the soldiers surprised my band in their haunt, I was on board a fast-sailing schooner, standing out to sea with a favourable wind."

"And what became of your companions?"

"Oh, they were shot down in about five minutes."

"Could you not have saved them?"

"I don't know. I didn't try."

"Well, go on."

"The ship in which I had taken a passage was wrecked, but again I was saved from destruction, and, together with the most valuable part of my spoil, cast ashore on a desolate, rocky coast."

"What happened to you there?"

"I was found lying stunned and bleeding on the shore, by some white-faced men, I believe to have been Portuguese settlers. They seemed sociable and friendly enough, but when I asked them for food and shelter, appeared frightened, and gave me to understand there was some great lord, without whose permission they dared do nothing."

"Who was this great man?"

"I cannot say."

"Did you never hear his name?"

"Never."

"Do you know anything respecting him?"

"Yes," lisped the negro, between his clenched teeth. "I know that if I could have his blood I should die happy !"

"How has he wronged you?"

"I will tell you. When he heard my story, or, rather, such a story as I chose to tell him, he received me into his house, treated me kindly, and appeared so friendly towards me, that I was fool enough to believe him."

"Did he betray you?"

"He would have done so, but that I overheard the plot."

"How was that?"

"I found that his cupidity had been aroused by the sight of the gold I had with me, and that he had formed a design to possess himself of my treasure, and sell me into slavery."

"How did you thwart him?"

"By flight. I gathered together all my portable wealth, stole a horse, and, by incessant journeying, at the end of two days arrived here. Feeling it was a safe retreat, and not daring to venture amongst white men, I built myself this hut, buried my treasure, and have now, as well as I can calculate, lived here eight years, daily increasing my wealth, and——"

"Increasing your wealth? By what means?"

"Within five hundred yards of this hut is a stream, the sand of which abounds with gold, which day by day I gather and add to my hoard."

"For what purpose? What use is it to you?"

"What use? Is there no pleasure, do you think, in turning over the precious metal—in plunging your hands into the glittering fragments—in the knowledge that those who call themselves my superiors have not the same weight of iron in their possession? That I have gold—that I could buy up kings and emperors? But I am old—very old," continued the negro, suddenly altering his tone, "and gold cannot undo the work of years."

For a long time the negro remained silent, and Owen, too, was busy with his own thoughts.

Was it true? he asked himself.

Had the black really stated facts, or had he been listening to the ravings of delirium?

The negro continued his narrative.

"Till yesterday, I had not seen a white face for eight years."

"And that was mine," observed Owen.

"I saw yours, it is true, but I saw others as well."

"What others?"

"The face of him I hate most upon earth—the man I told you of."

"You say you do not know his name?"

"I do not."

"How came you to see him?"

"I had wandered farther than is my custom from the hut, and suddenly found myself surrounded by white men, who seized and roughly dragged me before their chief, who appeared to be out on some hunting expedition. At all events, he had several Indians with him ; while, by his side, was the girl whose form and features you described last night."

Owen rose from his seat, and walked angrily across the hut.

"What is to be done?" he cried. "How can I, single-handed, cope with a band of armed men? Yet, to leave her in *his* grasp—oh, it is distraction! Go on with your story! Tell me quickly—how did she look—what did she say?"

"I cannot answer your questions."

"Why not?"

"Because, at a signal from the tyrant, she was removed, and he and I were left face to face He recognised me at once, and questioned me concerning my treasure. I evaded him—he threatened—angry words were spoken, and I was surrounded and tightly bound. Again and again I was promised liberty, if I would but reveal where I had concealed my treasure ; but the more they cajoled and threatened me, the more stedfastly I held my tongue."

"How did you effect your escape?"

"I watched my opportunity, and, by a violent effort, burst asunder the bonds which held me, tumbled down two or three men who stood near me, receiving in return this cut on the head with a sword, and then took to my heels, and ran across the swamp as fast as my legs would carry me."

"Were you not pursued?"

"Yes ; but those who followed did not know the track, and sunk deeper into the mire than they liked, so soon gave up the pursuit."

"You made your way to this hut?"

No. 7.—THE BUCCANEERS.

"Yes; and on arriving here, found a man, with a gun by his side, lying asleep on the floor. I did not doubt but that it was one of the band I thought I had escaped, who had discovered my retreat, and was on the point of strangling him as he lay there in his sleep, when the loss of blood, consequent upon the wound in my head, caused me to faint."

"Twice, then, I am indebted to that wound for saving my life; for afterwards, when your fingers were at my throat, and I was at my last gasp, I suppose it was again sudden faintness which caused your hold to relax?"

"It was."

"So I supposed."

"Now, in return for the story of your life, I have given you an outline of mine. An hour later you would not have heard it."

"Why not?"

"I could not have told it you."

"What do you mean?"

"I feel that my end is approaching."

"Nonsense!"

"It is the truth. I am a very old man. The shock, after so many years of excitement, has been too much for me."

"Don't give way. You'll be all right in a day or two."

"Never!"

"What makes you think so?"

"I am sure of it. I feel death approaching. Give me some water."

Owen did as he was desired, and then sat by the side of the dying negro, watching him gasping painfully for breath.

It was a strange scene. The wild, weird log hut, destitute of furniture, and into which, through the aperture which did duty for a window, the last rays of the setting sun streamed in, lighting up the two figures, leaving the rest of the interior in darkness.

Strange, too, were the figures.

The still athletic form of the old negro stretched upon the floor, his white beard straying about his swarthy visage, where it had escaped from the bandage which bound his head, and by his side the handsome young Englishman, with rude, travel-stained garments, supporting the black in his stalwart arms, and ever and anon moistening his lips with water.

This was the scene the sun witnessed, as he slowly sunk, like a ball of crimson fire, behind the luxuriant weeds and rushes of the dismal swamp.

Day gave way to night, and still the two remained in much the same attitude, the negro occasionally showing life still remained in him by giving utterance to low, feeble moans of pain.

Owen, wearied with his self-imposed task, dozed as he sat by the side of the negro.

It was scarcely sleep, for the least movement on the part of the sufferer aroused him; and when the old man spoke in low, quivering tones, Owen heard them and listened.

"Come close to me," said the dying one. "Be sure no one is listening, and I will tell you a secret."

Owen bent his head so as to catch the last words which fell from the lips of the dying man.

"I thought when I died," continued the negro, "my secret would die with me. I did not think a stranger would inherit my treasure, but you have been kind to an old man—you are the only person who ever did him a good turn, and you shall reap your reward."

He paused from exhaustion, and Owen again moistened his lips.

Then he continued: "The old hollow stump of tree where I kept my food—there you will find my treasure; dig deep down at the roots, and keep what what you find. I could almost bring the lips, so ter-

riably familiar with curses, to bless you for your kindness and charity to an old negro; but—but——"

He never concluded his sentence.

For some moments he struggled in vain to utter the words which rose to his lips, and then, with a groan, fell heavily back upon the floor of the hut.

Owen pressed his fingers on the old negro's wrist.

The pulse had ceased to beat.

He placed his hand upon his heart.

It gave no sign of life.

He was dead!

The whole night through Owen Redgrave sat by the side of the corpse, weaving plans for the future. Bright golden plans they were, in which the negro's hoard was to play a prominent part.

He longed for daylight, that he might make sure that after all it had not been a delusion; that the coins and gold dust were solid realities, not having sole existence in the disordered brain of the negro who now lay lifeless by his side.

At length day dawned.

As the grey light came stealing gradually over the swamp, Owen arose and searched for the pickaxe and spade.

These he easily found, and with one more glance at the black, to make sure life had in truth departed, he shouldered the implements, and went forth into the air to dig for his fortune.

_____

CHAPTER XXI.

OWEN REDGRAVE DIGS FOR A FORTUNE.

IN the pale light of early morning, Owen Redgrave dug manfully at the root of the old tree.

Down, down he went into the earth, until he began to suspect that either the treasure was a myth or else that he had mistaken the spot.

But, no—the latter could not be the case, for trees were few.

Around him on every side rose luxuriant, large-leaved plants; and there, at no great distance from the hut, stood the stem of what had once been a goodly-sized tree.

No other was near, so again he set too at his work with renewed vigour, only pausing occasionally to recover his breath.

Still there was no sign of the treasure.

The sun rose high in the heavens, and still he dug on, throwing out the earth, but the hole he had made was deep, and he had often to pause, for the sun was powerful and the labour great.

"Psha!" he exclaimed, "what am I doing! Slaving for a madman's fancy. I will do no more!"

So saying, he stuck the pickaxe hard into the soil.

The iron came in contact with some hard substance, and jarred his hand. Hope revived within him, and again he set to work.

Half an hour's labour disclosed a flat, white stone, and yet another half-hour, and he raised it with a pick.

The negro's words were true!

There, beneath the stone, lay gold in greater profusion than Owen had ever seen it before.

With a wild cry of delight, he plunged his arms into the glittering metal, drawing out handfuls, filling his pockets, his coat, his cap—in short, everything which could by any possibility be made to contain the precious ore.

While he was thus occupied, he was startled by the fall of some earth from the top upon his bare head.

Looking upwards for a moment, he saw a face gazing down upon him.

The glance he obtained was so momentary that he could form no idea as to who it was thus playing the spy upon him.

A cold perspiration stood upon his brow.

Great as the wealth was at his feet, the greed of gain was so strong upon him, he could not bear the idea of sharing it with any one.

For some little while he stood irresolute, not knowing what to do, and then slowly and cautiously he ascended from the hole he had dug, by means of steps he had cut as he went down.

He reached the surface, and there a sight met his eyes which, for the time, rendered him powerless with fright.

The negro he had left for dead in the log hut stood upright before him, his eyes glaring and distended, his whole air that of a lunatic.

In his hand he held a long, sharp-pointed knife, and as Owen gained the surface, with a frantic yell he rushed at him, brandishing the weapon above his head.

It was his last act.

Ere he could reach the spot where Owen stood paralyzed, his strength gave way, and he fell heavily backwards—this time, in truth, dead.

He had before been only in a stupor, from which he had awoke after Owen's departure from the hut, and then, bereft of sense as he was, instinct had led him to the spot he had most frequented.

In his delirium he failed to recognise Owen, only seeing in him a robber who would bear away his treasure; and had not Death claimed him the moment he leaped forward, it would have fared badly with Owen.

It was some time before he could convince himself that this time the negro was really dead; but having done so, he removed the body to the tent, and then sat down to reflect calmly upon the plan he should pursue.

To take away the vast wealth he had discovered upon his person was an utter impossibility.

Yet how else could he hope to do it without making others the sharers of the secret?

As aforesaid, he had brought up with him as much as he could conceal about his person; he therefore, after mature deliberation, resolved upon closing the hole, marking the spot carefully, and returning whenever opportunity occurred to obtain fresh supplies.

But whither should he go?

He knew not where to bend his steps.

However, he took the precaution before dark of filling up the hole, and laboured hard to remove every trace of a disturbance in the earth, so that if, by any chance, strangers should pass the spot, nothing might be visible to excite their suspicions.

So ended another day in the dreary swamp.

Owen Redgrave's sleep that night was disturbed by strange dreams.

He thought Drake had discovered his secret, and was clamorous for his share of the negro's treasure, and that his voice grew louder and louder, and his tone more and more imperious.

Then the voice resolved itself into a reality, as Owen started from his slumber.

It was a loud and continuous knocking, which had awakened him, together with a voice, which shouted, "Open the door, you infernal black scoundrel, unless you want the place pulled about your ears."

It was broad daylight.

Owen's exertions had made him sleep soundly, and for a moment he scarcely comprehended where he was.

A glance round the hut told him.

His eyes rested upon the ghastly corpse of the negro, around whose head the bloodstained cloth was still bound, and which gave to his ebony features a still more horrible expression than that stamped upon them by death.

The cries outside the hut became more impatient, but before Owen could collect his senses sufficiently to make any answer to the reiterated summons, the whole dwelling was shaken violently, and with a wild huzza, the rude door, which Owen had barricaded the previous night, fell inwards, and a band of some dozen ruffians rushed in.

Owen caught up his gun, but saw resistance would be worse than useless, for what could he hope to do against so many?

For a short time he remained unnoticed, for the ruffians rushed at once to the corpse of the old negro, and crowded round it.

An exclamation of disappointment, mingled with one or two hearty curses, showed their disgust at finding death had been before them, and baulked them of their victim.

They presented a curious appearance these dozen men, who had so rudely entered the log hut.

In their dress they affected somewhat of a military air, while the shoulders of one of their number were decorated with epaulettes. Though an attempt had apparently been made at uniform, it was more ludicrous in appearance than military, and altogether their attire seemed to accord ill with their personal appearance.

A low-looking, beetle-browed lot of ruffians they were, who swaggered, swore, talked loudly and coarsely, blustered about, making a great deal of noise, and doing very little.

Owen was not long to escape observation.

The negro having been proved to be dead, he was quickly discovered, seized, and dragged violently towards the individual with the epaulettes, who seemed to possess some slight command over the others.

"Who are you?" asked that worthy member of society.

"My name is Owen Redgrave."

"What brings you here?"

"By what right do you ask?"

"By the right of being able to compel a reply."

"What do you want to know?"

"First of all, where that old nigger hid his treasure?"

"How should I know?"

"No prevarication—search him!" cried the officer (for so we must call him) to some of his subordinates.

The order was promptly executed, and from Owen's pockets came tumbling forth the bright coins, the possession of which, a few hours before, had caused him so much joy.

"I tell you what," said the officer; "it's plain enough to me that you've murdered that old fellow, and stolen his hoard."

"I—murder!" cried Owen, indignantly.

"Oh, it isn't the killing we mind—a nigger more or less ain't of much account; but when it comes to stealing the gold, that's another matter. Our captain has been trying all he knows to get that black rascal to give up his treasure, but couldn't do it, and now you'd very nearly marched off with it. Why, it was only two days ago," continued the loquacious officer, "we got that old nigger hard and fast, as we thought, and just as we were going to give him a taste of the hot pincers, to make him disclose his secret, hang me if he didn't make his escape, spoiling one of our best men, by knocking him over like a nine-pin, and drowning another, who tried to pursue him over the swamp."

"What is that you say?" cried Owen, eagerly. "Was this negro taken prisoner by you two days ago?"

"He was."

"And led before your captain?"

"Exactly."

"Tell me, then, has your captain a young captive Indian girl with him?"

"How did you know that?"

"Is it true?"

"It is; and as haughty, disdainful a bit of goods as I ever saw; although I don't wonder at the captain taking a fancy to her, for she's as pretty a lass as I've seen in the country, and the artful little baggage knows——"

"Silence!" yelled Owen. "Hold your tongue!"

The officer was so amazed at this sudden outburst, as to sit for a minute or two with open mouth, staring in blank astonishment at the man who evinced so little respect for his epaulettes; but recovering himself, he gave orders that Owen should be bound and carried away prisoner.

Far from this being disagreeable to Owen, it was the thing of all others he desired.

He had no doubt that the Indian girl detained prisoner by this mysterious captain was she of whom he was in search; and he trusted, though a prisoner, his good fortune would favour him so far as to allow him at least one interview with her.

The ruffians, having searched every hole and corner of the hut, in the hope of discovering more gold, now made preparations to depart.

A mean, pitiful, and paltry revenge they took upon the old negro for baulking them of the pleasure they had anticipated in witnessing his tortures.

Placing a rope round his neck, they hung his inanimate corpse from the centre beam of the log hut, and then, piling what dry wood they could collect round the dwelling, they set fire to it; watched it till the flames caught the logs of the habitation; and then, with a fiendish yell, pursued their way, leaving the blazing hut behind them, as, pioneered by an Indian guide, they made their way along the intricate winding path which led through the dismal swamp.

As regards Owen, though a prisoner, he was not treated badly.

They believed he had murdered the negro, which rather raised him in their estimation.

They believed he had possessed himself of the whole of the old man's treasure, never dreaming that far beneath the earth lay ten times that they had found on his person.

Owen, discovering their belief that in taking all he had about him they had obtained all the old man's hoard, took care not to undeceive them; and thus the party trudged wearily on, lighted on their way by the blazing of the negro's hut, and beguiling the way with rude song and ruder jest, till the darkness warned them it was time to encamp for the night.

The following day the march was resumed, and it was not till the afternoon of the third day that Owen saw stretching before him the open sea, glittering in the sun, and the few rude huts which constituted the village where this lawless band resided, when not absent on some predatory excursion.

CHAPTER XXII.

CONCERNING CERTAIN ADVENTURES WHICH BEFEL OWEN REDGRAVE DURING HIS CAPTIVITY.

Owen hailed with delight the sight of the village towards which the band were rapidly escorting him.

Before long he would know his fate—before long the dreadful uncertainty which had been tormenting him the last three days would be at an end.

He had no complaints to make against his conductors, for their manners to him had been civil and obliging, but they had taken good care to avoid giving him the least opportunity for escape.

While progressing across the swamp, the morass which lay on either side of the narrow track which they pursued was sufficient safeguard; but at night, although they admitted him into the circle which collected round the camp fire, and permitted him to listen to their tales of wild, lawless adventure and ribald songs and jests, one of his feet was securely bound to that of a member of the gang, so that the slightest movement on Owen's part during the hours of repose would arouse his keeper.

When they left the swamp, and entered the depths of a gloomy forest, still greater precautions were taken.

As they neared the village of scattered huts after emerging from the wood, Owen noticed a marked change in the demeanour of his guides.

No longer did they straggle about at will, beguiling the tedium of the march with songs and shouts of merriment. They formed into a steady file of three abreast, and marched onward with the regularity of soldiers, maintaining a profound silence.

"Is that our destination?" asked Owen of one of them, pointing at the same time to the collection of huts.

"Silence, as you value your life!" growled the man he had questioned.

"But——" commenced Owen.

The cold muzzle of a pistol, pressed against his temple, warned him it would be more prudent to desist questioning, and the remainder of the journey was performed in rigid silence.

It was night when they reached the village (if such a wretched collection of huts deserves the name), and some difficulty appeared to exist in the minds of his guardians as to the manner in which Owen was to be disposed of.

In answer to the hoarse challenge of a sentry, the captain of the band, in the midst of which Owen was placed, rapidly spoke some words in a language which our hero did not comprehend; and the party still proceeded onwards, till they halted before the door of a small log hut, which, from its dilapidated condition, appeared to be uninhabited.

"Enter here!" said the captain, signing to Owen to advance. "Food will be brought to you presently."

"Why am I kept prisoner? What——"

"Remember," interrupted the captain, "any attempt at escape on your part, or any words spoken by you, no matter to whom, will be your death-warrant."

So saying, he thrust Owen forward into the hut, closed and bolted the door, and then marched rapidly away with his troop, in a direction contrary to that in which they had come.

One man, however, was left behind.

Owen heard him pacing regularly backwards and forwards in front of the hut, and knew it was a guard to prevent his escape.

Anxious and perplexed, he seated himself on a rough wooden bench he found in one corner of the sole apartment of which the habitation boasted, and gave way to his meditations.

Anxious and perplexed he was as to the meaning of his close confinement.

Who were these semi-military men who inhabited this remote village?

What was their object in guarding him so closely?

He was at a loss to answer either question; neither could he determine in his own mind what fate to anticipate.

He was interrupted in his thoughts by the sudden entrance into the hut of a queer, misshapen being, whom it was scarcely possible to believe human, so distorted were his limbs.

In height he was a mere dwarf, though his head would have been large for a full-grown man.

Coarse, rough hair fell in matted locks about a face so hideous and repulsive that no words can describe it.

His legs were short and bandy, but sturdy; and his long arms, covered with hair of a reddish colour, betokened immense strength.

This strange being entered the hut in which Owen was confined, bearing on his head a small wicker-work basket.

Placing his fingers on his thick, bloated lips, in token of silence, he left the basket on the floor of the hut, and disappeared.

Owen had fasted too long to allow the personal appearance of his waiter to take away his appetite.

He speedily removed the cover, and discovered the basket to contain bread, meat, and fruit, while in one corner lay a small flask of red wine.

To the dreary accompaniment of the monotonous tramp, tramp of the sentry's footsteps, Owen Redgrave made a hearty meal from the viands placed before him.

The whole affair appeared to him to abound in mystery; and as soon as his hunger was in some degree appeased, he again began turning over in his mind every probable and improbable story to account for the conduct of his captors.

Whether it was the wine, or the fatigue, or whether some soporific had been administered to him in the food, it is impossible to say; but certain it is, that no sooner had he finished his meal, than an almost intolerable sense of drowsiness came upon him, and almost ere his jaws ceased to masticate, he was in a sound slumber.

His sleep remained undisturbed all through the night, and when, in the morning, he awoke, it was but to be recalled to the sense of his position as a prisoner, by hearing still the pacing of the sentry before his hut.

Of the time he had no accurate means of judging, but the sun was already high in the heavens when the same ugly, misshapen dwarf who had brought him refreshment on the preceding night appeared, bearing a similar basket, which he again left on the floor, repeating, as before, the sign of silence.

His meal concluded, Owen began to wonder how much longer he was to remain a prisoner.

He was at a complete loss to penetrate the reasons of his captors for thus confining him.

While he still pondered, the door of the hut was again thrown open, and the chief of the band, who had surprised him in the hut with the dead negro, made his appearance, accompanied by half a dozen of the gang, fully armed and equipped.

By a sign, the captain gave Owen to understand he was to go with them.

He placed himself in their midst; and at the word of command the party started at a quick pace in the direction of the forest.

Though strict silence was enforced, Owen was not blindfolded, and was therefore enabled to look around him, and note carefully the appearance of this extraordinary village.

To his amazement, he discovered what, in the darkness of the preceding night, he had failed to notice—namely, that the whole village was strongly and completely fortified.

Nature had done much to render it impregnable, and art had supplied all that was wanting.

On one side the sea, on another the forest, which seemed impenetrable; and on the third a broad, rapid river and a large swampy tract of land rendered approach on those sides almost impossible; while the fourth, for which nature had done less, was fortified in a masterly manner, with trenches and earthworks which told of much knowledge of military defences on the part of their constructor.

Owen likewise noticed that at certain intervals sentries paraded the outskirts of the village, ready to give an immediate alarm at the approach of any hostile party.

Of every nation under the sun, from the Albanian to the negro, did this strange band of marauders appear to be composed.

Owen's conductors suddenly diverged from the broad track along which they had been proceeding, and struck off at right angles.

The path they were now pursuing led straight to the forest, at a part where the most practised eye could scarcely have detected an opening; indeed, so well was it concealed, that none but those intimately acquainted with the spot could have discovered it.

They turned rapidly into the wood.

The branches of the trees formed a thick canopy overhead, through which occasional glimpses of blue sky could be seen; but so thick were the leaves that the light of day was in a great measure excluded from the path trodden by Owen Redgrave and his guards.

Some distance they progressed into the forest.

The silence was unbroken, save by the chirping of the birds, or the cry of some startled animal as it fled away at the approach of the armed men.

Suddenly, and as if by magic, a man habited as those who guarded Owen, barred their further advance.

A few words from the leader of the band caused him to step aside with a military salute, and again they went onwards.

A second and a third time this happened, and then suddenly the band emerged into a large open space in the wood.

It was evidently of artificial construction, for in more than one place stumps of trees bore witness that not so long since the forest had been as thick there as in other places.

Now the clearing extended over the space of some two acres.

At one corner of it stood a large dwelling-place—whether house, mansion, or palace, it was impossible to say, so strange was its external appearance. Built mostly of wood, which the action of the weather had in many places rendered mildewed and rotten, it looked, with its bending beams and worm-eaten frame, as if at any moment it might fall to pieces.

In front of this tumble-down residence was a handsome paved terrace, with a carved balustrade in the Italian style.

But the weather had not spared that. The stone was crumbling away—the pavement was green and damp-stained—everything looked old, worn out, and decayed.

Yet not everything.

Some attempts had been recently made to impart a more genial feeling to the house and its immediate neighbourhood.

Part of the clearing had been formed into a flower-garden, with neat, well-trimmed beds, and flowers blooming in all the brilliancy of tropical vegetation.

At this the soldiers who conducted our hero glanced with supercilious disdain.

All this Owen noticed as he passed rapidly on.

Neither did it escape him that one portion of the house had been recently embellished.

The bending, tottering beams had been supported in this portion by strong trees. Some efforts to paint the mildewed window-sashes had been made, while four of the windows themselves were draped with bright crimson curtains, which only made the others not similarly decorated appear more drear and comfortless.

Surely it could not be fancy!

Owen gave a start of surprise as he saw, or fancied he saw, a small white hand—decorated with rings, the stones in which flashed and sparkled in the sun—draw aside one of the crimson curtains as he passed by, escorted by the savage soldiery.

It seemed so strange, so incomprehensible, that the owner of a small white hand should exist in this gloomy, mysterious house in the depths of the forest.

However, Owen had no more time to make observations. His conductors hurried him on—a door was opened—Owen entered, his guard following: with a sonorous bang, which echoed through the house, the door reclosed, and our hero found himself in a large, roomy hall, which presented a most forbidding aspect.

The ceiling was low, and supported by huge beams; the whole apartment was panelled with wood, so dark as to be nearly black. Upon these panels, arranged in perfect order, hung specimens of every conceivable weapon. Swords, guns, pistols, dirks and hangers; old-fashioned, lumbering firearms—calculated to do more injury to the person who fired them, than he at whom they were fired; shields and bucklers, Indian spears and arrows; the huge two-handed sword of the days of Elizabeth; the slight rapier of the later Hanoverian reign,—all were there.

This hall was but imperfectly lighted by two windows, at one end.

At the end opposite to these windows was placed a heavy, old-fashioned chair of dark wood, and over it swung a massive lamp, which sent forth a bright stream of light, illuminating a huge carved cabinet, and making the horribly grotesque figures with which the artist had embellished it, doubly hideous in its flickering, wavering light.

This was the apartment into which Owen Redgrave was ushered.

The guard fell back, taking up their position by the walls, as motionless as statues, leaving our hero standing alone, near the centre of the gloomy hall.

While he yet wondered what was about to happen, a door at the further end was thrown open, and the frightful dwarf, who had brought Owen his food in the hut, made his appearance, and took his stand upon one side of the chair already noticed.

Scarcely had he done so, when a tall man, clothed entirely in black, made his appearance through the same doorway, and took his seat amidst profound silence.

There was something about the mystery and solemnity of the whole affair, which impressed Owen with a sense of awe, which he strove to overcome in vain.

The tall man beckoned to Owen to advance, which he did; and as the light from the lamp shone full upon his face, our hero had a good opportunity of noting his personal appearance.

His face was thin, and of a pale olive colour, while the features were as perfectly cut, as hard, and as cold, as those of an antique statue.

A black moustache decorated his upper lip, the points of which, curling upwards, gave him somewhat of a sardonic appearance, which the expression of his eyes heightened.

His dress consisted of a dark tunic, descending to his knees, and fastened round the waist by a broad belt, the buckle of which was decorated with precious stones. This was the only ornament he wore.

"Your name?" he asked, in a stern, though not unmusical voice.

"Owen Redgrave."

"Where do you come from?"

"That is more than I can tell."

"Explain yourself," said his interrogator, sternly, fixing his piercing eyes upon him, as if to search out the truth.

"I have been tossed hither and thither, buffeted about from one place to another, till I no longer know even in what country I am."

"Relate your adventures."

Owen thought nothing would be gained by concealment, so narrated all that had occurred to him till his arrival in the negro's hut; with the exception that he made no reference to his meeting with the lovely Indian girl, and of the strange mystery attached to her.

"Have you told me the truth?"

"Yes."

"The whole truth?"

"Yes."

"Yet you have concealed something from me."

"To what do you refer?"

"I should hardly have thought you had forgotten yet the service you rendered an English girl, disguised as an Indian."

"You know of that?"

"So it appears."

"How did you learn it?"

"That does not matter. I knew as well all you have just told me."

"Then why did you call upon me to relate it?"

"Merely to ascertain if your word was to be relied on."

"Are you satisfied?"

"Yes."

"Was it for this alone I have been brought here?"

"No."

"For what then?"

"I have a purpose."

"What is it?"

"Do you expect me to confide in you—in an escaped convict?"

Owen began to lose patience, and stamped his foot impatiently.

"Tell me," said the tall man, authoritatively, "tell me all that passed in the negro's hut."

"If you know that as well," replied Owen, "there is no occasion for my doing so."

The other's brow contracted ominously.

"Do as you are told," said he, in a tone of command.

It is needless to say how little Owen relished this style of address, but prudence forbade him to resent it; so, swallowing his pride as best he could, he recounted all that with which the reader is already acquainted, only leaving his hearer to understand that he had abstracted the whole of the negro's treasure.

When he told, however, of the act of the band who had surprised him, of setting fire to the hut, the stern man's brow grew black as night.

"Who did the deed?" he asked, in a voice of thunder.

No one answered.

He repeated the question, at the same time rising from his seat and taking a pistol from the dwarf, who stood by his side.

One of the gang, who were ranged as statues along the wall, stepped forth.

"Were you the man?"

He bowed his head in token of acquiescence.

"Did you not take an oath to abide by the rules of the society?"

Again he bowed.

"Was not one of those rules that no property was to be wilfully or wantonly destroyed?"

"It was only——" commenced the wretched man.

"Silence!" cried the chief. "You have broken one of our laws. I alone am to be obeyed while you remain with me. Hold out your hand."

Tremblingly the man stretched forth his arm.

In a second there was a flash and a report.

The chief had fired his pistol, and the ball had passed through the hand of the wretched man.

"The next time of disobedience, death!" said the chief; then, turning to Owen, he continued, "You are right in supposing I should not have summoned you hither for the sake of merely listening to the story of your adventures. I have some terms to dictate to you before you leave this place."

"To dictate?"

"Yes. I am king and ruler here. I have absolute authority. Do as I tell you, or die!"

"Let me hear your terms."

"Although you *forgot* to relate to me the story of the Indian princess whose life you saved, I must trouble you to endeavour to remember the circumstance."

"Well?"

"You love her."

Owen was taken aback by the suddenness of the assertion. He was about to stammer out a denial, when his questioner interrupted him.

"Psha! Do not attempt to deny it. You told her so; besides, I can see it in your face."

"Supposing it to be the case, why should I not do so?"

"Because I do not choose it."

Owen was about to make a fierce rejoinder, but stopped himself in time.

"She told you her history."

"Part of it."

"That is all I want to know. Now listen to me. You must swear by everything you hold sacred never to repeat that history to any living person. You must swear that during the whole course of your life you will never seek her—never speak with her; and, above all, cease to love her. Will you swear it?"

"No."

"You refuse?"

"Decidedly."

The stern man seemed unprepared for this reply.

He had anticipated a ready acquiescence in his proposal.

He had expected that the solemnness of the scene would awe Owen into a ready compliance.

But he was mistaken.

His brow became livid, and he half drew the sword he carried from its scabbard.

Owen dreaded, from the fate of the man who had fired the negro's hut, that he might be murdered in cold blood upon the spot.

He determined to sell his life as dearly as possible, and with that intention rushed to the wall, where weapons of every description hung, and hastily seized a sword.

In an instant a dozen guns were levelled at his head.

"Ground arms!" cried their chief, rising from his seat, and advancing towards Owen, who stood in an attitude of defence. "This foolish boy is anxious to try a fencing match, and I will humour him."

As he advanced towards Owen there was a cruel glitter in his eye, and a smile of triumph on his lip.

"Once more," said he, "will you accept my terms? Take the oath, and you shall be conducted whither you will in perfect safety."

"I scorn both you and your offer," cried Owen.

"Then die!"

Their swords clashed together.

Owen was an expert fencer, but he felt at once he had this time met more than his match. His only chance was in keeping cool and watching his opportunity, but his antagonist was too powerful for him; in a few minutes Owen's sword was whirled from his hand with a force which almost dislocated his wrist, and he stood unarmed and defenceless.

His courage never deserted him, and he waited the death-stroke calmly.

His antagonist, with a low laugh, drew back his sword arm, preparatory to making the fatal plunge.

Suddenly he lowered the point of his weapon.

"No," said he; "this sword has never killed a man in cold blood, yet neither shall it begin it now."

Then, turning to his guards, who had throughout maintained a perfectly impassive rigidity at their several stations, he said, "Take this boy into the forest out of sight of the house, and hang him."

Owen was seized and led towards the door.

"For the last time," said his late opponent, "will you take the oath?"

"Never!" replied our hero, firmly.

With this determination on his lips he was led forth into the open air, and conducted towards the place of execution.

CHAPTER XXIII.

THE SIGNORA.

As Owen Redgrave was led onwards to execution, he could not but look around him with a pang of regret, to bid farewell to the earth where he had passed so chequered a life.

The trees, the grass, the sky—all seemed to him more attractive than he ever before had seen them.

For a moment it crossed his mind that it was but for a mistaken notion of chivalry he was about to surrender his life; but he scouted the idea as soon as formed, that by taking the required oath he yet might live.

No; he would die—die as became a man and a hero, rather than relinquish for ever the bright hopes he had once had of a happy, brilliant future.

In his heart he said farewell to every object he passed. He thought of his many sins, and uttered an inward prayer for forgiveness. He thought of the negro's hoard, and of the secret of immense wealth which would die with him; but it was with the calm, philosophical despair of a man who has voluntarily surrendered his life that he thought of these things.

They led him on some distance from the house—in fact, to the borders of the forest—where they fixed upon a tree which would answer the required purpose.

Calmly they completed all the necessary preparations as men well accustomed to their work.

The place they had fixed upon for the execution was a lovely spot.

Far away, the sea stretched, shining brilliantly in the sun, like a silvery belt encircling the land. Behind, the forest, in all the beauty of its tropical foliage; and high above, the bright, clear, blue sky. Nature all around, and nought to tell of man's guilt and crime except that one silent group, in the midst of which a young and handsome man, with a rope about his neck, stands pensive, but determined.

All was ready for the deed.

The rope had been adjusted, and thrown over a convenient branch. The men, who knew no will but their master's—who scoffed at mercy and jeered at death—were ready to twist Owen into mid-air.

Already they had taken a few steps. The rope was taut—Owen felt his last moment had come, and clasped his hands in silent prayer.

Suddenly the brushwood was parted beneath the trees, and a tall woman's figure stepped from the thick foliage, and raised her hand in an attitude of command.

"The Signora!" muttered the executioners, and paused, as if in doubt.

She did not long leave them in perplexity as to the cause of her presence.

Hastily drawing a small poniard from her bosom, she severed the rope with a few rapid strokes.

Owen, who had with closed eyes been awaiting his fate, knew nothing till he felt the tightness round his throat relax.

Then he opened his eyes, to see standing before him the perfection of grace and loveliness.

Though her face was completely hidden by a thick veil made after the fashion of a Spanish mantilla, Owen was at no loss to recognise the lovely Indian girl in his deliverer.

He would have fallen at her feet, and avowed his knowledge, but for her whispered words of caution.

"Recognise me, and *nothing* can save your life," she said. "If you are questioned, deny you have ever seen me, and all will be well. A life for a life. You saved mine: it is now my turn."

While she whispered these words hurriedly into his ear, the executioners drew round.

By the respect they paid the lady, it was evident the "Signora" was an important personage in their estimation—indeed, for no other would they have wavered in executing the orders of their chief.

"Don Pedro ordered it," said one of the men apologetically, when the lady ordered them to release the prisoner, at the same time upbraiding them for their willingness to cause the death of a fellow-creature.

She replied angrily, "Don Pedro is——"

"What is he?" asked the tall, stern man, stepping from the shadow of the trees where for the last few moments he had been watching the proceedings with a diabolical expression of rage on his handsome features.

The Signora looked him full in the face as she continued in a calm tone.

"Don Pedro is a harsh, stern, cruel man who abuses the power he might turn to good—who destroys life wantonly—and who suffers his evil passions to rule him."

The harsh man cowered before the imperious woman, who, as she spoke, drew herself up to her full height, looking majestic as an empress.

"Why do you take an interest in this man? Have you ever seen him before?" he asked, angrily.

"I only know him as one of the numerous victims of your cruel will. Release him!"

Don Pedro hesitated.

"Do you hear me? I say, release him!"

"Let him go," said the Spaniard, sulkily, to the men, who speedily unfastened the cords by which Owen's hands and feet had been bound.

"Now swear to me, Don Pedro," said the Signora, "that you will on no future occasion seek the life of this man."

"I swear it."

"Swear, also, that you will not cause others to murder him."

"Why are you so suspicious?"

"Because I know you. Swear it!"

"I swear."

"That is well."

"Are you satisfied?"

"I am. Let the young man go."

"Not so. I grant his life, but not his liberty."

"Do you mean to keep him prisoner?"

"That is my intention."

Owen, now liberated, came forward to tender his thanks to the Signora for preserving his life, but Don Pedro seized him by the collar of his coat.

"Not a step nearer, dog!" said he, in tones which he strove to make appear calm, but which showed the furious anger burning in him.

The Signora, who had been meditating for a few moments, now said, "Be it so, Don Pedro. Keep him prisoner, but remember your oath."

Without a glance to Owen, she turned and walked rapidly away.

The Spaniard's eyes followed her with a curious expression, in which a variety of passions appeared to be striving for the mastery.

The look he turned upon Owen boded him no good. Our hero read in it that the cruel Spaniard had formed some deep-laid plot, by which, without breaking his oath, he hoped to gain his ends.

A cunning, malicious smile played about his mouth, as he gave the men some directions in a language Owen could not understand, and then strode off rapidly through the wood.

Without roughness, the guards escorted him again into the forest, and halted, after a while, before a small log hut, into which they led him.

While two kept guard over his movements, the others hastily shovelled away the earth which formed the floor, till they came to a large, white stone, which, after much exertion, they removed, disclosing a flight of steep steps, descending apparently into darkness.

They signalled to Owen to descend.

Resistance would have been worse than useless, and our hero, resigning himself to his fate, did as he was told.

No sooner was he fairly on his way to the bottom, than the huge slab which served to cover the entrance fell, with a sonorous bang, and Owen was left in total darkness, uncertain whither the steps led, and only conscious that he had escaped the death of hanging, to suffer, perhaps, longer and more lingering tortures.

With a weary sigh, he seated himself upon the steps, to deliberate as to the course it would be best for him to pursue.

Certainly there was nothing to be gained by waiting where he was; but yet a fear of what might be before him for a time prevented his progress.

At length he summoned up courage to proceed.

Cautiously, and feeling his way with the greatest care, he reached the bottom of the steps.

A damp, mouldy smell, and a clammy moisture on the walls, told him the nature of the place in which he now found himself.

It was a small vault, constructed, doubtless, for the purpose of effectually keeping prisoners till such time as the Spaniard's cruel spirit relented; or, far more probably, till confinement, damp, and want of proper nourishment released the poor unfortunate from all earthly sufferings.

These were the thoughts which flashed through Owen's mind, as he stood in the darkness, uncertain whether to proceed or remain.

A sound, at some little distance, of splashing water told him that it might be unsafe to venture onward till he had obtained some knowledge of the size and shape of his dungeon.

He seated himself on the moist ground which formed the only flooring—not to bewail his fate, not to give way to useless sighs and groans, but to recall the adventures of the day, and to meditate on the possibility of escape.

Who was this girl who had rescued him from a violent death?

First, he had seen her in the guise of an Indian princess, and, as such, she had first inspired in him the pains and pleasures of love.

Then came her story.

According to that, she was an Englishwoman; but now, living among this strange troop of foreign marauders, her title was the "Signora," which would betoken her of Spanish origin.

Surely he could not be mistaken. Certainly he had not seen her face; but surely there could not be two such perfect forms of symmetry.

Then, did not the few words spoken in his ear give

him to understand she knew him, and would save his life, in return for the service he had rendered her?

Save his life! Was that all? Where, then, were the bright dreams of the future in which he had indulged, in which this dark beauty played so prominent a part?

His heart sank within him as he thought of the castles in the air he had built upon the foundation of the pleasure of the few short hours he had passed with her?

Then jealousy of the hard, cruel Spaniard made him clasp his hands savagely.

In what relation did she stand to him?

The negro had stated she was a prisoner, yet she apparently went whither she would, and certainly had more power than any other person over the chief of the marauders.

"It is too much to be borne!" he cried aloud, starting to his feet in anger; but, in another moment, the sense of his own impotency came upon him, and, with a groan of despair—the first he had uttered—again sank upon the ground, and buried his face in his hands.

When he removed his fingers, and placed them on the ground, they came in contact with something hard and cold.

What could it be?

Curiosity impelled him to examine it closely.

Feeling around him, he discovered that on every side these hard, cold substances lay. Of different shapes and different sizes, he was at a loss, in the complete darkness, to determine what they might be, till one of another form met his touch.

It was round and smooth, though on one side there were several indentations.

A thrill of horror ran through his frame, as the sense of touch revealed to him the nature of that he held in his hand.

It was a human skull!

Then he was at no loss to account for the other objects. He was surrounded by skeletons.

Horror at the thought of the terrible fate which in all probability awaited him, almost took away his breath.

These bones, on every side, were doubtless those of former prisoners, who had been cast into the gloomy vault, and there had languished away a miserable existence, without light or food.

Surely hanging were a better death than to die by inches in inexpressible torture!

Owen had no means of computing time. It seemed to him that he had been days in the vault. The pangs of hunger and thirst were dreadful.

He heard the trickling of water, and strove to reach it, feeling around the sides of the vault in which he was confined, but it mocked him.

Wherever he stood, it seemed close to him, but yet he could not reach it.

In the torture which he suffered from the intensity of thirst, he actually sucked the green slime from off the walls.

As he lay praying for death to release him from his sufferings, he heard a harsh, grating noise above him, and presently a solitary ray of light penetrated into the gloomy cell.

Owen was too much prostrated by hunger to do more than glance listlessly at it, and wonder if it were a companion in confinement.

To his surprise, after a few moments, he saw standing before him the figure of the misshapen dwarf, who had brought him food when confined in the hut.

Such now seemed his mission.

In his hands he carried a tray, upon which, in tempting profusion, were arranged hot meats, which sent forth a savoury smell.

Hunger overcame every thing, and Owen dashed at the viands. With the greatest ease, the dwarf, with one arm, held him off, while a broad grin upon his ugly face showed how much he enjoyed the torture he was inflicting.

At length he spoke, in harsh, grating tones.

"Our honourable Captain desired me to ask you whether you were prepared to take the oath?"

"Never!" cried Owen, excitedly.

"You are sure of that?"

"Yes."

"Then good morning, signor."

The dwarf remounted the steps, while a chorus of fiendish laughter showed that others above were enjoying the scene.

"Stay, stay!" cried Owen, scarcely knowing what he did or said, in the agonies of hunger. "Give me some food."

The dwarf halted, and with a diabolical grin, pointed to the white skeletons dimly discernible on the floor, and then disappeared with the smoking viands.

The stone was replaced, and Owen was again left in total darkness.

Madly he rushed up the steps, and knocked against the stone which shielded the exit, till his knuckles were red and bruised. Loudly he shrieked for help, but a faint, jeering laugh, dying away in the distance, told him how little mercy he was to expect.

Then his heart sank within him. A few minutes before, hope had revived in his breast, but only to give way to utter and complete despair.

However, it did not seem to be Don Pedro's intention to break his oath.

Later in the day the stone was again removed, and a small basket let down by means of a string.

To Owen's intense joy, this basket contained a small roll of bread and some water.

Hastily he broke the bread in half, when, to his surprise, there fell from it a folded paper. This he could tell by the feel, but the darkness was too great for him to discover whether, as he hoped, it contained any directions from the "Signora" as to escape.

However, he was too hungry to pay much attention to it at the time.

He gnawed the bread voraciously; but there was little of it, and long before his hunger was appeased, he had devoured it to the last crumb.

Still, it had been better than nothing, for it served to keep life in his body, while the piece of paper which had fallen from it, raised hope again in his breast.

Again and again he endeavoured to ascertain if his hopes were founded on substantial ground, and that there were really some written characters on the paper —but he failed in the attempt.

At last, worn out and wearied by all that he had gone through, still clutching the paper firmly in his hand, he fell into a restless, uneasy slumber, which lasted for many hours.

CHAPTER XXIV.

THE ESCAPE.

WITH a weary sigh, which showed the despair which was taking possession of his heart, Owen Redgrave sank back as he found all his efforts to decipher the writing were in vain.

It was a tiny scrap of paper, after all, and the marks upon it might not have been of any importance, yet the mysterious way in which it had reached his hands negatived this idea.

Could it be possible that the lovely girl, whose only name, as far as he could learn, was the Signora,—could she have further compassionated him?

Was it her doing?

Might he yet hope to be free?

Poor Grace was well-nigh forgotten in the blind intoxication of his new passion; or if remembered, only to be compared at a disadvantage with the Signora.

Yet Grace never faltered in her love. Far, far away, the deep, restless sea rolling between them, she remained constant and true to Owen, little knowing the scenes in which he was playing so prominent a part.

And so it was, and is, and will be. Women love and trust, while they upon whom they lavish their affection leave them after a while in pursuit of some new joy, to break their poor, tender, foolish, loving hearts, and to pine away and die, forgotten and forsaken.

Certainly Owen was visited at times by sharp pangs of conscience—pangs which told him he was surrendering the treasure of a good, virtuous woman's love for the glittering, meretricious attractions of the Signora.

He had not strength of mind to look the matter full in the face—to place the affair in a proper light. When conscience became troublesome, he dismissed the affair from his mind.

As Owen lay upon the damp floor of his dungeon, two scraps of paper crumpled in his hand, he heard the low, grating noise which signified the stone at the entrance was being removed.

Eagerly he glanced towards it; but no rays of light penetrated into the vault, though he fancied he detected the sound of light footsteps descending the steps.

A sudden gleam of light from a lantern revealed the presence of some one in his dungeon.

Some one whose form was enveloped from head to foot in a long cloak, and whose features were concealed by a large hood.

Owen's heart thrilled with delight as he fancied he detected, even through the cloak, the graceful outline of the Signora.

He was not mistaken.

She threw back the hood, and suffered the cloak to fall to the ground.

Owen uttered an exclamation of joy, and started forward with outstretched arms.

She stepped back a few paces.

"Thank you—thank you," cried Owen, "for this visit! I would undergo much worse for a similar reward!"

A cold smile played upon the lips of the Signora.

"I am indebted to you for my life," said she, "and am not ungrateful."

"Oh, do not talk of gratitude—it is a cold word! Anything I may have done for you has been more than repaid!"

"I come to talk to you of escape? You must leave this place."

"How is it to be managed?"

"I will arrange all."

"You? But are you not also a prisoner?"

For a moment the Signora seemed confused, and did not reply.

"Alas, yes!" she faltered, at length.

"Then——"

"You mean," interrupted the Signora, "if I am a prisoner, how am I able to liberate others?"

"Precisely!"

"Listen, and I will tell you."

"I am all attention."

"This man—Don Pedro—the captain of the gang of soldiers, freebooters, robbers—call them what you will—fancies he still has gentler feelings in his bosom. He professes to love me!"

Owen stamped angrily on the ground at these words.

"Though he keeps me a prisoner inasmuch as to prevent my leaving the place, he allows me liberty to go whither I will within certain boundaries. I know enough to set you free; but that is all."

"But you? Will you not accompany me in this flight?"

"It cannot be!"

"Why not? Listen to me. Escape from the thraldom of this monster! Fly with me—fly with one who loves you in all sincerity! Once clear of this accursed place, we may bid defiance to this haughty Spaniard and his ruffian horde!"

"No, no!" answered the Signora, sadly; "I must remain here! It is my fate!"

"Not so! I swear I will not leave the place without you! Once away from this vile place, we could speedily reach some town, where we might spend the remainder of our days in love and affluence!"

"Affluence?"

"Yes. Doubtless you are surprised to hear me talk of wealth; but I have a treasure which——"

"Ha! Then you——"

"What?"

"Nothing—nothing!"

"Why did you express surprise?"

"It was only at a thought of mine."

"What was that?"

"Is your wealth part of the negro's treasure?" she asked, earnestly.

"Why should you suppose that?"

"Only—only because it appeared possible."

As she spoke, she drew nearer to Owen, and at last placed her beautiful white hand upon his arm.

She suffered him to pass his arm round her slender waist.

Owen, intoxicated with love and joy at this unlooked-for happiness, poured forth a torrent of words of affection.

"Tell me—where is this treasure of which you speak?" said the Signora, almost before Owen had concluded his ardent speech.

These words aroused his suspicions.

Was it possible that, after all, she was but playing with him?

Could it be that her design was but to extract from him the secret of the negro's hidden wealth?

He dismissed the suspicion as soon as formed; but, nevertheless, determined not to reveal his secret, for the sake of prudence.

Had there been more light, he might have noticed an expression of baffled anger on the face of his lovely visitor, as he evaded her questions; but it was an expression which her words belied.

Softly fell the tender words from her lips on Owen's ears; yet, at the same time that she professed her love, she refused to share his flight.

Any one less in love than our hero might have entertained doubts of the truth of her words; but so infatuated was he, that no suspicions of her crossed his mind.

"I will not fly, to leave you in the hands of this Spaniard," repeated Owen.

"I cannot—cannot go with you," she sobbed.

"Then here I will remain. Only visit me at times, and I will endure any tortures that can be inflicted."

"It is impossible; I can never come here again. Fly, or remain, but for ever bid me farewell."

Ere Owen could reply, there was the noise of the stone at the entrance to the dungeon being removed, and a low whistle sounded.

"Too late—too late!" cried the Signora. "I cannot help you now; your escape must be of your own doing."

In a moment, the light vanished, and she was gone.

Owen passed his hand across his brow, to assure

himself that he was in reality awake, and that the interview had not been a dream.

So strange did it seem, that for some little while he was unable to form any opinion upon the words of his visitor.

Still, no doubts crossed his mind. He could not believe one so beautiful would stoop to deceit.

*   *   *   *   *   *   *

Days lengthened into weeks, and still Owen Redgrave dragged out a miserable existence in the dungeon.

As day succeeded day, and no visit or even message from the Signora reached him, he began to despair of ever again seeing her.

She had said it was impossible she could again visit him.

She had said his escape must be of his own doing.

These were her last words.

It was easy to talk of escaping, but how was it to be done?

None came near him but the wretched, deformed dwarf, and he maintained a resolute silence.

Owen determined to do his best to conquer all difficulties. "Liberty or death" should be his motto. He would make his escape, rescue the Signora, fly with her, possess himself of the negro's treasure, and lead a happy life with the lovely girl for his wife. These were the joyous dreams which occupied his mind in his more sanguine moments; but then, the sense of his utter helplessness and total inability to free himself, much less another, would pass through his brain, and, with a groan of despair, he would sink upon the damp ground, which formed the floor of his prison.

After mature deliberation as to the most likely means for effecting his escape, he determined upon endeavouring to bribe the misshapen dwarf who waited upon him—bribe him, not with money, for he had none, but with promises.

It seemed unlikely enough that the mere promise of gold would induce the dwarf to betray his master; but Owen was unable to think of any other plan, for what avail was the strength of one man against a whole colony?

It was sheer desperation which drove him to the attempt, but it was the only course open to him; and, accordingly, when on the following day the dwarf brought him his food in a wicker basket, he ordered him to stay.

"What do you want with me?" asked the dwarf, in harsh, grating accents.

"I am tired of confinement in this dreary dungeon," replied Owen.

The dwarf gave a hoarse chuckle.

"I don't doubt it," said he.

"Is there no way of escape?"

The dwarf grinned, and, by way of reply, lifted one of the numerous skulls from the ground, and cast it at Owen's feet, who could not but shudder as the ghastly emblem of death rolled towards him.

"Cannot I escape this dreadful fate?"

"You must ask the Captain."

"Is there no way of quitting this dismal dungeon alive?"

"Ask the Captain."

"I would enrich any one who would give me my liberty."

"You had better tell the Captain."

"Is he the only person who can set me free?"

"Yes."

"Surely others could do so if they were so disposed?"

"It is possible."

"Do you know any one who has the power?"

"I may."

"Yourself, for instance."

"I may have the power without the will. I shouldn't like to lose you. Day by day I look forward to visiting you."

"But if, instead of seeing me, you had the greater pleasure of bags of gold to look upon?"

"Ah, that might be different."

"I could give wealth to a large amount in return for liberty."

"Ha, ha, ha!"

"What are you laughing at?"

"You're talking as if you were Chancellor of the Exchequer."

"I do not promise more than I can perform."

"Say you so? Then show me the money—let me see but one piece of gold, and then I will discuss the matter of escape with you."

"I have none here."

"Ho, ho, ho! You're a comical fellow."

"What do you mean?"

"To expect trust. Oh, dear! To think the promise of gold is equivalent to the pleasure of day by day feasting my eyes on your body becoming gradually thinner and thinner—to watching your eyes as they sink deeper into your head—to seeing your bones every day becoming more prominent!"

"Why should you delight in this? What harm have I ever done you?"

"Harm? You, individually, none; but I am at enmity with the whole human race. I, because I am ugly and deformed, have been, so long as my memory serves me, laughed at, sneered at, made the point of rude jests, and all this because my limbs are crooked, and my features unsightly. I suffer this because of my inability to resent it; but when it becomes my turn—when I have the opportunity of torturing a fine, stalwart, handsome man, do you think I am likely to forget it? No—no, I tell you! I gloat over their sufferings; I delight to see them reduced to a condition in which they would willingly change places with me. Yes, with me—the dwarf, the hunchback, the cripple, whom they have mocked and jeered."

It was impossible to give an adequate idea of the concentrated hate and bitterness expressed by the tone in which the dwarf uttered this speech.

He had begun calmly, but had gradually worked himself up to a pitch of frenzy.

His arms swayed violently with excitement, his whole form trembled, and his eyes glared with the ferocity of a wild beast.

This outburst had not been without effect upon Owen.

It had revealed to him that to attempt to obtain the dwarf's assistance in his escape was worse than useless, and he determined upon another course of action.

"You refuse my offer?" he asked, at the same time stepping nearer to the dwarf.

"What offer? You have made me none."

"Psha! You understand me. Liberate me, and I will reward you well."

"Ha, ha, ha!"

"You despise my proposal?"

"No," chuckled the dwarf; "I do *not* despise it, for I know what it is worth. I know, from your words, that you possess the secret of the negro's treasure. The Captain has set his heart upon obtaining it, and will not stick at trifles to become its possessor. Rough and rude as is our colony, we possess instruments of torture which would make the dumb speak. Ha, ha! We'll tear the secret from you. Ha, ha, ha! The instruments are rusty for want of use; I must oil them on purpose for you! Ha, ha!"

With a fiendish grin, the dwarf took a few steps towards the exit from the dungeon.

"Stay!" cried Owen, at the top of his voice. "If that be your plan, I have but one course open to me!"

Saying this, with a bound like an infuriated tiger,

he leaped upon the dwarf, and then strove to hurl him to the ground; but he did not find his adversary so unprepared as he had anticipated.

The dwarf stretched forth one of his long, hairy arms, and caught Owen by the throat, as the latter sprang upon him. Owen, too, had seized his opponent in a like manner.

The shock of the concussion brought them both to the ground, Owen undermost.

For some moments, the two rolled over and over on the damp, slimy ground, neither gaining the advantage.

In grim silence, they tightened their hold upon each other, and exerted all their strength to gain the mastery.

Despair lent strength to Owen, but his frame was enfeebled by long confinement and want of proper food.

He knew he was struggling for life and liberty.

An unevenness in the ground gave our hero a slight advantage, of which he was not slow to avail himself.

The dwarf's hold upon his throat relaxed, while his was but the firmer.

In another moment, Owen was leaning on the dwarf's chest, compressing his windpipe.

"No, no!" he exclaimed; "I cannot murder him in cold blood!"

He rose to his feet, took the body of his antagonist in his arms, and then, exerting all his strength, hurled it with his full force to the opposite end of the dungeon.

Then, without waiting to see the effect, he rapidly mounted the steps which led up to freedom, and once more saw the clear blue sky above him, and inhaled the pure, fresh air.

To secure himself from immediate pursuit, and to guard against the dwarf giving the alarm, in the event of his recovery, he placed the huge stone firmly over the entrance to the cavern, and then looked about him to arrange his plans.

CHAPTER XXV

HOW OWEN REDGRAVE FARED AFTER HIS ESCAPE, AND THE STRANGE SIGHT HE SAW IN THE FOREST.

It will be remembered that the entrance to the dungeon in which Owen had been confined was in a half-ruined, dilapidated out-building, and it was in this hut our hero found himself on emerging from his prison.

The sudden glare of broad daylight almost blinded him at first, coming, as he did, from utter darkness.

He covered his face with his hands for a few minutes.

Gradually he became accustomed to the light, and then he set to work to effect his escape from the hut.

A horrid dread of being seen in the act of escape, retaken, and again cast into the den of horror he had just quitted, made him very careful in ascertaining none of the Spaniard's gang were in the neighbourhood.

Cautiously he opened the door, and then stood, joyous and happy, the green turf beneath his feet, the blue sky above his head—free!

Yes, he was free, but whither should he bend his steps?

To go towards the sea would be to pass by the fortified village, and to court death.

To go into the depths of the forest, alone and un-armed, was almost certain destruction: still, from the quadrupeds there was a chance of escape—from the men savages, none.

Accordingly, Owen Redgrave at once plunged into the gloomy depths of the forest, little caring whither his steps carried him, so long as he was far away from the haunts of those who had so cruelly treated him.

And the Signora?

Again and again his thoughts turned to her.

What was the reason of her strange conduct?

There was only one explanation, and that was that she had deceived him as to the position in which she stood with reference to Don Pedro.

Yet his mind and heart revolted against so base a supposition. He could not believe one so young and beautiful would stoop so low.

His passion argued against his reason, and he determined, come what might, to believe in her innocence and purity.

Still he went onward, plunging through the briars and underwood, over huge trunks of fallen trees, but as yet he felt not fatigue, and wildly he continued his career, only anxious to put as great a distance as possible between himself and his enemies.

It was not till the black darkness of night, rendering progression impossible, that he halted.

How should he pass the night?

To sleep on the ground was to expose himself to numberless dangers, yet it was necessary he should have rest.

The difficulty was soon solved. A huge tree, spreading out its branches above him, seemed to offer its friendly protection. He quickly mounted, and ensconced himself among its boughs as snugly as circumstances would permit, and was soon buried in the profound slumber produced by fatigue.

How long he slept he knew not, but he was awakened by a noise and flashes of light. For a few moments he was unable to recognise his novel position; but presently he recovered himself, and was able to take note of what was passing beneath him.

A band, numbering about a dozen, bearing torches, and completely armed, had halted beneath the tree in the boughs of which he had taken shelter, and were holding an animated discussion.

"The search is useless," said one. "It is looking for a needle in a bottle of hay."

"The Captain ordered us not to return without him," said another.

"Then why didn't he come to look for him himself? For my part, I am sick of this life of obedience."

"You'd better tell the Captain so," sneered a third speaker. "That's to say, if you're ambitious of forming food for the birds."

"Well, anyhow, I'm going no further to-night."

"Nor I—nor I!" chorussed several.

"I must say, for my part, I don't admire the life we lead. Where's all the fun and jollity of a lawless life? We toil like slaves in order that the Captain and the Signora may enjoy themselves."

"Come, come, no mutineering," rejoined one, in a voice of authority. "We'll camp here for the night, and resume our search to-morrow."

"Why should we? Leave the Indians or the wild beasts to do the work."

With some grumbling the men gathered materials for a fire, which they lighted, and then proceeded to cook their food.

Owen had listened with trepidation to their conversation.

It was plain his escape had been discovered, and that the men now carousing a few feet beneath him had been sent in pursuit by the Captain.

To remain where he was would be almost certain discovery in the morning light; yet how to escape?

His pursuers had bivouacked around the trunk of the tree in which he had taken refuge, and though sleep soon overcame them, two throughout the night remained sentinels, waking their comrades at stated times to take their places.

To descend, or to remain where he was, seemed certain discovery. However, he determined to wait patiently till morning in the hope some chance would offer itself.

At early dawn the band aroused, rekindled their fire, and, with some joking and some grumbling, prepared to resume their search after him who for the last six hours had been within a few feet of them.

A light wind, coming from the sea, had arisen during the night, and went sweeping over the tops of the trees, sending showers of leaves and twigs whirling to the ground, and causing the bough on which Owen rested to sway violently.

Had he only been more prudent, and selected his resting-place with greater caution, he might have remained securely behind a leafy screen till the band had departed; but the branch he had chosen was but little covered, and, with his pursuers beneath, he dared not venture to alter his position.

At length fortune favoured him.

The men withdrew to some little distance to prepare their breakfast, and Owen quitted the branch on which he had rested during the night, slid noiselessly down the smooth stem, and plunged into the thick, dry brushwood; but not before he was perceived. The band of robber soldiers were gifted with good eyesight, and the sharp crack of a rifle, and the whiz of a bullet in unpleasant proximity to his head, told him he was discovered, and that there would be a race for life.

With shouts and yells, accompanied by the report of fire-arms directed blindly at the spot where he had been discovered, the band started in pursuit of our hero, who, with but a short start, ran, leapt, and stumbled with all the speed he could muster, through the thick forest.

At times, in more open places, they caught glimpses of his flying figure—a fact which was announced by a shower of bullets; but good fortune, and the trunks of the trees, preserved him scathless, and still he continued on his course, his pursuers close at his heels. Rapid progression was, of course, impossible; but the same obstacles which lay in our hero's way baulked the robber band, and they gained little or nothing upon him.

Owen was fully alive to his own danger. He knew the odds were strongly in favour of his death or capture; still, the prize of life and liberty for which he struggled, nerved him to efforts at which, had he had time for reflection, he would himself have been astonished.

Already he fancied that the chase had been too severe for some of his pursuers, and that their number had diminished; but the cries of those who still followed, warned him not to relax in his exertions, and still he plunged frantically onwards.

The wind had increased almost to a tempest, and the sky was obscured by thick clouds. The foliage made it almost pitch dark in places, but that was in his favour.

Suddenly a violent gust of wind bore a cloud along with it—a thick, black cloud, which almost took away his breath.

A cry from his pursuers, far different to any they had yet uttered, made him turn his head.

It was a dreadful, yet grand sight, which met his gaze.

The forest was on fire!

The cloud which the wind had driven after him was smoke.

Thick, black smoke it was, which, as it rolled along, threatened to suffocate him.

His pursuers had, in their hurry to give chase, forgotten to extinguish their fire; the wind had scattered the embers amongst the dry brushwood, and soon fanned it into a flame.

Owen heard the roar of the fire, the crackling of the wood, and the crashing of the forest trees, as they toppled over into the flames; but, as yet, the thick smoke, brightened occasionally by a lurid gleam, was all he could see.

He had a worse enemy now to contend with than man.

His pursuers abandoned all thoughts of seizing him in desire for their own safety, and fled hither and thither, in the hope of reaching some place of refuge.

Vain, delusive hope!

The wind and the fire were both behind them, and the flames were advancing with tenfold the rapidity they could run.

Almost without hope, Owen still fled onward. More than once the thought crossed his mind of lying down, and waiting for the end which he made sure must come; but the love of life was strong, and while he had yet the power, he could not but struggle against death.

Onward, onward he went, almost choked by the dense volumes of smoke in which he was enveloped.

The roar of the fire momentarily increased, the heat became almost insufferable; but just as Owen gave up all hope of preserving his life, the trees became thinner, the brushwood lower, and at last, with a bound, our hero found himself in a large open space in the forest.

It was one of those clearings which nature sometimes forms in her largest forests—a large, open space, with trees on every side, but yet destitute of their massive trunks itself.

No words can describe the inexpressible delight of Owen. Rapidly he ran across the plain, till stopped midway by a rocky gully, through which a narrow river tossed and tumbled among the stones on its way seawards.

Parched, hot, and all but suffocated, Owen threw himself upon the stones, and drank a long, long draught from the stream, the while the smoke rolled in thick volumes over his head.

But the gully saved his life.

There the smoke did not come—the wind bore it rapidly above him; but the heat was almost unbearable, and but for the copious draughts of water which he swallowed, must have been fatal.

Momentarily, the heat increased, till, with a sudden thought, he threw off his clothes, and plunged into the water.

The sudden reaction, the excitement, the fatigue he had gone through, asserted themselves, and Owen fainted.

Luckily, the stream was shallow, and a friendly rock saved his head from immersion; and there he remained, in cool and quiet, while the devouring element swept on its way, surrounding the plain with a band of fire.

Lying there insensible, he saw nothing of the grandest sight which human eye can behold.

He did not witness the forked flames leaping from branch to branch of the mighty monarchs of the forest; he saw not the massive trees tremble as the fire devoured their roots, and then, with a terrific crash, fall into the blaze beneath; he beheld not the devouring element licking up the undergrowth of bushes in its insatiable course, but lay unconscious of the dreadful conflagration raging around him.

When he recovered his senses, it was to no pleasant consciousness he returned.

The fire had long since passed the spot where he lay, and he was safe from that; but another danger threatened him.

A death even more appalling than that from which he had been so miraculously preserved.

Death by starvation!

In making his escape into the forest, he had trusted to being able to live upon the fruits and berries he might find, but where was that hope now? The fire had devoured all!

But the fire, after all, had provided him a better repast than he had ever hoped to make.

Wandering on the plain, he found lying about numberless birds, which had fallen victims to the heat and smoke. Scorched, and in many instances burnt though they were, hunger made him seize them with ravenous joy.

The fire, still smouldering round the clearing, made them speedily fit for food, and Owen gnawed them with the appetite of a man who has fasted for thirty-six hours.

The following day our hero had a new fright. As he lay in the gully, which, for the time being, he had constituted his home, fresh volumes of smoke rolled over his head.

What could it mean?

Surely the fire was burnt out, at all events, in his immediate neighbourhood. Watching the suffocating vapour as it was wafted above him, though not in such dense clouds as on the first occasion, he noticed that its direction was contrary to that of the previous day.

Then the joyful fact occurred to him.

The wind had shifted, and now headed the fire, and if it only continued in that direction, the flames would burn themselves out, and after some little while, the ground would be passable.

For several days Owen remained in the gully, subsisting on the birds he could find about him. At the end of that time, the smoke had entirely abated, and the ground had become moderately cool.

It was time he should think of what steps he should take for making his escape. The birds would not last for ever, and it was desirable that before this supply of food altogether ceased, he should make his way, if possible, to some part of the unburnt forest, where he could obtain the fruit and berries upon which he had expected to subsist.

His mind made up on this point, he collected together as much food as he conveniently carry, and then, in order always to have water at command, started off to follow the course of the river.

For many days he walked before he arrived at the spot where the fire had terminated. Through soft, yielding wood-ashes he strode; but the walking required much circumspection, for every here and there beneath the white ash lay smouldering and hot the charred wood; but without any more serious accident than some blisters, and a few trifling burns, he at length arrived once more in the forest, just as his stock of provisions was exhausted.

Not to protract the narration of his wanderings to a tedious length, let it suffice that, for many days, he followed the course of the stream, feeding upon whatever chance threw in his way, till an incident occurred which altered the whole of his plans, and changed the entire tenour of his life.

He had left the burnt forest many miles behind him, and was walking onward beneath the shelter of the enormous trees, and surrounded by the full luxuriance of tropical vegetation. It was nearly dark, and our hero was about selecting a favourable tree in which to pass the night, when a faint, glimmering light appeared in the distance, shining through the trees.

The sight at first filled him with alarm, for his mind indistinctly associated human beings with enemies; but a moment's reflection convinced him that at this distance he had nothing to fear from Don Pedro and his gang.

With some caution, he approached the light, and found it proceeded from a fire kindled on the banks of the stream.

Around this fire was seated a most picturesque group. Men, clothed in garments of every shape and colour, lounged about, smoking and drinking, while near them, piled in confusion, lay a large assortment of fire-arms.

Who and what were they?

On that subject there could be little doubt. Their whole appearance bespoke them freebooters, or, as they named themselves, "adventurers."

But what could be their object in the depths of the forest?

They were evidently upon some expedition. Was it possible, Owen asked himself, that he was in the neighbourhood of some town or village?

After reflection, he deemed it better to come forward openly, than to endeavour to play hide-and-seek with this gang, and run the chance of discovery and an ignominious death.

Putting his resolve into execution, he advanced boldly towards the fire.

At first he was unnoticed; but suddenly one of the number, seeing him, shouted "A spy!" drew a pistol from his belt, and fired.

Luckily for our hero, the aim had been too hasty to be accurate, but yet death menaced him on every side: for, in a second, the men had started to their feet, and presented guns and pistols at him.

"Stay, stay! Do not fire!" cried one of the number, who, by his dress, appeared to be of higher rank.

The men reluctantly lowered their weapons.

"A pretty fellow you are!" growled one. "Always preaching mercy! Shoot a spy first, say I, and question him afterwards!"

"Who are you, and from whence?" asked he who had interfered in Owen's behalf.

"Owen Redgrave is my name. I have recently escaped from a dungeon, since which I have been wandering through the forest."

"A likely story!" interrupted a coarse-looking ruffian. "Hang him at once!"

"Not so. At all events, we will keep him till morning, and question him closely. Should he prove a spy, you will hear no word from me to save his life!"

"*Prove* a spy! When he has betrayed us, you mean?"

"Silence!" cried the other, angrily. "Do you dare dispute my word?"

The man grumbled to himself, but obeyed.

Owen, who had stood calmly by during this short conversation, in which he was so deeply interested, now stepped forward, and begged to be allowed to tell his story; but the chief of the party refused to hear it till morning.

Though again saved from death, at all events, for the time, measures were taken to prevent our hero from making his escape during the night, even had he been so disposed. His hands and feet were securely bound, but, otherwise, he was well treated. Meat and drink were given him, and one hand partially liberated, in order that he might feed himself, and afterwards he was allowed to draw near the fire; and then, wearied out, he followed the example of those around him, and composed himself to sleep.

When he awoke, the fire had partially died out, but there was still sufficient glimmering light for him to see that, although surrounded by recumbent forms, there were others seated near him who, far from being asleep, were engaged in an animated discussion.

Without giving any sign that he was awake, Owen listened, in the hope of discovering from their conversation where he was, or whither the band was bound.

The first whole sentence which reached our hero's ears was spoken by a rough-looking, burly man.

"If we were only sure of the way," said he, "we would push on at once and attack the village, and then I would settle accounts with this Don Pedro."

"Don Pedro!" exclaimed Owen, involuntarily, as he started up.

With a loud oath the man who had spoken darted upon our hero, and drew a sharp, glittering dagger from its sheath.

Owen closed his eyes, convinced his last moment had come; but what was his surprise to hear his own name pronounced in a surprised tone.

"Owen Redgrave!"

By the flickering firelight he scrutinized the man's face.

"Drake!" he cried, scarcely less amazed.

CHAPTER XXVI.

TREATS OF CAPTAIN DRAKE AND HIS FOLLOWERS.

"You here?" cried Drake; "I never thought to see you again."

"I, too, can say the same. How did you escape?"

"Psha! never mind that story now. Tell me how you got here. There never was much love between us, but I don't want to stick a knife into you in cold blood."

"I have escaped from the man whose name you just mentioned—Don Pedro."

"Take care—beware what you say. I believe you come from him; but by all the saints, if it is as a spy, no power on earth can save your life."

"I am no spy."

"Prove it."

"That will I, readily; for if, as I suspect from the fragments of the conversation I overheard, this expedition is directed against him, I will serve you by guiding you to his encampment."

"Serve me!" said Drake, with a sneer. "You weren't always so willing to do me a service. Is that your only reason?"

"No, it is not. I have long accounts to settle with this Don Pedro; he has to answer to me for much; and as I live, if I get the opportunity, he shall have cause to regret the day he first saw me."

"Would you kill him?"

"Ay, that would I! in the manner he doomed me to die—a long, lingering death, without the hope of mercy."

Drake withdrew, and consulted a few moments with his companions.

"Well, Redgrave," said he, after a pause, "we have determined to trust you. You know me well enough to have no doubt as to your fate if you attempt to deceive me."

"And you ought to know me well enough not to think me capable of playing the part you suspect."

"Well, well, never mind what has passed; in this matter of revenge on the haughty Spaniard we are one—so let us be friends."

Drake held out his coarse, rough hand as he spoke, and Owen had no choice but to grasp it.

"Tell me," said he, "what is the cause of your enmity with Don Pedro?"

"That I can easily explain. You must know I am

captain of these brave men you see around me, and of many score like them."

"What—what——" stammered Owen, uncertain in what way to frame the question, without giving offence.

"What profession are we, eh? Is that what you mean?"

"Yes."

"Well, I don't mind confessing: people readier with their tongues than their purses, call us Buccaneers."

"Buccaneers?"

"Precisely so."

"Then what brings you roaming through these forests?"

"I was just going to tell you when you stopped me with your questions."

"Go on."

"Well, you understand, we confine ourselves usually to naval engagements: this Don Pedro, on the contrary, attacks small towns; seizes caravans; and, in fact, carries on the same game on land we do at sea."

"Well?"

"This Spanish rascal, hearing some of my men were bringing a large amount of treasure over land, sent a party of his soldiers to attack them. My party was surprised, and almost before the men could draw their cutlasses to defend themselves, they were all slain, and the treasure carried off."

"Just what I should have expected from him."

"You may easily imagine I will not allow an outrage like this to go unpunished. We have all sworn to have revenge, or to die in the attempt. I chose a body of faithful followers from the crew of my ship, and we have been now five days' march on our way to attack the Spaniard's camp."

"Why did you do that? Do you not know it is on the sea-coast, and that you might have sailed round to it?"

Drake glanced at Owen contemptuously.

"Yes," he replied, "I know we might have done that; and I also know that while our ship was drawing near shore, the gang would have recognised her, and would have time to prepare for defence. However, my ship is on her way there now."

"What are your plans of attack?"

"You're a cool hand to expect me to let you into our secrets."

"I only ask, in order that, if possible, I may, by my knowledge of the place, assist you."

"Well, then, my ship will keep out at sea till a certain signal from us directs my lieutenant to put in towards shore. When Don Pedro's men recognise Captain Drake's flag floating at the peak, they will know what is coming."

"I thought you said you wished to surprise them?"

"Can't you hear a fellow out?"

"I beg your pardon—go on."

"Naturally, there will, at first, be much bustle and confusion at the discovery of the impending attack, of which I intend to take advantage, by rushing full pelt into the place. The engagement will soon be general; but I shall have the advantage on my side, though they will outnumber me."

"I think I can be of service to you," said Owen.

"I'm glad to hear it."

Owen Redgrave then proceeded to recount his experience of the camp-village; describing the earthen fortifications and the regular posting of sentries.

"Ah! all that is for my benefit," said Drake; "they are expecting an attack."

Owen further narrated how the Spaniard lived away from the others in the forest.

Drake ground his teeth.

"When I get face to face with that treacherous

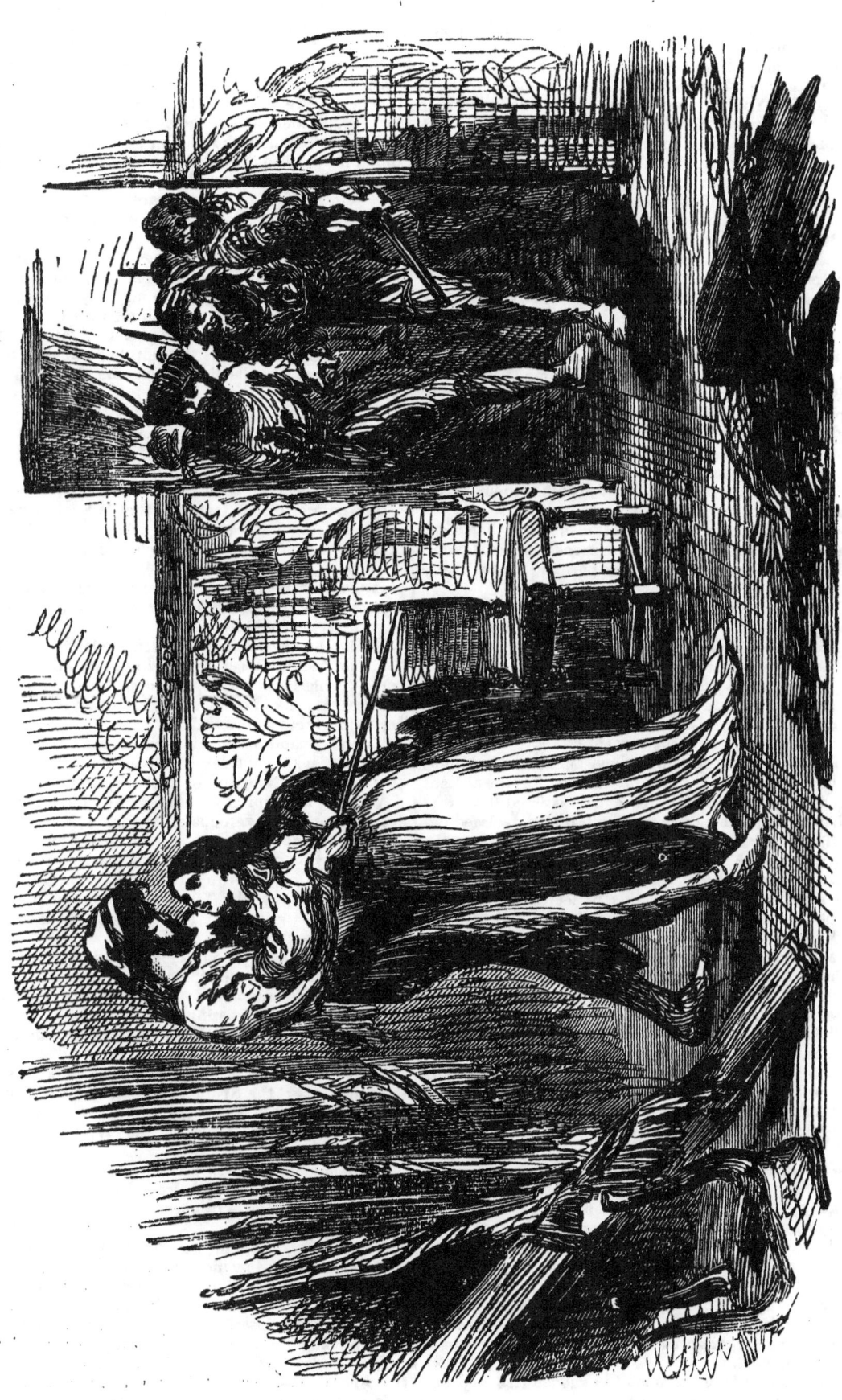

No. 9.—THE BUCCANEERS.

scoundrel, he shall find out what it is to insult Captain Drake."

" Hold !" cried Owen ; " I claim as my right to settle accounts with Don Pedro."

" You may claim what you like ; but I tell you there's no one but myself will have first set-to with the Spaniard. You may have him when I've done with him !" continued he, with a diabolical grin ; " that is, supposing any of him to be left !"

Owen made no reply to this speech, though an angry one rose to his lips ; for, for prudence sake, he deemed it better to avoid, if possible, an open rupture with this man.

Drake's character and disposition are already known to the reader, as is the manner in which he and our hero regarded each other ; but as fate had united them in common cause against the same enemy, they both appeared, for the while at least, to forget their own feuds, and join cause against Don Pedro.

The morning repast concluded, the buccaneers, at the word of command, prepared to resume their march.

Before they started, however, Drake, in a few words, explained to them that he whom they had taken for a spy was in reality a joint hater with themselves of the cruel Spaniard ; and that, having just escaped from his hands, he was both able and willing to give them much useful information, and to guide them to his stronghold.

Public opinion, which the previous night had been so sorely against our hero, now turned in his favour, and with the rough band he now met with much ready sympathy.

He was supplied with new clothes, which, however incongruous in their mixture, he sorely needed. A cutlass and pistol fell to his share ; and the whole party started on their march.

A strange but formidable-looking band were these followers of Captain Drake. Their movements lacked the caution and precision of the Spaniard's troop ; but they were a far finer class of men.

Men whose strong proportions and muscular limbs might have qualified them for models for the ancient Hercules. Men whose bronzed and scarred faces told of hardships and blows, whose knit brows declared determination, and whose whole appearance bespoke they really were " awkward customers."

As they assembled at their Captain's call, and formed into some semblance of a line of march, Owen could not help contrasting the stalwart figures and signs of hardihood with the comparatively puny forms and effeminate faces of Don Pedro's followers ; and without wishing to underrate the Spaniard's band, he had no doubt that he would find Drake's men formidable adversaries, though not numbering half so many.

The march was kept up throughout the day, with only one hour for rest and refreshment ; and towards evening the band again encamped upon the bank of the stream, the course of which Owen had for so many days followed upwards, without a notion that he should ever retrace his steps in company with his deadliest enemy.

Without chronicling the progress of the buccaneers day by day towards the stronghold of Don Pedro and his gang, let it suffice that their route lay over the same ground as Owen had previously traversed.

They were not many days in reaching the spot where the devastating fire had laid low the monarchs of the forest ; but still they pushed on with, if anything, an increased rapidity, for if the Spaniard once obtained tidings of their approach, he would be ready to receive them, and it might go hard with them, for they would be outnumbered.

Everything depended upon the suddenness and unexpected nature of the attack.

At last, after many days' marching, they found themselves within a few miles of the fortified village where the Spaniards lived in fancied security.

Before them stretched the broad expanse of the ocean, and upon its bosom, though at a considerable distance from land, the experienced eye of Drake at once discerned his ship.

The sun went down into the sea, tinging all with his lurid glare, and tipping the clouds with a deep crimson, as if to foreshadow the coming struggle. But no such thought occupied the mind of Drake's followers.

Bloodshed, war, and pillage were their trade ; and they but bestowed a more careful examination than usual upon their various arms and accoutrements before seeking rest in sleep.

Prudence forbade the lighting of fires, and the noisy carousals with which time had been beguiled on former evenings ; and before long the majority of the marauding band were buried in deep slumber.

Early the following morning a council of war was held. During the night the ship had stood in to land, and now awaited the signal from the shore to advance still nearer.

To make this signal was no easy task.

Projecting far into the sea was a rough, rocky point, at the end of which it had been arranged by the Captain a fire should be lighted, the smoke of which would be seen on board.

The danger of the task was that it might attract the notice of Don Pedro's band, in which event the lighter of the fire would stand a poor chance of escape.

With such devil-may-care fellows as composed this party of buccaneers, however, such peril was accounted a pleasure as well as an honour, and there was no lack of volunteers for the job.

Drake, however, silenced all their claims.

He professed himself unable to decide upon the comparative merits of the applicants. To avoid dispute and jealousy, he announced his intention of himself undertaking the dangerous duty.

The command of the land party was entrusted to a big, burly man, considerably over six feet in height, broad in proportion, and of gigantic strength.

With a few words of caution and direction, Drake departed on his hazardous enterprise.

The buccaneers, by his orders, advanced stealthily and quietly as near as they could venture without discovery to Don Pedro's stronghold, and there lay crouching among the brushwood, anxiously awaiting the signal—a gun from the ship—to make their onslaught upon the village.

From the position in which they were ensconced they were unable to see the columns of smoke rising in the air which announced their presence to those on board ; but by the hoisting of a flag, and by the vessel standing in still nearer to the shore, they knew it had been seen.

They also knew, by the shouting and confusion in the village, that the Spaniard's gang had recognised an enemy in the ship, and were preparing to give her a warm reception as soon as she approached within range.

Thus far Drake's plan was a success.

Suddenly there flashed from one of the ports a stream of light, and a quantity of white smoke curled upwards.

The heavy boom of the gun fell upon the ears of those in ambush after a few moments of suspense ; and at the long-expected signal the band started to their feet, and, led by their burly lieutenant, dashed over the land fortifications, now deserted, with a yell of triumph.

The result was as had been anticipated.

Don Pedro's gang were thrown into confusion by this unexpected onslaught, and many were cut down before they had recovered from their consternation ; still, however, when the assaulted perceived the paucity of numbers who had ventured to attack them, they grew bolder, formed themselves into something approaching a square, and steadily withstood the savage charges of Drake's men.

The loss of life was great.

Blood flowed like water.

Yet every comrade fallen seemed but to nerve those who remained to fresh energy.

The ground was covered with dead and dying.

The cries of the wounded rose above the clamour of battle.

The sharp report of pistols and muskets—the clanging of swords as they met in hand to hand encounter—the oaths, the groans, the shrieks, the cries—all told the deadly nature of the conflict.

Owen had done his share.

Amid the diabolical uproar and confusion he had been calm and collected.

His weapon was never raised but in defence; but when the blade *was* raised, no matter by what opposed, a few moments sufficed to lay his adversary low.

He had one great object.

He longed to be once more face to face with Don Pedro, and for that struggle he reserved himself.

The Spaniard and his sword were, in truth, fully employed.

Hither and thither went the Captain of the attacked, dealing death and destruction wherever his stalwart arm was raised.

Again and again Owen pushed and fought his way towards him.

But without success.

He could not find the opportunity for which he sought.

For a long time the result of the combat was doubtful; but, at length, the Spaniard's gang wavered and gave way.

The fact was, they had not the trust and confidence in their chief the others had in Drake.

At the first signs of giving in, Don Pedro, with oaths and shouts, re-formed his band, and placed himself at their head.

Hitherto they had contented themselves with repelling their assailants; but now, headed by their Captain, they rushed headlong on their foes, and a fearful hand-to-hand combat took place.

The burly lieutenant found himself matched against Don Pedro.

With envious eyes, Owen noticed this, and strove to force his way to the front; but swords flashed around him, and it was but slow progress he made.

Almost mechanically, he cut and thrust, doing right good service; but, with his eyes fixed upon the spot where the respective leaders were opposed to each other in deadly conflict.

It was with feelings of rage and despair he saw Drake's powerful lieutenant disarm his antagonist, and shorten his sword preparatory to running him through the body.

But Don Pedro was not yet to meet his fate.

With a gasping moan, the lieutenant, in the moment of victory, sank back—stabbed through the heart—dead.

The dwarf, whose career our hero had so nearly terminated, had crept, unperceived, behind him, and just as he was about to deal the fatal blow, had plunged a dagger into his body.

The Spaniard laughed aloud at his escape; but he was unable to reward the dwarf who had done him such good service, for as his dagger entered the lieutenant's heart, a pistol-bullet crashed through his brain.

Don Pedro recovered his weapon, and glanced around him.

On every side his men, despite their numbers, were getting the worst of it, and he formed rapidly a plan by which he hoped to retrieve the fortune of the day.

With his powerful voice he called out a few words, in Spanish, to his men, who, at the word of command, formed themselves into a compact body, and then set off, with rapid, measured tread, in the direction of the forest.

Several of Drake's band followed in disorderly pursuit; but the folly of the movement was soon apparent, for they were shot down by the retreating party.

Owen, who alone knew of the house in the wood, guessed Don Pedro's plan.

He saw his enemy escaping him at the last moment.

Waving his sword above his head, he shouted to the men, who had already began their pillage, to form themselves into a body, and take him for a leader.

They all responded, more or less eagerly; and at his command, started in pursuit of their enemy in the nearest approach to order and regularity they could maintain.

CHAPTER XXVII.

THE HOUSE IN THE FOREST.

ARRIVED at the borders of the forest, Owen halted the men, and, in a few words, explained to them the reason of his conduct.

He told them that far from the enemy having flown from them into the depths of the wood, they had only retreated to another stronghold, in order to reorganize their forces to renew the battle.

He urged the great advantage of following up their victory, and routing the enemy before they had time to re-form.

He held out promises of far richer plunder than that in the village; and by his well-chosen words and impassioned manner so impressed the men, that they professed their readiness, with a wild cheer, to follow wherever he led.

Crashing through the underwood, they followed Owen, whose quick eye did not fail to recognise the different marks which served to guide to the house in the forest.

Don Pedro's retreat had been well planned.

He thought one of two results must ensue, either of which would turn the tide in his favour.

He thought that either Drake's band would be led by their ardour to pursue him into the wood, where they would speedily lose themselves, and then be easily picked off; or else that they would at once set about pillaging the village while he reorganized his band, and that at dusk he might make a successful attack upon them.

The plans were good, but were foiled by one circumstance.

A circumstance of which he had no inkling.

He did not know Owen Redgrave was with them.

He never doubted that he had perished in the burning forest.

He little thought his enemies possessed a leader who could guide them through the intricacies of the wood to the house.

That was more than he had calculated upon.

Owen advanced steadily and cautiously through the wood, keeping a careful look-out, dreading an ambush.

But the Spaniards, feeling secure in their secret, even neglected all ordinary precautions, and it was not till the men were within sight of the house that their presence was discovered.

It must be confessed that another feeling besides revenge actuated Owen.

A feeling which has caused many a wise man to do a foolish action.

A feeling which has caused much pain and misery. Love!

The Signora inhabited this house; and if he was victorious he might rescue her from her prison.

Doubts, as already stated, would arise from time to time of the candour and truthfulness of the lovely girl he so much admired; but he steadfastly pushed them aside, and strove to convince himself by arguing that one so lovely could not be false.

Time will show whether or not this argument was correct.

No sooner were the assailants perceived besieging the house than a perfect shower of bullets were rained upon them from the windows.

Owen ordered those under his command to retreat to the shelter of the trees.

They did so; and then commenced an interchange of shots, which both parties seemed to consider vastly amusing.

The appearance of a figure at a window was sure to be the signal for half a dozen balls to go crashing through the glass; while from the house the same compliment was paid whenever a man emerged from his hiding-place behind a tree.

After a while a figure appeared full in one of the windows, which, by its hat and dress, Owen had no difficulty in recognising as that of Don Pedro.

A shower of bullets pierced the windows on every side; still the figure remained apparently untouched.

Volley succeeded volley; but still the Spaniard never moved.

The buccaneers. ever inclined to superstition, stood amazed and irresolute.

"I'll fight with any man that ever breathed," exclaimed one, after taking deliberate aim, firing his gun and producing no result; "but I can't fight the fiend in person!"

His speech was but the impression of them all.

Even Owen could not repress a vague feeling of awe at the invulnerability of the Captain of the enemy.

In addition to this superstitious dread, which was unnerving many of the men, the ammunition was almost exhausted; and Owen determined upon commanding an attack upon the house.

It certainly was a bold attempt; and successful or not, must sacrifice very many lives; but it was a question of some or all; and when our hero announced his intention it was received with cheers on every side.

For danger, these men cared little or nothing.

The plan was bold, dashing, exciting, and adventurous, and as such, met with the approval of the reckless spirits, whose greatest pleasure was to be engaged in hazardous enterprises.

Owen formed the men under his command into two small and compact bodies, leading one of them himself, and entrusting the other to a man named Chaffers, of whom more anon.

With surprising energy the buccaneers rushed towards the house.

Shot fell about them like hail; but though it thinned their numbers it did not deter those who remained unhurt from endeavouring to force the door of Don Pedro's house.

They threw themselves with full force against the door.

They made battering rams of their own bodies.

At last the door showed signs of giving way.

A wild cry announced the fact.

Then, with a mighty crash, it fell inwards; and the buccaneers, led by Owen, thronged into the gloomy hall, where our hero had been received on the occasion of his first visit.

A sardonic smile of triumph lit up his face momentarily, as he thought how different was his entrance as a prisoner and as a conqueror.

His work was not yet at an end.

Don Pedro, with a handful of picked men, stood ready to receive his enemies.

The sight of the Spaniard gave renewed energy to Owen, who dashed towards him sword in hand.

"You—you here!" cried the Spanish Captain, in tones of astonishment, for it appeared to him that nothing short of a miracle could have saved our hero from the fire in the forest.

Strange and unnatural as it was to him, Don Pedro was betrayed into an exclamation of surprise when he found himself face to face with Owen Redgrave.

For a few moments the two regarded each other fixedly, and then, as if by common and tacit consent, they raised their weapons.

For a second time their swords met.

Now stood forward the Spaniard, tall and sinewy, prepared for combat.

His features were smeared with blood—his hands black with gunpowder.

In his face, however, there was an expression of haughty security as he parried his assailant's thrusts, waiting for the opportunity of returning them with interest.

Owen was cool and collected.

His brow was knit, but otherwise he showed no signs of the passion which was raging within him.

Still he did not suffer his anger to overcome prudence, for he had a far from pleasant recollection of the manner in which Don Pedro had on the occasion of their previous encounter made his weapon fly from his grasp.

So fierce and deadly was the nature of their conflict, that it attracted attention, and the men on both sides instinctively drew back to become spectators of the duel.

Owen had received two slight wounds, but he was unconscious of them.

He felt no pain. The fight was to the death. The swords flashed with lightning-like rapidity.

The clashing of the weapons, as they met, reverberated through the hall, but no other sound was heard.

These two men, about an equal match in point of strength, were fighting, with savage energy, for life.

Don Pedro's superior skill gained him a slight advantage.

He saw it, and determined to avail himself of it.

He pushed eagerly forward.

In doing so he neglected his guard.

In a moment Owen leapt forward, and plunged his sword almost to the hilt in the Spaniard's body.

With a cry, between a moan and a gasping sob, he fell heavily backwards, his teeth clenched, his hand still firmly grasping his weapon.

But the hand was powerless — the muscles were useless—the body a senseless lump of clay.

Don Pedro would never again move or speak.

He was dead.

His followers, for a moment, were dismayed at their Captain's fall; but they had little time for thought.

No sooner was the combat ended, than Drake's band raised a shout of triumph, and dashed upon their foes with renewed energy.

The resistance they met with was but trifling, for the men were discomposed at the loss of their leader, and a few minutes sufficed to place the house at the disposal of Owen and his followers.

It was in vain that our hero endeavoured to call the men together to maintain something like order and discipline.

They were intoxicated with success.

Victory was theirs, and they rapidly dispersed themselves over the house in search of plunder, preparatory to destroying it by fire.

Owen Redgrave dreaded the Signora might fall into the hands of the ruffianly band.

He shuddered as he thought of what her fate might be before he could rescue her.

The dread of evil befalling her sent him rapidly through the house, in the hope of discovering her hiding-place.

A small door, which, owing to its being partially hidden by some tattered tapestry, appeared to have escaped the notice of the plunderers, attracted his attention.

He tried it, but it was locked.

A vigorous push from his broad shoulders, however, burst it open, and he rushed in.

Chance had led him straight to the room he sought.

There, in one corner, crouching amidst the ruins of broken furniture and torn embroidery, was the Signora.

Clad in a long, flowing robe, which but partially concealed her exquisite form, with her luxuriant hair floating over her beautiful shoulders, was the object of his search—the lovely girl, for whose sake he had endured so much.

"Spare me—spare me!" she cried, in piteous accents, extending her arms in the attitude of supplication.

Owen advanced close to her before she raised her eyes to his face.

When, at last, she looked up, she scarcely appeared to recognise him, and no wonder. The alteration in dress, the blood-stains, the disorder of his whole appearance, prevented her from knowing, for the moment, who it was standing by her side.

"Owen Redgrave!" she exclaimed, after a moment's pause.

Though she recognised him, there appeared, by her tone, to be some doubt in her mind as to the usage she might expect from him.

Could it have been she was conscious of treachery on her own part, and feared it might have been discovered?

"Owen!" she exclaimed.

"My own darling!"

In another moment, reassured by his tones and words, she was close to him, her head resting on his shoulder, while his arm encircled her slender waist.

A hoarse shout of laughter caused them both to turn.

In the doorway stood some half-dozen of the buccaneers, who seemed to enjoy the sight hugely.

"The young 'un knows what he's about!" laughed one. "He's got the best prize of the lot!"

"Something like a girl, she is!" said another, advancing, and roughly holding up the Signora's head, the better to examine her features; but a tremendous blow from Owen sent him staggering back, growling to himself, while a discontented murmur rose from the others."

"Come, come, Captain, share and share alike is our rule. You don't mean to keep her all to yourself?"

"Let one of you dare to lay a finger on her," said Owen, savagely, "and I will mark him in a way he will never forget!"

There was some murmuring; but Owen's resolute appearance, as he faced the men, and the remembrance of his strength, and the deeds of daring he had done, speedily checked it.

Just then Chaffers, attracted hither by the noise, entered the room.

Owen had turned, so that he did not perceive his entrance; but the Signora, whose face was towards the door, noticed it, and a shudder passed through her frame.

"Marie!" exclaimed Chaffers, in a tone of intense surprise.

"Hush!" cried she, in a low whisper. "Do not recognise me, as you value your own life and mine!"

Chaffers took the hint, and left the apartment, without any one being the wiser for this short, whispered conference besides the parties concerned.

For some minutes, Owen gave himself up entirely to the intoxicating delight of holding the Signora in his arms, and whispering soft words in her ear.

He—the man who had endured innumerable hardships, who had suffered so much, who had acted so bravely—forgot all, in the transport of once again meeting her whose image for many months had occupied the foremost place in his mind and heart, to the total exclusion of poor, trusting, loving Grace.

He was recalled to a sense of his duties as present commander of the band of buccaneers, by the sound of their half-drunken whooping and yelling outside the house.

What did it mean?

Owen, looking from the window, perceived they had piled heaps of dry brushwood against the house, and had set it alight.

Already the smoke rose to the upper room in which he was.

There was not a moment to lose.

As it was, it was almost too late.

Owen took the slight form of the Signora in his arms, and rushed frantically down the steep stairs, around which the sharp tongues of flame were already playing.

The huge hall was completely filled with suffocating smoke; but Owen dashed through it, holding his breath.

He threw open the door, and once more felt the fresh, pure air upon his face.

Sternly he reproved the men for their folly and carelessness, and then directed his attention to his lovely burden.

She was insensible.

Water was procured, with which he moistened her lips and bathed her forehead, and shortly he had the pleasure of perceiving she was gradually returning to consciousness.

The buccaneers, before setting fire to the house, had loaded themselves with all the portable valuables upon which they could lay hands; and now the question arose as to what was to be done next.

It had been arranged by Drake that the ship was to be signalled after the battle, and that they were to sail away with as little delay as possible, in case superior forces might be brought to bear upon them; but Captain Drake was missing, and both his lieutenants had been killed, and there was not any authorized person to take the command of the marauding band.

Nearly half the men were in favour of remaining, and searching the place for hidden treasure; but Owen and the remainder all strongly counselled leaving the spot at once.

After a stormy debate, this latter plan was decided upon.

The ship was signalled, boats were sent ashore, and, before evening, the whole band, including Owen Redgrave and the Signora, were on board.

CHAPTER XXVIII.

THE BUCCANEERS RETURN TO THEIR ISLAND HOME.

WHAT had become of Drake?

The question was asked by all, but none were able to answer it.

From the moment he had left the band to signal his ship to stand closer in, he had not been seen.

That he had safely reached the rocky extremity was proved by the fire having been lighted; but, beyond that, nothing was known.

A boat was despatched to search for him.

They reached the rocky point; they found the ashes of the fire, and, near it, a pistol, but it had not been discharged. They called and shouted, but met with no response. As it grew dark, they burnt blue lights and fired guns, but all without success.

Had the Captain been alive, he must have heard and answered these signals.

The following morning, as soon as it was light, they searched among the dead bodies on the field of battle, but Drake's corpse was not among them; so, at last, they were compelled reluctantly to abandon the search, and return to the ship.

No sooner were they on board, than the anchor was weighed, and the sails set, and, with a fresh breeze, they stood out to sea.

Owen had gone on board without knowing whither the vessel was bound.

He had no wish again to brave the dangers of the forest; indeed, with the Signora, such a proceeding would have been impossible, and to separate himself from her he could not: so, little caring whither he went, so long as *she* was by his side, he stepped on board with a light heart; and as the white sails were spread to the wind, and the ship went cleaving through the blue waters, he felt some of his old happiness returning.

The buccaneers welcomed him gladly amongst them, for he had shown the strength of his arm in a way which had won admiration from them all.

And now for a word or two respecting the vessel in which he had embarked.

She was called the Black Cloud, and was a low, rakish-looking craft, schooner-rigged, her hull was painted black, and, on board, everything was arranged with the scrupulous neatness of a man-of-war. And so it need be; for again and again had she saved the lives of her crew by her speed and constant readiness for sea.

There was not over much room on board; and when Owen demanded a separate cabin for the lady, a loud laugh broke from all who heard the request.

They treated it as the harmless fancy of a lunatic.

No sooner was the Black Cloud well out at sea than quarrels and disputes arose among the buccaneers.

Their Captain was missing, their lieutenants were dead, and consequently there was no commander to the fierce band.

All brought forward claims which entitled them to the vacant post; but no one was inclined to give way to others. Indeed, so far did the quarrel extend, that two rival claimants agreed to decide their respective merits by mortal combat.

Owen, perceiving a gathering of men together upon one portion of the deck, went thither, and, to his surprise, found the two men stripped to their shirts and trousers, facing each other, cutlass in hand, while the majority of the crew gathered round to see the sport.

Owen pushed his way through, and seized each of the combatants in his powerful grasp

In vain they struggled to escape, for he held them with a grip of iron.

"Fools!" said he, in his clear, ringing voice. "Are you mad? Keep your swords for enemies!"

So saying, he hurled them violently apart.

Murmurs of indignation rose from the lookers-on.

"Who dares question my right?" asked Owen. "Once destroy discipline, and your band will be at an end!"

"He's in the right, lads!" cried Chaffers. "We must choose a leader at once, and take the oath to obey him, and what better Captain can we find than Owen Redgrave?"

"No, no!" shouted the majority.

"But I say, yes! If we choose one of our own number, it will lead to endless bickering and jealousy. The one man chosen will be pleased, but all the rest will be dissatisfied!"

"There's something in that!"

"Well, then, let us elect a man who is not one of us—a man who has shown by his whole conduct since he has been with us that he is worthy of filling Captain Drake's place. Redgrave for Captain, say I!"

A few echoed the words, "Redgrave for Captain!" but the majority expressed their disapprobation.

"It seems to me," said Owen, "that I might be allowed to speak a few words on this subject I had no idea of joining you, much less of becoming your Captain; but if I can serve you by filling that office, I will do so; but remember, as I do not seek it, I will refuse it, unless it is the universal wish!"

A perfect uproar - a Babel of tongues arose, as he finished this speech; and leaving them still talking in an excited manner, Owen walked aft, to whisper words of love in the ear of the Signora.

It was a long time before the buccaneers could arrive at any decision; but, at last, a party of them, headed by Chaffers, came aft, and, addressing Owen, hailed him as their chief.

Owen, in a short, manly speech, thanked them, declaring he would do all in his power for them, but should in return expect perfect obedience.

His words were loudly cheered by the crew, who willingly, for the most part, took the usual oath of obedience, while our hero, on his part, bound himself solemnly to serve the band in every way.

Since the occasion of their first meeting, no word or sign of recognition had passed between Chaffers and the Signora, though it was evident, from what had then taken place, that they had met previously.

While the choice of Captain had been made, the Black Cloud had been progressing rapidly under easy sail. Owen, though nominally appointed Captain, and, as such, appealed to on all points, was ignorant of the coast which the ship he commanded was approaching, neither did he know whither they were bound, beyond that it was "home."

On the morning of the tenth day after leaving the ruins of Don Pedro's stronghold, the head of the Black Cloud was turned towards the shore, and, before noon, they were sailing slowly up a broad river.

Owen had not allowed the time to pass idly. He had learnt particulars from Chaffers of the island home of the buccaneers, and had already settled upon the line of conduct he would pursue.

The Signora had been during the voyage almost all the ardent lover could wish; but there was one thing which at times caused Owen some uneasiness, and that was the imperfect way in which she accounted for her presence in the Spaniard's house.

True, she had a story which fell glibly from her tongue, but it was full of inaccuracies; and Owen felt, even while she related this strange tale, that it was not wholly true.

Yet he was still infatuated, and could not bring his mind to doubt her.

She professed, with many a sigh, that Owen alone possessed her love; and her eyes were too lustrous, her hair too glossy, her whole form too beautiful, for him to deem her words untrue.

As night fell, the Black Cloud was brought to an anchor under the lee of a large, well-wooded island in the middle of the river, which was the home of the buccaneers.

It was too dark to venture ashore then, but early the next morning there was bustle and confusion on board; for boats were going rapidly between the ship and the island, conveying the buccaneers with their spoils from their sea to their land home.

Owen was not sorry to leave the Black Cloud, but he did not do so until he had seen her towed to her anchorage, which was a small creek running into the island; and which, owing to a sudden natural curve, and the thick foliage, so completely hid her from view, that no one in passing the spot would have imagined so large a vessel could be screened there.

These arrangements completed, Owen and the Signora were rowed ashore, and conveyed to the log-hut formerly occupied by Drake.

The hut, though rough and rude as to the exterior, had some pretensions to comfort inside.

Rich, heavy drapery, the spoils of various predatory excursions, concealed the rough logs, while some handsome furniture was placed about. Of mere ornament there was little; indeed, space would not allow of it; but, when in the evening, a large bronze lamp, which swung from the roof, was lighted, and spread its glow upon the dull crimson curtains, and caught the gold upon the furniture, the hut presented a far from uncomfortable appearance; and to Owen, after the places he had inhabited for the last few months, it seemed a perfect palace.

Leaving the Signora for a while, though much against his will, Owen paid a visit to the cavern, where the band of buccaneers, who called him Captain, were carousing.

It was a large chamber, formed by nature in the solid rock, and would have been gloomy enough but for the blaze of light which illumined every corner.

Lamps of every shape, size, and description diffused their bright rays around, making even the hard rock look warm and comfortable, and lighting up the picturesque group of adventurers who rested themselves around the fire, or who gambled away their hard-earned booty.

It was strange the way in which shawls and draperies of the richest description lay heaped about, while massive silver cups were thrown about like pewters in a pot-house.

This was the scene which presented itself to Owen's eyes as he entered the cavern.

He was warmly greeted by the men; for during their short voyage he had found means to ingratiate himself with them, and there was not one who doubted they had done well in choosing Owen Redgrave for their Captain.

It was but rarely that this band of buccaneers put to sea. Their spoil was principally derived from passage-boats passing up the river; though when any good prize was likely to be the result of the cruise, they did not hesitate to make the attempt.

The number of boats which passed up the river was small, but from all of them the buccaneers extracted a heavy tribute. They fixed the toll at a certain sum, and if it was paid, the party were allowed to proceed; but if money and goods were not forthcoming, or if resistance was offered, force was employed to compel compliance with their demand.

It was well the rocks and trees could not speak, for they might have told many a tale which would have made Owen regret having linked himself with the band.

Weeks passed away without any adventures of note. The buccaneers were well supplied with food and liquor, and spent their time in drinking and gambling. No boats passed up the stream; and as the band had sufficient of everything for the present, there was no temptation to them for the present to risk their fortune on the high seas.

Owen's office, hitherto, had been a sinecure.

One glorious day, tired of a life of inactivity, the Captain announced his intention of proceeding down the river in a boat, to reconnoitre.

Some half-dozen men accompanied him; but they had not proceeded far when the gathering clouds and the increasing wind warned them of an approaching storm.

They hastened back to the island; the boat was secured just as the storm burst in all its fury; the men hurried to the cavern, and Owen bent his steps in the direction of the hut, which was his by right of office.

As he was about to push open the door, he heard the sound of voices in the interior.

One he recognised as that of the Signora, the other was Chaffers.

Something told him to wait and listen.

He did so.

"You do not, then, love this Owen Redgrave, Marie?"

"Love!" And a clear, silvery laugh, which Owen knew too well, fell upon his ear.

"Why, then, do you stay with him?"

"Why did I stay with Johann? Why did I stay with Pedro?"

"Because it served your turn."

"Precisely."

"Well?"

"Do you not understand that I may have similar reasons for assuming love to this Englishman?"

"What are they?"

"That is my business."

"Surely, I have a right to know."

"A right! What right?"

"The right of a husband."

"Pshaw! Have you not yet forgotten that silly ceremony we went through together?"

"No," answered Chaffers, in a surly tone.

"It pleases me," continued the Signora, "to make a dupe—a fool of this Owen Redgrave, the while I amass treasure, which will enable me to live in affluence the rest of my life. Twice already have I done so, and each time, at the last moment, it has been snatched from my grasp."

"But your heart?"

"What of it?"

"Where is it?"

"Yours!"

Chaffers drew the lovely girl towards him, and imprinted a kiss upon her lips.

Owen was well-nigh beside himself with rage.

To have been thus tricked and deceived—to have gone through so much for this worthless woman—it was indeed galling to his proud spirit.

He drew a pistol from his breast, and cocked it; then stole quietly round to the window of the hut.

The sight which met his eyes did not allay the demon which was raging within him.

The Signora was sitting lovingly by the side of the man Chaffers, her head resting on his shoulder.

Owen bent forward, and rested the barrel of his pistol upon the window-sill, and took steady aim at the heart of the faithless girl.

Even then, some return of the old affection stayed his finger as he would have pulled the trigger; but at the very moment that he relented the lips of those he watched again met.

In an agony of rage and jealousy he pressed the trigger.

The cap exploded; but the rain, which was falling fast, had damped the powder, and it did not go off.

The noise of the cap, however, had been sufficient to attract the attention of those inside the hut; and Owen, scarcely knowing why, turned and fled.

Fled through the pouring rain—fled into the thick wood, and at length threw himself down upon the wet grass in an agony of wounded pride and despair.

Like a panorama, the events of his past life appeared before his eyes. For her sake he had endured torture and confinement—for her sake he had been faithless to one who loved him truly; and now the mask was removed, and he saw how worthless was she in whom he had trusted—how depraved was this woman upon whom he had wasted his love.

For many hours he lay upon the grass, neither heeding or caring for the moisture which soaked his garments; but at last, when the shades of night began to fall, he rose to his feet, and strode moodily towards his hut, revolving in his own mind what course he should pursue with the faithless girl.

His most passionate feelings were calmed in some measure; still, he felt he hardly dared face her.

He entered the hut, pondering in his own mind how they would meet.

Would she greet him lovingly, as of old?

If so, what should he reply to the words of affection?

He was spared the meeting.

The hut was deserted.

He looked round, and saw to his surprise that every article of value had been removed. The rich hangings had been torn down, revealing the rough logs in all their ugliness. The curiously-wrought golden ornaments which had decorated the room were removed The box containing all his worldly wealth was gone!

For a moment he remained thunderstruck. Then, with an oath, he darted from the place to the cavern where the buccaneers were carousing.

"Where is Chaffers?" cried he, in wrathful tones.

The men looked up amazed.

Before them stood their Captain, the wet dripping from his garments, his hair floating wildly about his face, his eyes glaring fiercely upon them, and his whole aspect like that of one distraught.

"Where is he?" he asked, impatiently.

No one had seen him.

He was not in the cavern, and had not been there for some hours.

Without another word, Owen rushed to the place where the boat had been made fast on his return that morning.

It was gone.

Stooping down to examine the rope, Owen's eyes rested upon a small, delicately embroidered pocket-handkerchief.

In a moment he recognised it as one he had seen in the hands of the Signora.

It settled the matter.

There could no longer be any doubt respecting her disappearance.

She had gone off with Chaffers.

Owen rent the handkerchief with savage fury, and threw it from him.

And then with rapid steps returned to the cavern.

He entered it, and with quick strides advanced to the fire, around which the buccaneers were seated.

All looked up as he approached, for so wild and strange was his appearance that it was evident something out of the common had happened.

"Listen to me!" cried Owen, in loud, harsh tones. "I have been duped and fooled by a woman! I have been robbed by her and her lover! I was idiot enough to believe the softly-spoken words of the Signora; but I have discovered the folly of believing or trusting any one. She has eloped with Chaffers!"

"Gone?" chorussed the gang.

"Yes, gone! But you may reap the benefit. Listen to my words. I have been leading a life of idleness and inactivity since you chose me Captain, but now it shall be the reverse! I make a solemn vow to devote my life to you, and swear by all that is sacred to spare neither man, woman, nor child who fall into my hands!"

"Hurrah for the Captain!" shouted several.

"Are any of you afraid to join me?" continued Owen; "if so, let him leave at once before it is too late. To-morrow we will hoist the black flag; and may heaven help those who come across my path, for their life shall be a forfeit! I want no plunder—all shall be divided amongst you! I want revenge—revenge on the whole human race! Who joins me?"

"I!—"And I!" resounded on every side; and to a man they caught their chief's enthusiasm.

"Then prepare your arms; for at daybreak to-morrow my vow commences; and if I spare the life of any one—no matter their age or sex—may I myself fall victim to death—death at your hands!"

"Three cheers for our noble Captain!"

They were given with unwonted vehemence; and as the sound reverberated through the cavern, Owen's face lit up with a fiendish joy, his eyes sparkled, and his fingers quivered, as he drew forth his sword and held its blade high above his head.

"Death to all who cross our path!" he shouted; and the buccaneers echoed the cry.

CHAPTER XXIX.

THE LOVES OF A COUNTRY LAWYER.

IT is necessary that, for a time, we should change the scene of our story, and treat of others of our *dramatis personæ*, whom for some time past we have neglected.

Accompany me, then, kind reader, on board a steamboat, which is slowly working its way onwards, down one of those fast-flowing rivers which abound in the land of wild and wonderful adventure our history treats of.

The sun has long gone down, and the moon shines brightly on the dark and rapid waters, save when, at times, the drifting clouds dim the lustre of the Queen of Night, and cast black shadows o'er the far-stretching plains which lie on either side of the river.

The water gurgles melodiously from the paddles, and forms a kind of accompaniment to the low chorus chanted by the sailors lolling idly over the boat-side.

Every now and then the cry of the coon, shrilly and mocking, comes from the shore; and large cat-fish, leaping from their cold bed, glitter for a moment like silver in the moonlight, ere they fall back with a dull plash into the water.

Far ahead, large drifting trees, the growth of hundreds of years, stretch their giant arms across the stream, towards their murmuring brethren upon the opposite side; and beyond, a deep silence reigns over the river, which has something ominous and threatening, even in its unbroken gloom and quietude.

There were a large number of passengers on board the steamboat of which I have spoken; but the greater part of them were composed of the poorer classes of Scotch and Irish emigrants, who, for the most part, sat huddled together down below, grumbling and groaning, and bewailing their hard lot in being obliged to leave the land of plenty, where they had starved, and the dear home which had seen them through years of misery and squalor.

There had been a great deal of sickness on board; and, at one period of the voyage, there had even been a question of putting back, but this was overruled by the person who had organized the expedition, and whose good sense and sound judgment smoothed away all difficulties, and restored confidence when it seemed almost shaken beyond hope of recovery.

The same influence was even quietly at work below among the malcontents, endeavouring to cheer them

in their moments of gloom, and to point out the bright prospect that beamed ahead.

Many and many a time did a few well-spoken, kindly words bring smiles to tearful eyes, and cause the most gloomy and despondent to brighten up, and be as cheerful as circumstances would admit of.

Not that all on board were in any way discontented with their lot, or that any had joined the expedition without their own consent, and at their own eagerly expressed desire.

The object of the voyage was this—to find a new home in a land of plenty, where there was room enough for all.

Among the habitations of the poor and miserable, a bright angel had one morning paid a visit, bringing with her words of comfort and other gifts more costly, in a material point of view, than the flimsy little tracts with which the visiting ladies, who had often made calls upon them, were in the habit of inundating these dwellers in narrow courts and crooked alleys.

This lady had brought with her stories which were absolutely wonderful to those poor benighted ones, of a land beyond the seas, and a happy home to be won by honest labour.

Would they cast away their rags, and go with her? she asked.

Would they leave the squalor and misery of the hard, struggling life they lived here in the crowded city, and go to the land of plenty which she described.

If they would agree, she would pay their passage there. She would start them all in life, when they reached their journey's end. They would all have a fair chance in a new field, and it depended upon themselves whether or not success was theirs.

Need you ask whether there were many volunteers?

All to whom the offer was made were only too eager to accept the terms she made them.

She, on her part, though, did not gather together her flock without proper consideration.

Many incorrigible ne'er-do-wells were there, who would not have worked when they reached the new land, any more than they had worked here in the mother country.

Many were there who were their own determined enemies, and who would not be helped to aught but their own destruction.

These she prudently refused to take with her, but not without well weighing the reasons pro and con, and doing all in her power to arrive at a just estimation of their character, before making a refusal when it was absolutely necessary.

And then, too, it was only when she had conferred with a shrewd man of business, whose services she had enlisted in carrying out the practical part of this great work of benevolence.

" And who was this good lady?" the reader may ask.

An old friend of ours, whom I trust you have not altogether forgotten.

A rich young lady she was, whom the world wondered had never yet got married.

It was not because she had no offers, certainly, for she might have married into any of the best families in the county.

She lived a somewhat lonely life, in a pretty little rose-covered cottage, far away in the country—far away among the rich pasture land of one of the most beautiful English counties. She lived there, where she had lived since she was a little girl, before all those whom she loved had died or left her.

Some were there who wondered how it was that she could endure a residence in an abode which must have such painful associations; for there was a grim and ghastly story of crime attached to this picturesque

little cottage, standing in its garden of sweet-smelling flowers, and almost hidden from the high road by its high hedges of laurel and holly.

A dreadful story was this, which was faintly whispered about—never, though, in the young lady's hearing—of a mother's death at the hands of her unnatural son.

Strange to say, the young lady herself strenuously defended the character of the son—earnestly pleaded his cause, and asserted her conviction of his innocence, and wrongful accusation.

Those who heard her, though, did not alter their opinion. Some thought her eccentric; and those who knew her best, knew that, her life through, she had never given an unkind word to living creature. It was not, therefore, to be wondered at if she endeavoured even to shelter a villain, if he were persecuted.

He had been tried for burglary, and sentenced to transportation for a long period.

Though morally guilty of murder, he had escaped the hangman's rope. It was not with an assassin's knife that his mother had perished. She had died, the doctors decided, a natural death.

She awakened in the dead of the night to find her son rifling her chamber — to find him, perchance, threatening her with upraised dagger.

Then, screaming in terror, she had burst a blood-vessel, and died.

It could not, then, be said that he murdered her, and yet it was very certain that she would not have died thus suddenly had it not been in consequence of his misconduct.

When the son was sent for trial, this young lady had exerted herself to the utmost to save him.

After he had been transported, too, she relaxed not in her efforts; but still, they were all unavailing.

Time rolled on.

She lived in anxious hopes of his return.

Alas, hopes that were doomed never to be realized!

Long, disheartening accounts arrived from the penal settlement.

Tales of outrage and violence, of attempted escape, fire, and shipwreck. Then came a long interval of silence and uncertainty, during which the fond, loving heart left in England fluttered like a caged bird in its grief and terror.

It was at this time, though, that the young lady, instead of abandoning herself entirely to grief, as other young ladies might have done in her place, worked harder than ever in the cause of local charity, which she had long ago espoused.

For some years past, she herself had lived with great frugality, saying that all that she could save, belonged to the poor; but still refusing to touch, and allowing to accumulate, all the property which had belonged to the old lady.

This property was not hers, she had persisted in, in spite of all the reasonings of her legal adviser. It must be saved until the son returned to claim it.

" He never will return, my dear young lady."

But the young lady only shook her head, and smiled faintly.

" We will wait and see," said she.

" But, in the meantime——"

" In the meantime, let the property accumulate. It will be all the more for him when he does come. Has he not long enough been wrongly deprived of it? Surely we ought to try to make it worth his acceptance when he does return at last."

" You always will maintain that Owen Redgrave is innocent?"

" I always will refuse to ague the point with you, Mr. Hardstaff, and I claim a woman's privilege of keeping her own opinion, in spite of argument——"

"And in spite of reason."

"Most certainly."

When Mr. Hardstaff walked away that afternoon, he turned upon the hill-top, from which he could look back at the little cottage, took off his hat, and pondered.

"How obstinate all women are!" said he. "They don't argue according to what they think is, but what they think ought to be. How unfair they are, and Miss Grace Atherton is altogether the most unfair I I ever came across; and yet——"

Mr. Hardstaff did not go on with his remarks for a few moments.

Then he looked long and earnestly at the pretty little cottage, and heaved a sigh.

"That woman is an angel!" said he—"a downright angel! I'll be hanged if she isn't!"

He set off at a brisk pace down the other side of the hill, after having thus delivered his opinion, as though he feared that somebody might stop him, and demand an explanation of his very singular behaviour.

One day, some little time after this, Mr. Hardstaff went down to the cottage.

For some reason and another, he very frequently went down to the cottage. They were, of course, all of them, very good and weighty reasons, mind you. I do not for a moment intend to dispute that, or throw any doubt upon the necessity of his frequent attendance upon Miss Grace Atherton. Understand me aright. I only say he very frequently went down to the cottage.

Upon this occasion he went at an early hour. Miss Atherton was an early riser, but she had not yet taken her breakfast.

He raised the latch of the garden gate, and walked quietly up the lawn. He found the house door open, and as he was not a stranger, he thought he might venture inside without knocking.

He was always a very quiet walker, and he made no noise in passing across the little hall. The door of the parlour stood ajar, and he peeped in.

He could see nobody there.

The breakfast-table was laid, and upon it were scattered some letters and newspapers, which had been opened.

"She is down," thought Mr. Hardstaff to himself. "Where is she, I wonder?"

He drew back again into the hall, and looked out into the garden, where sometimes he knew she was in the habit of walking before breakfast. But he could see nothing of her.

Somehow or other, Mr. Hardstaff appeared not to be altogether displeased by her absence.

He heaved a little sigh of relief, and sat down in an easy chair close to the door.

He had something he wanted to think of, and he sat down with the resolute determination of turning the matter over in his mind.

"I will do it," said he, aloud. "The question is, how to begin."

This had been the question which had been troubling him for some days past; but as yet he had arrived at no satisfactory solution of the difficulty.

How was it to be done?

He had gone to bed over night, thinking of it.

He had lain awake thinking of it. He had thought of it so long, and with such unsatisfactory results, that he had determined to give up thinking until next morning.

However, this was not so easy to do.

The slightest push will set a wheel rolling upon the top of a hill; but stand half-way down, and try and stop it!

Mr. Hardstaff passed a sleepless night, and rose a little before the lark, determined to take a walk, and see what fresh air would do towards improving his mental faculties.

Fresh air, however, did very little towards bringing him to a satisfactory conclusion respecting this question which had been agitating him.

This question, which was nothing more nor less— of course you ladies guessed it ever so long ago—than how he should propose to Miss Grace Atherton.

You see, there are, after all, only a few ways of proposing. Either it is verbally, or by letter.

If by letter, some composition is required, and the words have to be picked very carefully, for they are, you may be sure, well read and conned over by the fair one; and at the same time that the proposal should not come too suddenly, there should not be too much beating about the bush.

Now, a verbal proposal is decidedly the easiest, although some of you nervous ones may be inclined to prefer the epistolary style. If the young lady only helps you a little, two or three incoherent words are quite sufficient to express your meaning.

According to the most learned authors, when once the ice is broken, a flow of impassioned language at once comes to your assistance, and you carry all before you in a flood of eloquence.

You see, therefore, that the sooner the ice is broken the better, and I have no doubt but that the words will follow; though certainly, if they do not, your situation would be rather awkward.

As to the manner of breaking the ice, I must leave that to your discretion.

At the theatre, they generally go down on one knee. They do so in valentines, and point to a church conveniently situated in the background, at the end of a trimly-kept gavel walk serpentining up to it.

But upon this subject I must refer you to those useful little books on the etiquette of courtship and marriage; which will give you full instructions how to act.

It is with Mr. Hardstaff's case, though, that I have to deal, and not with yours, however great the interest may be which I take in your love affairs.

Mr. Hardstaff had made up his mind to do a desperate deed. He had determined to propose marriage to Miss Grace Atherton.

He did not think he stood a very good chance. How could he, indeed, when so many better men than he had been refused?

But he was resolved to risk all, and he went with this determination to call upon Miss Atherton on the morning I have described to you.

He had been trying to make up his mind to how to break the ice; and at last, fairly to do so, he had resolved to go, and trust to chance.

He was very thankful, though, when at length he arrived at the cottage, for a few moments' repose, so that he might gather together his scattered thoughts.

He sat down in the arm-chair by the door, as we have seen, and for the hundredth time began to think the matter over.

For the hundredth time he asked himself the question, "How shall I begin?"

He could not find any answer to this, and therefore sat puzzling for a very long time in silence.

At length, however, it struck him that the time was very long indeed.

What could have become of the young lady?

Perhaps she had gone out. After all his arrangements, after all his consideration and deliberation, the young lady had gone out, and he was, therefore, just where he had been at the commencement.

It was, certainly, extremely annoying. This obstacle now thrown in his path was such an unexpected one.

What was to be done? He rose with the determination of ringing the bell, and making some inquiries of the servant.

He all this time, as I have already told you, had been sitting in an arm-chair close to the room door.

As yet, he had not penetrated more than a yard and a half, at most, into the apartment.

To reach the bell, it was necessary that he should go round the table.

With the bell-pull in his hand, he cast his eyes accidentally upon the floor on the other side of the table, close to the window, and some object lying there attracted his attention.

He stood for a moment transfixed with amazement, wondering what it was.

He took a step towards it, and the truth was revealed to him.

In another moment, a wild terror possessing him, he fell upon his knees with an inarticulate cry for help, and strove to raise from the ground the senseless form of poor Grace Atherton.

"Was she dead?" he asked himself. This, at first, he feared was the case, for she lay so white, and still, and motionless.

He raised her in his arms, and laid her gently down upon the sofa.

He rang the bell, and called for assistance.

He ran breathlessly out in search of medical aid.

Then, failing to obtain it, returned, and in a hundred ways tried to be of service; though, in all he did, but hindering the servants—who, knowing what was requisite, worked steadily to obtain the desired result.

But when, at length, the young lady, having shown signs of returning consciousness, was conveyed upstairs to her own room, Mr. Hardstaff remained below, and asked himself what could be the cause of the strange scene at which he had just assisted.

What had occasioned her sudden indisposition? How was it to be accounted for?

He paced slowly to and fro in the little parlour, taking particular care to step exactly in the centre of the small squares which composed the pattern of the carpet.

"It's something about that fellow, Redgrave!" he exclaimed, at last, coming to a sudden pause as he uttered the words.

He paced to and fro again, now more rapidly than before.

Suddenly, again he came to a stand-still in front of an open newspaper which he saw lying upon the ground.

He had not previously noticed it, he thought; and yet, when he began to reflect upon the occurrences of the past hour, he most certainly had seen a newspaper of some kind lying upon the ground by the side of the girl's insensible form.

She, then, had been reading it.

What was there in it which could account for her indisposition?

He opened the paper and turned it over and over, without, however, being able to discover any passage which he could suppose would be likely to cause any emotion to the young lady; who, nevertheless, he felt convinced, had been deeply affected by the perusal of some portion of the news.

It appeared to him, as he scanned its contents, to be almost destitute of intelligence calculated to be of any interest to anybody.

It was a country paper, and there were one or two slip-slop leaders, expressing no particular opinions in very indifferent English. There was a correspondent's letter from London, with the latest fashionable, literary, and dramatic gossip to be picked up from the London newspapers. There was a Paris letter, very evidently written in the little country town where the newspaper was published, by somebody who never in his life had crossed the Channel.

Then there followed a few police reports of local orchard robberies, wife-beating, and trespass. Then a separate article about a serious charge against a licensed victualler; a brief account of a recent battle in foreign parts; and three-quarters of a column about an enormous gooseberry.

A shower of frogs turned up on the last page, and a letter from "A Constant Reader," observed upon the remarkable clemency of the season.

Then followed a number of advertisements; births, deaths, and marriages; quotations from the latest London market-prices, and from the *London Gazette*; and then the printer's name.

"Nothing in it," said Mr. Hardstaff, as he turned the paper over and over in his hand. "Absolutely nothing in it; and yet what could it have been that affected her?"

He could not answer the question. In like case, how many of every day readers, take up the broad sheets, and say, after a careless glance over the printed matter which they contain, "There's nothing in it;" and yet, heaven only knows what unutterable anguish may lie there hidden for some eyes unexpectedly to find out.

Mr. Hardstaff was determined, though, to find out the secret, and still pondered over the columns of the country journal.

While thus employed, the door opened behind him, and Grace Atherton, calm, but deadly pale, entered, and advanced towards him.

He did not hear her coming, and until she stood by his side, was unaware of her presence.

He started forward to take her hand in his when at last he perceived her, at the same time uttering an exclamation of surprise.

"My dear young lady," he said, " are you—are you sufficiently recovered to——"

"I am not ill," she answered calmly. "I was a good deal shocked by the news."

"The news, Miss Atherton! What news?"

"You hold the paper in your hand."

"Yes," replied Mr. Hardstaff, throwing a despairing glance over its contents. "I have been trying in vain to find something to account for——I really don't see anything in it."

Grace stretched forth her small white hand, and took the newspaper from him.

Then returned it, pointing silently to a tiny paragraph in one corner, which the old gentleman had hitherto overlooked.

There, however, was a brief account of the capture of an American buccaneer, who had confessed to the existence of a band of pirates, many of whom were escaped convicts—among others, a man named Owen Redgrave, supposed to have escaped from Norfolk Island about two years before.

This latter, the paragraph went on to say, had been slain during a skirmish with the military, and had been recognised by certain papers found in his possession, relating to the rewards which from time to time had been offered for his apprehension.

Mr. Hardstaff read the account through to the end without making any observation. He did not place too much faith in the statements there made, and was, at first, upon the point of saying so, when another thought occurred to him.

Would it not be best for Grace to think her old lover dead? Was he not, at any rate, dead to her? Could she ever, with any show of probability, look forward to, or hope for, a happy meeting, after what had passed?

There was no selfish motive prompting the old man to this decision. He thought only for her good—for her happiness alone was he anxious.

Upon one thing he had very soon made up his mind.

This was not a proper time to make any proposal. He must put that off till a more favourable opportunity.

A few days elapsed after these occurrences before he and Miss Atherton met again.

When he called at the cottage, she was too indisposed to see him. She nevertheless, though, sent down soothing messages, thanking him warmly for his kind inquiries; and so this consoled him to some extent, and at the same time prevented his hopes from altogether sinking beyond all chance of recovery.

One morning, though, Miss Grace's servant brought him a letter to say that she was very anxious to see him.

It need not be said that he lost very little time in obeying the summons.

He was at breakfast at the time, but I rather doubt whether he stayed to break the shell of his second egg.

He was generally rather particular about his personal appearance; but this morning he went out without brushing his hat, and only half-buttoned his gaiters.

He walked at a great rate out of the little village, and reached the cottage almost out of breath.

"How can I be of service to you, Miss Atherton?" he asked, as soon as he entered.

"In many ways," she replied. "One is, to prepare my affairs in such a way that I can leave England."

"Leave England!" gasped Mr. Hardstaff.

He was much more out of breath now than all his fast walking had made him.

"Leave England!" he repeated, after a pause.

"Yes," said his companion, "and at once."

"At once!" echoed Mr. Hardstaff, if possible, more astonished still.

"And for good!" continued Miss Atherton.

But the worthy lawyer had no more astonishment left in his composition, and so he could express no greater surprise than he had done already.

He therefore took his pocket-handkerchief out of his pocket—he always resorted to it in moments of difficulty—rubbed his nose-end to a high state of polish; and putting it—the handkerchief, not his nose—back into his pocket again, simply observed—

"To be sure."

It was then that Miss Atherton unfolded a grand scheme of emigration which she had long since conceived, and which she now hoped to be able to carry out.

Mr. Hardstaff listened attentively, and offered to lend all the assistance in his power.

He, may be, did not think the scheme was quite as rational as it might have been.

If it had been anybody else's scheme, he would probably have called it folly.

But upon this occasion he offered no objection. What was there that he would not have done for this young lady, who ruled him with a wave of her little finger? She might, I am sure, as easily have robbed him of the last sixpence he possessed in the world, as she had already robbed him of his heart.

He therefore went, heart and soul, into the necessary preparations for the voyage.

There surely never was anybody who packed so well, so much, and so quickly. He was indefatigable, too, in the trouble he took in effecting proper arrangements, and in making the proper purchases in the right markets.

A rich gentleman who lived in that part of the country where Grace Atherton resided. and who had been one among her numerous but unsuccessful suitors, had died about eighteen months previous, and had bequeathed her all his fortune and estates; among the latter, some land upon the banks of the Mississippi, which report proclaimed to be in a high state of cultivation, and capable of amply rewarding any labour bestowed upon it.

At this place it was Miss Atherton's project to establish a colony, and the praiseworthy scheme showed every sign of being successfully carried out, if it was possible to judge of the result from the business-like steps which were taken in the matter at the commencement of that which all her friends denounced as an absurd enterprise.

So very rapid were Mr. Hardstaff's movements when once he set to work, and so very much occupied was he by his various duties, that the time seemed to him to pass with astonishing rapidity, and at length the week before the time fixed for the start came round, and all at once the old gentleman grew very uneasy.

He was standing in front of the fire in his office, looking at the office almanack hanging upon the wall, framed and glazed for reference, when, all at once, a thought struck him.

"By Jove!" he cried.

Out came his pocket handkerchief, which he used profusely.

"I'll do it!" he cried.

And putting on his hat, rushed out of the office.

He hesitated not a moment this time; there was no deliberation and consideration.

He walked rapidly over the hill. He knocked briskly at the door. He asked whether Miss Grace Atherton was at home.

She was, and was delighted to see him.

"I have come to speak to you upon a matter of some importance—to me!" he began.

"A matter of importance?" she repeated.

"To me!" replied Mr. Hardstaff.

"Won't you be seated?" she asked.

"No, thank you," replied Mr. Hardstaff. "I am not tired. In point of fact, I'd rather not sit down while I asked you this question."

"What question?" inquired Grace, opening her beautiful eyes in astonishment.

"I hardly know whether this is quite the right time to ask it, after all."

"To ask what?"

"I don't know that I ought not properly to have waited until you had finished tea."

"I have finished."

"Oh, I beg pardon! I thought you were taking tea."

"I had done."

"That makes it different, to be sure. In that case, then, there can be no reason why I should not——"

"Certainly not."

"In that case, then, I will delay no longer. To come to the point, then, at once. Miss Atherton, will you marry me?"

* * * * * *

An author has always the privilege of dropping the curtain when he thinks fit. Perhaps my lady readers will be of opinion that I should have given this interview at length, while some of my male readers may be very much obliged to me for sparing them the details.

I think that the most satisfactory way of explaining the rest of all that was said upon both sides, on this and various other occasions, by these two persons, is not to report one word of it, but merely record what took place eight days afterwards, upon the day that the ship was to set sail with Grace and her little colony on board.

The passengers' friends had left the ship's side, and the boats were dropping astern, amid the mingled cheers and tears which are always the accompaniment of these parting scenes, when somebody in another boat was heard hailing the vessel with all the strength of his lungs, which were tolerably powerful.

"Who's that?" asked the captain of the mate.

"I don't know," replied the latter, after taking a long observation through his glass of the vociferous person who was doing his utmost to attract their attention.

"Have we all our passengers on board?"

"There is one missing."

"Who is that?"

"There is one of the name of Smith."

"Does he belong to Miss Atherton's company?"

"No, a cabin passenger."

"That, no doubt, is Mr. Smith; we had better wait for him, I suppose."

The cabin passenger in question only just managed to save his passage.

He, however, came up in time, and was taken on board, where the captain received him without any great demonstration of affection.

He was a very affable gentleman, was this Mr. Smith; and in spite of his making the officers and passengers' acquaintance under such extremely disadvantageous circumstances, he was not very long before he contrived to ingratiate himself with everybody on board—everybody except Miss Atherton, by the way, who kept her cabin almost all the first day of the voyage, and so was not brought in contact with the procrastinating passenger.

At last, however, she did meet him, face to face.

Then she opened her eyes, and uttered an exclamation of astonishment.

"Mr. Hardstaff!" she exclaimed. "You don't mean to say that that is you?"

"All that's left of me, Miss Atherton," responded the country solicitor, cheerfully. "I never was intended for a sailor; I haven't found my sea-legs yet, and I've pretty well knocked my head off against the side of the cupboard they call my cabin. I should be awfully ill, too, if I had only time enough, but there are——Coming, coming!——There are, in point of fact, so many claims on my attention, and——Coming, I say!——How everybody does keep on calling, to be sure! I ought to be quartered, to be of any use in this ship! And so I hope you'll excuse the liberty I have taken in following you."

"Why have you followed me, Mr. Hardstaff?"

"Do you really want to know, Miss Atherton?"

"That was one reason which prompted me to inquire."

"It is, then—now don't be offended—because I absolutely adore the ground you walk upon. I had some idea of remaining at home and adoring the ground you had walked upon there, but it did not appear to me to be quite as satisfactory, so I ventured——"

"You gave me your promise, Mr. Hardstaff, that you would let this matter drop between us. I told you that I could never—never——And what do you propose doing?"

"Following you to your new home, working with you and for you until you are hard-hearted enough to send me about my business."

"But Mr. Hardstaff, I am sure I cannot find employment——"

"Oh, yes, you can. At least, try; ever so little or ever so much, quantity no object, and no wages expected."

"But how about your practice?"

"I've sold it."

"And your home?"

"Given it up."

"And your old servant?"

"Pensioned her."

"And you have done all this for my sake!"

"Why not, pray? Am not I old enough to do what I like with my own?"

"I shall never forgive you."

"Never?"

"Never!"

"And yet that is a long time!"

"Never, till you grow wiser, at any rate!" said the young lady, turning away with a laugh.

CHAPTER XXX.

THE APPROACH OF DANGER.

THE colonists journeyed onwards; and, for some length of time, the novelty of the life they led on shipboard was sufficient to distract their attention, and keep them from quarrelling among themselves.

Very soon, however, little dissensions arose, and little misunderstandings, which grew into great feuds in an incredibly short space of time. It was then that Mr. Hardstaff's presence on board ship was found to be of such service.

Towards the end of the journey the pining for land seemed to sour the temper of all; and had he not many times exerted himself to the utmost to calm the malcontents, the murmur of dissatisfaction must inevitably have broken forth into an open mutiny.

But all this wore off when land was reached, and things began to be tolerably comfortable during the short rest which followed the first landing in the new land.

But the delay allowed here was necessarily very short; and then came the wearisome and monotonous journey up the river.

Unhappily, too, some of those who had landed had brought back fever with them, which soon was communicated to the other passengers, and ran round the boat.

The journey, too, up the river was only to have occupied two or three days; but a variety of accidents occurred to cause the voyage to be of much longer duration.

An accident occurring to the engine was one of the misfortunes—the incompetency of the captain, the greatest.

At last, they came to that part of the river where, when our last chapter began, we found them.

At that place there were a number of small islands covered with reeds, willow, and tall cotton trees; and the river, at places, was scarcely navigable by large boats.

An intricate collection of fallen trees, with wide-spreading branches lying beneath the water, impeded the progress of the boats, and it was only a river pilot, acquainted with these dangers, who could safely guide a steamer past them.

In one of the villages upon the river's bank a pilot was found to take charge of the boat which contained the colonists.

They were a curious race of persons those found in the village, with a strangely hang-dog look about their sallow faces.

The man who offered his services was not a very favourable specimen even of these; but he had been declared by his fellows to be the man for the job, and the Captain had therefore engaged him without question.

"He may do his work very well, in spite of his being so ill-looking," said Mr. Hardstaff.

The Captain was of the same opinion, and went into a lengthy harangue, tending to show that it was necessary for a man to be born upon the banks of the river, and to pass all his life almost upon its waters, before he could know anything of its navigation in these parts.

"It's rather dangerous hereabouts, I suppose?" said Mr. Hardstaff.

"There are many dangers—snags, for instance, and sawyers."

"To be sure!" said Mr. Hardstaff, who, however, was by no means certain what snags and sawyers might be.

"Yes," continued the Captain; "and worse, too!"

"Worse than snags?" asked Mr. Hardstaff, incredulously.

"Much worse. There are pirates!"

"Impossible!"

"Perhaps so; but it is nevertheless the fact. You know that steam-vessels haven't very long run here. The trade with the interior used to be carried on by means of large, heavy boats, called arks. They used to be often stopped and robbed."

"Were there many of these pirates?"

"There was one little island, called Crow's Nest, where there was a regular organized band of robbers, who not only murdered and plundered all who fell into their hands, but forged bank-notes, which were extensively circulated in the West."

"But they are all sent to the right-abouts long ago?"

"Not so. There are several of these islands which serve as a retreat for horse thieves, robbers, murderers, and escaped convicts; and, in spite of all the attempts that are made to capture them, they have hitherto escaped, and set all laws at defiance!"

Mr. Hardstaff listened uneasily to this account, which, however, he trusted might prove in a great measure to be exaggeration.

"Look there!" said the Captain, pointing ahead. "That looks very like one of their strongholds!"

He alluded to a dark island, thickly studded with large trees. There were many like it to be found thereabouts; and little would the heedless landsman have thought, as he floated past this gloomy isle, what danger lay concealed in its shadow.

All around there were artificial snags and sawyers, artfully contrived, and the stubborn branches projecting over the water were sufficient to keep off the general run of boatmen, who expected no danger. Had a landing, however, been effected, the intruder would have had to seek his way for several hundred yards through the most formidable thicket.

Trees, torn up by the roots, were heaped confusedly together, so as to render advance almost impossible.

Nevertheless, there lay concealed here a complete settlement, so cunningly secreted as to deceive even the sharp eyes of a North American hunter.

It was formed of several block-houses, a tolerably large store and stables, the latter joined together, and communicating with each other.

They were built upon the plan of the Indian forts surrounding a court, so that they might easily be defended against a sudden attack even of superior force.

The store and one of the block-houses stood in the middle; and, in a semicircle to the east, the stables formed a solid wall, provided with loopholes, surrounding the cave already described.

On the western or less exposed side, high double fences connected the block-houses with one another.

A long brass swivel on a post was placed on the flat roof of the store-house, and was considered by the islanders as one of the best means of defence, with which they could scatter death and confusion among their assailants.

Two practicable paths alone conducted to the robbers' retreat.

One of these paths led from the shore towards the centre of the island.

It was, to all appearance, well worn and much used; but this was intended to lead the luckless intruder into a morass, in which he would inevitably perish.

The path which the robbers really used turned off at a sharp angle, and was artfully concealed by boughs.

It led into the fort, and was kept in good order, and passing the fort, came to a kind of bay, where boats were kept, as a means of retreat in the last extremity.

The object of the robbers was not so much to defend their stronghold when it was attacked; they only desired to keep their assailants off for a short time, until they were able to make good their retreat.

What they depended upon most was secrecy; and this, at all hazards, they must preserve.

Once discovered, they were lost.

But the band was bound together by the most fearful oaths, and it was not probable that any of them would dare to play his companions false.

These details, however, are all that I need to add to what in another place I have already described to you, except to state that the existence of the buccaneers' retreat, though hinted at, as we have seen, by the Captain of the steamboat, was nevertheless known only as a certainty to members of the band themselves.

As Mr. Hardstaff now strained his eyes to pierce the intense obscurity of the forest which covered the side of the island nearest to them, so deep was the darkness and silence, he could scarcely believe it possible that there could be any one living there in that wild and apparently deserted spot.

His attention, however, did not very long remain fixed upon this object.

On the contrary, his attention was attracted by the expression of the pilot's countenance, towards which his eyes, many times during the conversation, had been irresistibly attracted.

Was he to be trusted?

Mr. Hardstaff blew his nose vehemently—his energy increasing with his perplexity; but failed to arrive at any satisfactory conclusion on this point.

To treat a man as a criminal on suspicion merely, was certainly unfair; but still, doubts having once entered his head, he could not rid his brain of them, and he feared to leave the steamer, with its precious burden, entirely under the control of the villanous-looking pilot.

Their progress against the strong current was of the slowest—indeed, with the damaged engines, they were scarcely able to make way at all, and the island, which the Captain had pointed out as the pirates' haunt, still loomed hazily through the evening mist.

"We can go no further to-night," said the pilot, sulkily.

"No further! What do you mean?" asked Mr. Hardstaff.

"I spoke to the Captain," replied he of the evil countenance.

"Spoke to me! Bless me! what is it? Nothing the matter, mister, I hope?"

"No, not yet. I only said it would be imprudent to continue our course till daylight."

"Certainly, certainly! Very imprudent! Quite right—stop by all means! Decidedly!"

"But why cannot we go on?" interposed Mr. Hardstaff. "It won't be dark for another hour."

"You ain't much of a sailor, I fancy," said the pilot.

"Well, no, not exactly. Still, it is my opinion——"

"Perhaps you'd better keep your opinions for them as like to pay six-and-eightpence a-piece for 'em. I prefer to talk over the matter with one who knows something about it."

"Certainly! Very natural! Oh, yes!" said the Captain.

Mr. Hardstaff drew forth his large pocket-handkerchief, and waved it defiantly, and then used it vigorously ; but before he returned it to his pocket, he was forced to confess to himself that, after all, he was profoundly ignorant on nautical matters, and it might be as well to leave the guidance of the steamer to those who understood the business.

"If that pilot didn't look such a confounded scoundrel !" he muttered, as he walked to another part of the vessel, and leant over the bulwarks to watch the eddying waters sweeping by.

It wanted no very subtle powers of reasoning on the part of the pilot to persuade the Captain that the best and safest course to pursue was to lay to for the night ; and, accordingly, the steamer was soon secured by stout ropes to the trunks of some large trees which grew close down to the water, on an island scarcely a quarter of a mile higher up the stream than that which formed the stronghold of the buccaneers.

Mr. Hardstaff, with a few quiet words, explained to Grace that, in the opinion of both the Captain and the pilot, it was advisable for them to remain where they were for the night ; but he at the same time took particular care not to let her suppose, from his words, that he doubted either the honesty of the pilot or the skill of the Captain.

Almost before they were safely moored, night had closed in.

It was not one of those brilliant tropical nights when myriads of stars illumine the firmament, for it was black and foggy.

From the river and adjacent marshes rose a thick mist, which every hour grew more dense.

The passengers, and the greater portion of the crew, took shelter from the moist vapour in their cabins ; but Hardstaff still remained on deck, following all the movements of the pilot as a cat a mouse.

Once only Mr. Hardstaff went below, and that was only for a few seconds.

As he appeared on deck he was carefully placing "something" in the breast-pocket of his coat.

That "something" was a neat, well-made six-shooter, which he had taken from its case in his cabin, in order to carry it about with him in case of emergency.

"What an old idiot I am !" muttered the lawyer to himself, as he paced backwards and forwards on the wet, slippery deck. "As if it wasn't bad enough to have a chronic cold, without running the risk of catching an ordinary one on top of it. Whatever they call influenza in this country, I'm safe to have ; and then who's to nurse me ? I don't believe there's a creature on board that can make gruel as I like it ; and as for mustard plasters——Well, well, I'd do a deal more than this for Grace's sake. No harm shall come to her if I can prevent it."

He resumed his march up and down, grumbling outwardly, but inwardly rejoicing at having an opportunity of serving her he loved so well.

The ill-looking pilot was evidently annoyed at the pertinacious manner in which Mr. Hardstaff paced up and down.

He stamped his foot, and evinced other signs of impatience ; but still the lawyer did not seem disposed to go below.

"It's getting rather late," said the pilot, approaching and accosting the lawyer.

"So I suppose."

"This night air is rather trying to those who are not used to it."

"Ah, for my part, I like it !" said Mr. Hardstaff, blowing his nose violently.

"Many's the man these fogs have struck down with marsh fever and ague !"

"In-deed! Poor fellows !"

The pilot was disconcerted.

He altered his tactics, and resumed.

"Don't you think, sir, it would be more prudent if you went below ?"

"Not at present. In fact, I think I shall probably remain on deck all night."

"Confound the old blockhead !" growled the pilot, beneath his teeth.

"I beg your pardon—did you speak ?" said Hardstaff.

"I must say it's regular madness for you to stay on deck !"

"I don't see that. Why ?"

"Because of the fogs."

"I don't care for them."

"The damp !"

"I am used to it."

"The night air !"

"It won't hurt me."

"You'd better go below."

"You seem very anxious about it."

"Only for your good."

"You're very kind !"

The pilot muttered a curse between his teeth, and strode away, leaving Hardstaff chuckling at his success.

In the course of another hour he again approached the lawyer.

"You're not gone below yet !"

"No !"

"Are you going ?"

"No !"

"You'd better !"

"Now, look here—for some reason best known to yourself, you want to get me out of the way ; but I tell you candidly I'm not going ! I mean to stay and keep watch !"

"Of course, you can do as you like," growled the pilot ; but no sooner was Hardstaff out of hearing, than he gave vent to his passion in a string of oaths. "I'll do it, though, in spite of him !" he muttered as he went forward.

Stealthily he crept towards the rope which kept the steamer stationary.

He drew a large knife from its sheath, and with a few rapid strokes of its sharp blade he severed the strands.

The lawyer, though watching him, failed to perceive what he was about ; but, fearing mischief, approached him softly.

The cable alone now held the steamer.

The pilot was on the point of cutting it also, when a voice at his elbow observed, "A good thick cable that !"

The pilot was completely taken aback. He had no idea any one was near him. Rapidly he put the knife up his sleeve, and answered the observation in as quiet a tone as he could assume.

Mr. Hardstaff's suspicions had a foundation. He had seen enough to be convinced the pilot was treacherous ; but he was not aware that all the ropes but one had been already cut.

"I mustn't let that man out of my sight," said he to himself, "or he'll be after some mischief !"

For two whole hours the cunning lawyer kept by the pilot's side, notwithstanding all his efforts to get rid of him.

Together they paced the deck ; and Hardstaff had fully made his mind to continue to do so till morning.

"Mr. Hardstaff !" called a voice from one of the cabins.

"There's some one calling you," said the pilot.

"I think not," said the lawyer, blandly, determined to ignore the voice, though he recognised it as that of Grace Atherton.

"Mr. Hardstaff ! can I speak to you for a minute ?"

He was drawn two ways. He did not know what to do. While he yet deliberated, he was called a third time.

No. 11.—THE BUCCANEERS.

He sprang to the hatchway, only to whisper a few words of explanation; but the moments occupied in doing so were taken advantage of by the pilot, who leaped forward, knife in hand, and severed the sole rope which bound them to the shore.

Mr. Hardstaff looked up, and saw the traitor at the cable.

Without a moment's deliberation he drew his revolver from his pocket, levelled, and fired it.

The aim was true.

With a loud cry, the pirate pilot threw his arms wildly above his head, and disappeared over the bulwarks.

A loud splash in the river told his fate.

Aroused by the sound of the pistol-shot, the Captain and several of the crew rushed on deck.

"Only manslaughter," cried Hardstaff, excitedly. "There isn't a jury in the United Kingdom would bring it in murder!"

"What is it? Who was it? What have you done?" cried a score of voices.

Hardstaff told his story; told how he had seen the pilot about to cut the rope—how he had prevented it; and not wishing to proceed to extremities, had determined to keep him in sight all through the night; how chance had favoured the villain; and how, as a last resource, he had been obliged to shoot him just as his knife passed through the cable; "But, thank goodness," said the lawyer, as he concluded his story, "there are half a dozen other cables to keep us fast."

The words were scarcely out of his mouth, when a wild cry told of the misfortune which had befallen them.

The steamer was adrift!

Hardstaff had not seen the pilot sever the other ropes.

The one he thought to be the first cut through was in reality the last.

The steamer had slowly swung round, been caught by the stream, and was drifting rapidly down the river towards the pirates' haunt, before half the crew were aware of what had happened.

The engine fires had been suffered to get low, and there was not sufficient steam in the boilers to work the engines.

There were no means by which the course of the boat could be stayed.

The Captain was worse than useless. He wrung his hands, and bewailed his fate, but did no more.

The cries and confusion speedily brought all the passengers on deck.

Frightened, and almost paralyzed, they huddled together. Some few fell upon their knees, others did what little they could to help the crew in their vain efforts; but the majority only lamented noisily.

Grace alone, of the women, retained her presence of mind.

She was perfectly conscious of the imminent danger, and well knew the fate which awaited them; still, though she could not hold out much hope, she went hither and thither like a ministering angel, striving to comfort and quiet those who gave themselves up to useless lamentations.

The fog was so thick as to render it impossible to see more than a few yards ahead of the boat, which now, in the centre of the stream, was swinging along with the full force of the current.

Ignorant of how soon their fate might come, the emigrants huddled together in an agony of despair.

Some, unable to bear the dreadful suspense, jumped overboard; others attempted to lower the boat.

They succeeded in doing so, but so many leapt into her, that she was speedily swamped.

A sudden shock!

A harsh, grating noise!

A rush of water!

The steamer was hard aground!

But where?

As if to answer the question which arose in the minds of all, a diabolical yell of triumph rose through the fog, and smote upon their ears.

There could be but little doubt, for though those on board could see nothing, the shouts of joy told them they had fallen victims to a preconcerted plot, and were in the hands of the buccaneers.

CHAPTER XXXI.

THE OATH OF VENGEANCE.

THE suspense to those on board the steamer was indeed frightful.

Their vessel hard and fast aground—a band of savage pirates on shore—and a rushing, roaring torrent around them.

After the first yell of triumph from the buccaneers, all became silent.

Those on board waited in an agony of suspense to learn what their fate would be, but the pirates, knowing they were secure of their prey, preferred to wait for daylight; and, accordingly, the steamer was left to grind upon the shingle till sunrise.

"Is there any chance for us?" asked Grace Atherton of Mr. Hardstaff.

The lawyer blew his nose, but the sound was far different to the usual defiant trumpet-note. It was wavering, undecided, and dejected.

"Cannot we save some of these poor people?"

"I fear not."

"Are there no small boats?"

"There was but one, and that was swamped an hour ago."

"Cannot we reach the shore?"

"Yes; the shore of the pirate island."

"No other?"

"None."

"Then what is to be done?" And for the first time there was a tone of despair in Grace Atherton's voice.

"Not much, I fear."

The lawyer drew his revolver from his pocket, and patted the barrel.

"Of these half-dozen balls," said he, "five are for the buccaneers."

"And the sixth?"

"Is for you."

"For me?"

"Yes."

"What do you mean?"

"Better death a thousand times, than that you should fall into the hands of these ruffians. They are a band of miscreants, without a particle of feeling in them. A woman in their hands! I cannot bear to think of it!"

Grace shuddered.

"You understand me?"

"Yes," she answered, faintly.

"Then is it not better to be as I say?"

"Oh, yes, indeed it is!"

"You can trust me, Grace?"

"Yes. Death is indeed preferable, but it is hard to die thus! Oh, if I could but see Owen once again—if I could but tell him, ere I died, that my love had never wavered—that my heart was truly his, I could die happy; but I shall never see him again!—never—never!" And she buried her face in her hands, and sobbed in an agony of grief.

As the sun rose, the fog was dispelled, and those on board the steamer were able to see their frightful position.

The Captain proved himself totally unequal to the emergency, and did nothing but pace the deck, wringing his hands.

Hardstaff essayed to collect a band to endeavour to repel the pirates; but they were but few who would enter into his plans, and they were imperfectly armed.

With the knowledge that a few minutes would decide their fate, they watched the buccaneers putting off from shore in small boats, and rowing towards them.

As they approached nearer, they could perceive they were all fully armed, and as desperate-looking a band of ruffians as ever escaped the gallows.

"We'll startle them a little, I think!" said Hardstaff. "Reserve your fire till I give the word!"

The first boat was already alongside—the second was only a few yards behind.

"Now, then!" said Hardstaff, coolly. "Each your own man! Fire!"

As he spoke, a dozen guns were discharged full into the boats.

Hardstaff was right. He *had* startled them, for they were totally unprepared for resistance; still, the sight of their dead and dying comrades only excited them the more, and with wild, savage yells, they jumped on board the steamer, before any had time to reload.

With clubbed muskets the more resolute of the crew strove to repel the buccaneers; but the struggle was short. They were rapidly overpowered, and their lifeless bodies thrown into the river.

No sooner had the pirates made good their footing, than Hardstaff hastened to the side of Grace Atherton.

With cocked revolver in his hand, he waited the aproach of the ruffians.

As they advanced to where he stood, with his arm around Grace's waist, he raised his pistol.

Five shots were fired in as many seconds, and five lifeless bodies lay upon the deck.

Still there was no chance of escape from the pirate horde.

A fresh reinforcement, headed by a tall, stalwart man, who, in spite of the powder which smeared his face and hands, and the wound on his forehead, from whence the blood trickled, seemed of a somewhat superior grade, rushed upon them.

In pursuance of his plan, Hardstaff raised his pistol again; but this time it was directed towards the fair girl who stood by his side.

Her lips moved as she uttered an inward prayer.

The lawyer's finger was upon the trigger.

In another moment Grace Atherton would have been far, far away from all earthly sorrows and troubles; but ere the bullet from Hardstaff's pistol could speed upon its errand, she uttered a wild cry, and sprang forward towards the man who, with upraised cutlass, was leading the buccaneers towards them.

"Owen, Owen! don't you know me?" she cried, in heart-piercing accents, as she seized his arm, as he was upon the point of cutting down Hardstaff.

For a few moments, Owen—for it was indeed he—seemed troubled and confused.

He passed his hand once or twice over his brow.

"Grace!" he muttered, half to himself—"Grace! No, it cannot be!"

"It is I, Owen! Surely, you have not forgotten me!"

"No—no!" muttered Owen, as yet hardly able to realize that it was indeed Grace Atherton, his early love, who now stood by his side.

"Oh, Owen! have you nothing to say to me? Can you not spare one word of love?"

Owen placed his arm around her, and as one bewildered, led her from the scene of strife and carnage into one of the cabins.

"To think," she sighed, "that after all my prayers, that I might once more see you, that *this* should be our meeting!"

"What brings you here?"

A few words explained that which is already known to the reader.

It was evident something was preying upon Owen's mind, which prevented his feeling any pleasure at the meeting.

He pressed his hands to his forehead, and a low moan escaped from his lips.

"What is it, Owen? Why are you so distressed? Are you sorry to see me?"

"I am, indeed!" groaned he.

"Sorry! Oh, Owen!"

No words can describe Grace's lovingly reproachful tone as she spoke.

"Yes, Grace," he hissed between his clenched teeth; "I would rather never to have seen you again, than meet you now!"

"Why?" she asked, startled by the earnestness of his manner.

"Do not ask me!" he exclaimed, passionately. "You will know too soon!"

"What do you mean?"

"Your life is forfeited! Heaven knows, I would give you mine right willingly to save it, but I fear it is of no avail!"

Owen shuddered as he spoke. The remembrance of the solemn oath he had taken to spare neither man, woman, nor child who fell into his grasp, seemed to him like a hideous dream.

*   *   *   *   *   *

But it is time we should return to the deck of the steamer, where a dreadful scene had been enacted.

All who had offered resistance to the buccaneers were massacred in cold blood, and their bodies tossed into the river. The others had been bound hand and foot, and were being conveyed to the island; but their respite was short, for death was to be their fate, in accordance with Owen's oath of vengeance.

Hardstaff, too, had escaped immediate death, on account of his stubborn resistance; for the devilish malice of the pirates suggested that the slayer of so many of their comrades should meet with a slow, lingering death by torture.

The buccaneers had been so busily engaged in their slaughtering, that no one had noticed Owen's absence; and it was not until the bodies of the dead had been cast overboard, and the prisoners removed to the island stronghold, that the question of "Where's the Captain?" began to be asked.

No one could answer it.

He had not been seen since the first attack.

The only conclusion they could arrive at was that he had fallen overboard, and been drowned.

Bestowing but little thought, however, upon that matter, they commenced plundering the steamer of all the valuable merchandize she contained.

They had not been long at this task when they entered the cabin in which Owen and Grace sat side by side.

A loud peal of laughter burst from the ruffians as this sight met their gaze.

"Trust the Captain to find out the prettiest girl!" cried one.

"Don't they make a pretty picture!" sneered another.

"It's all very fine," growled a third, "for him to leave us to do all the fighting while he enjoys hisself!"

"Those big talkers never do much!" resumed the first speaker. "Perhaps the Captain felt a little bit frightened!"

"Silence!" cried Owen, starting to his feet. "I will give sufficient proof of my courage, if need be!"

" We don't want a Captain who gives all his time to girls and such like trumpery, do we, mates?"

" No, no!" was chorussed on every side.

" At all events, we don't want a coward!" said one bolder than the rest.

But he never spoke distinctly again; for, with one blow of his powerful arm, Owen crunched his lips and teeth, and laid him at full length upon the deck.

Murmurs rose from the men; but Owen's strength and resolute attitude awed them into silence.

" Shall we take the prisoner ashore, Captain?" asked one, after a pause.

" What prisoner?" he inquired, fiercely.

" That young woman?"

" No; I will see to that myself!"

" Remember your oath!" said a burly ruffian, in Owen's ear.

" I am not likely to forget it!" he replied, bitterly as he helped Grace on deck, and assisted her into the boat which was waiting to convey them ashore.

While they were being rowed to land Owen did not speak a word.

He was revolving in his own mind different schemes by which to preserve Grace's life.

That it should be saved, at whatever cost, he was resolved; but, as yet, it seemed almost an impossibility.

He would not suffer her to be placed with the other prisoners, but had her removed to his own hut, notwithstanding the murmurs and remonstrances of the buccaneers, who began to regard their Captain in a far from favourable light.

Indeed, when the cargo had been removed from the steamer, and the buccaneers were assembled together in their cavern, the question was openly discussed as to whether it would not be advisable to depose Owen, and give the command of the band to another.

" He must be compelled to keep his oath."

" Certainly."

" He swore that all, regardless of age and sex, who fell into his hands should perish."

" He did."

" He must be made to fulfil his vow."

" What if he refuses?"

" He must be compelled to keep it."

While this conversation was being carred on, Owen was moodily pacing backwards and forwards before his hut, forming plans for the rescue of Grace, and abandoning them as soon as formed, on the score of their impracticability.

He was not long in discovering that he was watched.

The buccaneers had no longer any confidence in their Captain, and had agreed amongst themselves never, if possible, to let him out of their sight.

Thus another difficulty was placed in the way of Grace's escape.

Luckily for the other prisoners, the buccaneers were too much exhausted with their day's work to carry out their threats respecting them that night; and, by common consent, they had obtained a respite of four-and-twenty hours.

Poor Grace, alone in Owen's hut, had but gloomy reflections upon which to rest.

To her the whole affair was buried in impenetrable mystery.

The whole affair was wonderful in the extreme; and she could hardly persuade herself that it was not all a dreadful dream.

She had prayed to see Owen once again before she died. Her prayer had been granted, but in a way she little expected.

How little she thought that he she had idolized in in her heart had become the chief of a band of miscreants famed for their sanguinary deeds.

Oppressed by these gloomy thoughts, and over-shadowed by a dread of evil to come, no wonder she passed a sleepless night.

Owen, after long deliberation, determined to attempt a plan which, wild and improbable of success as it appeared, still seemed to him worthy of a trial.

His distress of mind was great. He cursed his folly in having ever suffered the Signora for one moment to occupy the place in his heart which belonged by right to Grace; but the past was irrevocable, and he could only deal with the present; and as for the future, he dared not look forward for as much as a single day.

He knew the character of the men with whom he had to deal, and was positive it was but little mercy he could hope to receive from them.

That they would not absolve him from his oath seemed very certain; but yet he determined to make the attempt, and accordingly he entered the cavern where the buccaneers were as usual drinking and gambling, and advanced towards them till he stood in their midst, noble and erect.

CHAPTER XXXII.

FOILED.

" It ain't often the Captain comes among us," whispered one to his companion.

" What's in the wind now, I wonder?" cried a second, and all left off their occupations to look at Owen, who, with an expression on his face that they had never seen there before, stood in their midst, proud and defiant.

One of the buccaneers handed him wine, but he refused it.

" No, no!" he exclaimed; " it is not for merrymaking I have come amongst you. It is upon a matter of serious import."

" What is it, Captain?"

" Some short time back, in a moment of passion, I took a solemn oath——"

" To kill all who fell into your hands!" roared a buccaneer; " and we mean you to keep it!"

" I implore mercy for one—only one! Spare that fair girl whom we took prisoner to-day?"

" No, no! Why should we?"

" Have none of you—ruffians that you are—known what it is to have a tender, loving heart wholly yours? Men, years ago, in old England, this girl and I loved; accident separated us—accident has thrown us together again! By my vow, I am bound to cause her to be put to death; but it was an oath made in the heat of passion, and I will not keep it!"

" Well, look here, Captain——"

" Stay! I am no longer your Captain! I renounce all connexion with you! Do what you will with me, but spare her for whom I intercede! If you consider my life forfeited, take it, but not that of the innocent girl whose cause I plead. I had thought all soft feelings had withered in my heart, but it is not so."

One of the buccaneers, who seemed by common consent to act as spokesman, rose, and spoke thus: " There is not one amongst us that has not remarked your conduct, Owen Redgrave. Since you have been our Captain, you have led a life of inactivity, and cared nothing for those over whom you held command. She in whose delusive smiles you basked deceived you, and in your rage you swore an oath which you now must keep, or die!"

" I tell you I will willingly forfeit my life for hers. Swear to me to set her free, and do what you will with me."

"You are both in our power. What can either you or she do against us?"

"By what right do you speak?"

"By the right of being Captain in your place. You have resigned your command, but before that we had disposed of you. I was elected in your place."

"Spare her—it is all I ask."

The newly-chosen Captain turned to the buccaneers gathered round him.

"What say you, mates? Shall her life be spared?"

"No, no!" they answered, in chorus.

"What harm has she ever done you that you should slay her?" asked Owen.

"We have taken a vow of blood, and we will keep to it!"

"You are determined?"

"We are!"

"Then do your worst! My life, I know, is forfeited!"

"Nonsense!" cried the new Captain. "We know you are brave, by what you did in attacking Don Pedro. We do not wish to lose you. In a short time you will get over this grief, as you did the other. Pshaw! there are girls enough in the world! What signifies one, more or less? Come, be a man, cheer up, and remain with us!"

Owen was about to make an indignant refusal, but the thought occurred to him that, by feigning acquiescence, a better opportunity might present itself for assisting Grace.

Were he to refuse, what chance would he have of again seeing his first love again? None.

There were some signs of dissent from the buccaneers at the speech of the new Captain, for many of them looked upon Owen as a traitor, and would willingly have assisted at his execution; but Captain Baldock (that was his name) had experienced some kindness from Owen, and determined, if possible, to save him.

Even had he been so disposed, it would not have been in his power to save Grace Atherton, for the whole band were set upon her death, if only to spite their former Captain.

After a few minutes' deliberation with himself, Owen answered Baldock's proposal in a calm voice which told nothing of the fever which was raging within him.

"I have reflected," said he: "I see you will not be turned from your purpose of shedding the blood of this innocent girl, but as you are still willing to retain me in your band, I will remain. I only beg you to grant me one favour."

"Remember your oath."

"I do. It is not for life I crave."

"What is it?"

"This girl is to die?"

"Yes."

"Can nothing alter your determination?"

"Nothing."

"Then I claim to be her executioner!"

"You?"

"Yes. Grant me but this; I ask for nothing more."

The buccaneers seemed undecided.

"Surely you will not refuse me this? If I falter, there will be many hands ready to complete the deed."

"That's true."

"Do you agree?"

"Remember your oath."

"I will keep it."

"Then we agree."

"At sunrise to-morrow I will fulfil my vow. I go now to prepare her for her fate. Let who will accompany me to see that I do not attempt escape."

Some three or four of the buccaneers rose and went with Owen to the hut where Grace Atherton, confused and bewildered, was confined.

"Wait outside and watch," said he; "I shall not be long."

When the door of the hut was opened, Grace started to her feet, scarcely knowing what to expect, but she was reassured by seeing Owen's noble form before her.

She ran to him, and nestled her head upon his shoulder, the while she told him of her griefs and sorrows, and gently upbraided him with remaining so long away.

"I have been doing my utmost to save your life, Grace," said he, in a loud tone.

She looked up into his face inquiringly.

"But without avail. To-morrow at sunrise you must die."

She could not repress a shudder as she heard her death-warrant.

"More has to be told. I, Grace, am to be your executioner."

"You?"

"Yes. They were bent upon your death, and I obtained this permission as a favour."

"Owen, Owen!" she sobbed, clinging to him frantically, as the force of her dreadful position and impending fate smote upon her.

The sound of footsteps moving away from the door of the hut caused a sudden alteration in Owen's manner.

"My darling Grace," he exclaimed, in a hurried whisper, "they were listening, and I had to act a part. Behind that curtain is a secret door, unknown to any besides myself. In two hours' time, from now, escape by it. I shall be there to meet you."

"But, Owen——"

"Hush! There is no time for explanation. If I stay longer, their suspicion will be roused."

As he said these words, he opened the door.

The pirates were lounging on the grass a little distance off. As Owen thought, they had suspected treachery on his part, and had listened, but the words they had heard him speak satisfied them.

As Owen left the hut he turned.

"To-morrow at sunrise," said he, in a melancholy tone.

"To-morrow at sunrise," repeated Grace, mechanically.

Her brain was in a whirl. The numerous events of the last twenty-four hours had followed each other with such wonderful rapidity, and had been so startling in their character, that there is little wonder she was unable to disentangle them.

That her life was in danger, and that Owen was planning her escape, she fully realized, however; and anxiously she glanced at her watch, which she still retained, in order that she might know when the appointed two hours had elapsed.

Owen Redgrave returned to the cabin with those who had accompanied him on his errand.

The answers of Owen's companions completely satisfied the buccaneers that our hero was well disposed towards them.

They shook Owen by the hand, and congratulated him on his firmness of purpose; while he was inwardly congratulating himself, and turning over in his mind the various plans he had partly formed for escaping from the cavern, and furthering the release of Grace from captivity and the prospect of death.

"Come, mates!" cried Owen, enthusiastically, seized with an idea; "you sit there as glum as if you were at a funeral! Drink, my boys!—drink the health of our noble Captain! Although he has deposed me, I bear him no malice!"

"Here's his jolly good health!" hiccuped some half-dozen, rising to their feet, and pouring more wine down their throats.

Owen had not planned to make them intoxicated;

for, from past experience, he knew such an endeavour would be useless. He knew, however, that, after copious libations, the buccaneers would sink into a species of stupor, from which it would be difficult to arouse them.

To this state of sleepy indolence he wished to bring them.

He had not long to wait for what he desired; for on board the steamer there happened to have been some wine, which was particularly palatable to the pirates, who tossed off glass after glass, totally heedless of the consequences.

Before the two hours had elapsed, Owen had the satisfaction of seeing the majority of the buccaneers lying senseless on the ground.

Slowly, and with as little noise as possible, he edged away from the sleeping, semi-conscious crowd, and in time he reached the entrance to the cavern unperceived, thanks to the caution he had taken.

On his way he had possessed himself of everything eatable and drinkable which he could come across.

The articles thus obtained he placed in a large canvas bag, which, as luck would have it, lay empty on the ground.

Thus provided, with one hasty glance round to make sure he was not observed, he left the cavern.

In the stilly quiet of the night, he stole away from his companions.

Once out of the cavern, he did not proceed straight to the hut where Grace was confined, for he had still a quarter of an hour to spare before the time he had appointed to meet her.

With gentle tread, and looking around every minute to make sure he was not followed, Owen bent his steps towards the river.

Arrived at the bank, he was able without difficulty to find the spot where one of the small boats belonging to the pirates was usually moored.

The boat was there, and only fastened to the shore by a single rope.

Into this boat Owen hastily flung the bag of provisions, and then carefully and silently inspected the fittings of the boat, to make sure she was in fit condition for the trip he proposed to take.

All was satisfactory.

With a deep indrawn sigh of relief he left the shore, and with the same precautions he had used before, advanced stealthily towards the hut where Grace Atherton was confined.

A sentinel had been placed before the door, but so careful was Owen to prevent the sounds of his footsteps being heard, that the watcher remained totally unconscious of his approach.

Owen had to pass within a few yards of him.

Holding his breath, he stepped with the greatest caution.

His heart gave a great leap of joy when he found he had passed the sentinel in safety.

It still wanted some few minutes to the time at which he had appointed to meet Grace; he, therefore, concealed himself among the neighbouring trees.

At last he saw the small door — the position of which he knew so well—gently opened, and there, in the space, stood the beautiful figure of Grace Atherton.

She looked around half-frightened, and as if uncertain in what direction to proceed.

"Grace!" whispered Owen.

She started at the sound of her own name.

"Hush! not a word!" continued Owen, as he signed to her to advance to where he stood.

"The least noise is discovery and death!" said Owen, in her ear. "Follow me."

Their progression was very slow, for branches of trees and long grass impeded them; but at last the sentinels were all passed, and Owen and Grace stood side by side on the banks of the broad river to which they were about to trust themselves.

Without a word, Owen conducted the lovely girl to the place where the boat was moored, and assisted her into it.

The bag of provisions was there, the oars, the small mast were just as he left them; and, as if to congratulate them on their success so far, the moon, which had hitherto been concealed behind a thick bank of clouds, burst forth and shed its brilliant light upon the rapid, rushing river.

"Now we are safe, Grace," cried Owen, exultingly, as he reached from the boat to unfasten the rope which bound her to the land.

A mocking laugh answered him.

From some neighbouring bushes, half-a-dozen of the buccaneers rushed down to the river, and before either of the fugitives had fully realized the misfortune which had befallen them, they were dragged from the boat and were being conveyed to the cavern.

"Foiled," cried Owen, bitterly, "at the very moment of success! Disguise is henceforth useless. Do not despair, Grace; we may yet effect our escape."

The buccaneers laughed in a mocking, jeering manner.

Grace and Owen were removed to a hut inside the fortifications, from whence escape was impossible.

Owen, despite the cheering words he had spoken to Grace, had but little hope.

He threw himself upon a rough wooden bench which stood in one corner of the hut, and covered his face with his hands.

Grace did her best to cheer him.

"It is not for myself, darling, that I care," said he. "I have too long lived facing death. It is for you. The thought that, after all, you will fall into the hands of these ruffians, is more than I can bear. But what am I saying? They shall not have you, come what may. I swear it. Do not despair, darling; we will escape or perish in the attempt!"

CHAPTER XXXIII.

A BOLD STROKE FOR LIBERTY.

OWEN REDGRAVE'S surprise was great to find that his captor was no other than the long missing Drake.

The Captain of the band of pirates again appeared upon the scene, and, for Owen, at a most inopportune moment.

As he and Grace were marched into the cavern, closely guarded by those who had taken them, they were greeted with threats, oaths, and jeering laughter; and it was not till afterwards that Owen learnt in what way he had been discovered, and how his old enemy, Drake, had been mainly instrumental in preventing his escape with her he loved so well.

After leaving his men, on the eve of the attack upon Don Pedro's camp, he had proceeded safely, and without interruption, to the extremity of the rocky peninsula, where it had been arranged the signal for the Black Cloud was to be made.

He gathered together all the wood and dry seaweed he could find, and set light to it.

The smoke rose upward in a straight column, and the Captain saw with pleasure his flag hoisted at the masthead, which showed his signal had been observed by those on board.

But, as had been feared, the Spaniards had perceived the smoke, as well as those to whom it served as a signal.

Four of Don Pedro's gang had been sent to reconnoitre.

Carefully and cautiously they had advanced along the promontory, screening themselves from observation behind the huge masses of rock, until they had arrived within a few yards of Drake, unperceived by him.

A few moments sufficed to show them that he was alone.

His back was towards them, for he was eagerly straining his eyes seawards, watching the movements of the Black Cloud.

With a yell of triumph, they threw themselves upon him.

He was totally unprepared for the attack.

They were four to one. But his great strength served him well.

He drew his revolver, but ere he had time to fire it, it was struck from his grasp.

Determined to sell his life dearly, he drew his cutlass.

So eager were his antagonists, that the foremost one rushed upon it.

The sharp blade passed completely through his body, and with a gasping sob, he fell back dead.

The Spaniards, though possessed of firearms, did not use them; for it was their object to take Drake alive, and learn from him, if possible, some particulars respecting the force which menaced them.

Before long, another of the Spaniards met his death from Drake's powerful weapon.

He had now only two to oppose him.

Made more wary by the death of their comrades, they advanced cautiously, and Drake, seeing but little chance of victory, rushed forward upon them, and seized the first in his iron grasp.

They both rolled together on the ground, but the pirate Captain's hold upon the other's throat did not lessen.

His companion came to his assistance, but their united strength was as nothing, when compared with Drake's muscular powers.

There was but one course open to them.

The Spaniard drew a pistol, and pointed it at Drake's head; but the buccaneer appeared to possess a charmed life; for, as the weapon was discharged, a sudden wrench from his antagonist forced his head from out the line of fire.

But he did not escape altogether.

The bullet intended for his brain shattered his elbow, and his right arm fell powerless by his side.

Freed from the grasp, the Spaniard, who had been upon the verge of strangulation, staggered to his feet. The two, without much difficulty, succeeded in binding the wounded Hercules.

With stout ropes they secured his hands and feet; while to prevent his cries for assistance being heard, a large silk handkerchief was stuffed into his mouth.

Just as this task was completed, a gleam of fire darted from the Black Cloud, a puff of white smoke eddied upwards, and the boom of a gun sounded over the water.

Drake—bound and helpless as he was—could not altogether refrain from showing his exultation at the success of his plans thus far.

His victors appeared uneasy.

They consulted together in a low tone; and at last one of them addressed a question to him in Spanish, removing the gag at the same time.

Drake understood sufficient of the language to comprehend what they required; but he deemed it the best policy to affect total ignorance.

Again the two consulted in a low tone.

Just then the rapid interchange of gunshots, the noise, the shouting, and the confusion, heard afar off,

revealed to Drake that his band had surprised the village.

He writhed as he lay on the ground in vexation at his inability to join in the fight

Could he but have burst his bonds, wounded as he was, he would have hastened to cast himself into the thickest of the combat.

In vain he struggled.

The cords only cut his wrists and ankles, and he was forced to desist from his attempts to free himself, from pain and exhaustion.

The two Spaniards who guarded him seemed perplexed at the sound of firing in a contrary direction to that in which they expected it.

They wavered, and showed signs of uncertainty as to the course they should pursue.

The firing became more frequent—the shouts and cries louder.

With a loud oath, one of them seized Drake by the feet, calling upon the others to assist him, and the two bore the pirate Captain into a cavern formed apparently by the washings of the sea against the rocks.

Here, having re-gagged him, they left him, and hurried away.

Chafing and impatient, Drake lay helpless, but " eager for the fray."

Again he essayed to free himself; but he had been too securely bound.

The pain and the loss of blood weakened his strong frame, and he fell into a swoon.

When he returned to consciousness, all was still.

He had no means of ascertaining in whose favour the battle had been decided.

For long he waited, expecting every minute the Spaniards would return; but they never came.

At last he heard the sound of approaching footsteps.

They came nearer and nearer.

From where he lay, unable to move or speak, he saw some human forms darkening the entrance to the cavern.

They were a party of his own men, sent expressly in search for him.

He heard himself called by name.

He strove to answer; but the handkerchief prevented articulation.

A dreadful despair seized him as he saw the men turn away without entering the cavern, and heard their footsteps dying away in the distance.

He heard the guns fired as signals to him; he heard his name shouted by well-known voices; but he was totally unable to give the least sign of his existence.

His men being there to search for him, told him the victory had been theirs, and that imparted a small ray of comfort; still it was dreadful to look forward to a slow, lingering death by starvation in the gloomy cavern.

After a while, silence reigned supreme, and Drake knew that those sent to look had failed to discover him, and had returned to the ship.

The torture which he suffered from hunger and thirst were more than those occasioned by his wounds.

To lie and die there without an effort seemed too dreadful.

He knew from sad experience it was useless to endeavour to burst asunder the bonds which held him.

A new idea occurred to him.

Disregarding the intense pain caused him by so doing, he raised his bound hands to his mouth, and after many failures succeeded in removing the gag.

His wounded arm gave him such exquisite pain he could hardly carry out his intention, but he persevered.

Holding his bound hands to his mouth, he set resolutely to work to gnaw through the rope.

It was a long, tedious, painful job, and ever and

anon the agony he suffered compelled him to relinquish his efforts, but only to set to work again with renewed energy.

Strand by strand, he gnawed through the rope, till, with an exertion of his powerful unwounded arm, he freed his hands.

To unfasten the cords which bound his feet was, now that his arms were free, an easy task, and ere long he once more stood erect—a free man!

The first thing was to make a sling for his wounded arm.

This he accomplished by means of tearing up his shirt.

This done, he left the cavern, and made his way towards the village.

The corpses strewn in every direction told him how severe the battle had been.

Of dead bodies there were plenty, but not a living person was to be seen.

They had all taken refuge in the forest.

In one of the ruined, deserted huts he found food.

He ate ravenously, and filled his pockets with the remnants; after which, arming himself with some weapons he found upon the field of battle, he started off to retrace the course of the river on foot, hoping thus ultimately to reach the island stronghold.

It took him very, very long to accomplish the journey, for he was weak from loss of blood; but at last, after many weary weeks of tramping, he found himself on the mainland near the island, but separated from it by a mile of rapid-flowing water.

How to cross he knew not.

Had he had the use of both arms he would have attempted to swim it; but with one limb disabled, and his whole frame exhausted by fatigue and want of proper nourishment, it would have been madness to try to do so.

Fortune favoured him.

As he sat on the stump of a fallen tree, he heard the sound of oars.

It was night; the moon had not risen, and he could see nothing; but he hailed the boat.

He heard, with unspeakable joy, a cheery response, and, as it pulled in to where he awaited its arrival, he recognised six of his own men.

They greeted him with rapturous enthusiasm, for, despite his faults, he had always been a great favourite with the band.

From them, as they pulled rapidly towards the island, he heard all the events which had taken place during his absence, and with which the reader is already acquainted.

As they neared the shore of their island home, two figures, those apparently of a man and a woman, were dimly discernible.

From what he had just heard, Drake had no doubt that they were Owen Redgrave and Grace Atherton; and so they proved to be.

Drake ordered caution and silence, and directed the boat to be put in shore some little distance above the spot where they had seen the two figures.

This was done.

They landed, hurried along the shore, and were just in time, as we already know, to prevent the escape of our hero and his first love.

After Owen and Grace had been led to the respective huts in which they were to pass the night, guards were placed over them to prevent their escape, and a lengthy and somewhat stormy discussion took place in the cavern as to the fate of the prisoners.

They must die.

In that they all agreed; but the difficulty was to settle the mode by which their earthly pains were to be ended.

Though Owen had turned traitor, and attempted to escape them; there were many to whom he had shown small acts of kindness, and these stood out steadfastly against the slow, lingering death by torture, which some of the more diabolical-minded proposed.

Next to Owen, the anger of the buccaneers fell upon Hardstaff, on account of the resolute defence he had made.

At last, a decision was arrived at.

Grace, Owen, and Hardstaff, were to die.

A death of dreadful agony was chosen for them.

A death which caused many of the martyrs of the olden time to shriek with agony.

A death which had caused cries of intense suffering to break involuntarily from lips kept resolutely closed.

They were to be burnt alive!

Sunrise was to be the signal; and as it was late at night before this dreadful decision was arrived at, a party of the pirate fiends set to work at once to prepare for the execution.

In the centre of the wood which almost covered the island upon which the buccaneers had made their home, was a large, open space of green turf.

There was a legend of a dreadful deed committed there years and years since by a former pirate chief, since which time no tree would grow upon it.

This was the place selected for the frightful scene which was about to be enacted.

By the light of pine torches, some dozen of the men worked upon their dreadful task; and as the wavering, ruddy light fell upon their rough, hairy faces, and muscular forms, they resembled the fiends of the nethermost hell busied about their master's work.

Three posts were driven firmly into the earth, at a distance of about six feet apart.

Around these posts was piled a vast quantity of dry brushwood; and as the sun rose upon the accomplished task, the three victims were led forth amidst the yells and hootings of the buccaneers.

All were calm and collected.

They expected death, though the form in which they were to meet it might have appalled stouter hearts than theirs.

Hardstaff, watching his opportunity, drew near Owen.

"Redgrave!" he whispered.

"Well?"

"They have not deprived me of my revolver!"

"Good! Is it loaded?"

"Yes."

"That is well—I, too, have mine!"

"Can we do anything?"

"Yes."

"What?"

"Escape!"

"I fear it is impossible."

"At all events, we can make the attempt."

"Certainly."

"If they cannot overtake us, they will shoot us; but that is better than being burnt."

"Most assuredly."

"If they do overtake us, why then we shall only be in the same predicament we are now."

"That's true."

"Well, then, when the time comes, startle those nearest with a couple of shots. Keep the other four bullets for the most eager of your pursuers, and then run for the shore."

"That's all very well; but what direction shall we take?"

"Follow me."

"And when we reach the shore?"

"Trust me to arrange the rest."

It is not to be supposed that this conversation was carried on continuously.

Questions and answers were whispered as opportu-

No. 12.—THE BUCCANEERS.

nity occurred during their progress towards the place of execution.

For one moment only, Owen was near enough to Grace to speak to her.

"Courage!" he whispered in her ear; "we have yet a chance of escape."

She would have asked him more, but she had not the chance, for guards came between them, and not another word was spoken during the march.

Arrived at the place of execution, the three were taken to the posts prepared for them.

Grace was placed in the middle; Owen and Hardstaff on either side.

The buccaneers formed a semicircle in front of them.

In the rear, only some half-dozen of the pirates and the thick wood intervened between them and the river.

It has already been mentioned that both our hero and the lawyer still possessed their pistols.

It was negligent on the part of the buccaneers not to have searched their prisoners; but so confident were they in the strength of numbers, that it had never occurred to them to do so.

They made no allowance for the desperate nature of those with whom they had to deal.

To the doomed three every moment was fraught with anxiety.

Their hearts beat violently.

And well they might, for in the space of a few short minutes their fate would be decided.

In a few short minutes they would be dead or—free!

They were led to the posts.

Behind them stood men with cords to bind them tightly to the spot.

Before them stood others holding flaming torches, wherewith to set fire to the piled up brushwood as soon as all the preparations were completed.

The moment for action had arrived.

Now to make the final struggle for life and freedom.

Owen glanced anxiously at Hardstaff, and was in some measure reassured by his confident appearance.

With the rapidity of lightning Owen drew his revolver from his breast.

Before any one could perceive what he was about, he had turned, fired, and sent a bullet crashing through the brain of the man who, cord in hand, was in the act of binding him to the post.

Another bullet disposed of the one who guarded Grace, and before the buccaneers had realized what had happened and recovered from their surprise, our hero had seized the beautiful girl in his arms, and was bearing her rapidly away towards the wood.

Neither had Hardstaff been behind-hand.

He had disposed of the pirate who guarded him, in the same way Owen had done, and then had taken to his heels.

He overtook Owen just as he reached the border of the wood.

All this had been the work of a few moments.

In less time than it takes to read these words, it had happened.

Three lifeless bodies lay stretched upon the green turf.

Those whose death the buccaneers had assembled to witness, were free, and speeding as fast as possible towards the shore.

Ere the fugitives entered the wood, a multitude of shots rained around them, but the aim had been too hasty to be effective, and the three pursued their way unscathed.

But the pirates were not disposed to let their prey escape them easily.

They started in pursuit.

But for Owen's knowledge of the forest, they must have been speedily retaken; but he was well acquainted with its intricacies, and hurried on without a moment's pause, still bearing Grace upon his shoulders.

Hardstaff followed close behind.

"Do not waste a shot!" cried Owen to him. "Fire only when you are sure of your aim, and then at the nearest!"

The advice was good, and Hardstaff followed it.

Thanks to the thick growth of the trees, it was next to impossible for the buccaneers to get a fair aim at those they pursued.

Again and again the branches of trees were shattered, and the bark sent flying, by the bullets of the enraged pirates.

But, as yet, neither of the three were wounded.

The buccaneers gained upon them.

There was no doubt of the fact.

Grace encumbered Owen in his flight; but to all her entreaties to be allowed to follow by herself her lover turned a deaf ear.

Already four of those who had approached nearest to them had fallen victims to the lawyer's aim.

But they flocked on in numbers, and it was a question of speed.

With a bound, Owen cleared the forest, and with his lovely burden hastened along the shore to the spot where he knew a boat was moored.

Hardstaff but lingered a moment to discharge the last barrel of his revolver in the face of the foremost of their pursuers, and then hurried after them.

The boat was reached.

"In, in—for your lives!" said Owen, pushing Grace and the lawyer with but little ceremony into the boat.

A hatchet lay on the shore.

With one blow, Owen severed the rope which bound the frail bark to land, and then leapt in.

A wild yell of baulked vengeance echoed along the rocky shore, as the pirates saw their prey escaping.

Owen forced his two companions to lie down at the bottom of the boat.

Then he seized an oar, and, with a few vigorous strokes, sent the boat fairly out into the middle of the current.

As he did so, one of the disappointed pirates took deliberate aim at him, and fired.

With fiendish delight, those on shore saw him stagger.

His hand let go its hold upon the oar.

Then, with a low cry, he sank back.

The boat was now fairly out in the stream; and through several shots were fired at it as the current bore it rapidly seawards, they did no harm.

One shot alone had told.

That one had done mischief enough.

At the bottom of the boat lay the senseless form of Owen Redgrave, his face ashy pale, while from a wound in his shoulder flowed a copious stream of blood, which Grace, bending over him, strove in vain to staunch.

"Heaven grant my life has not been spared at the expense of his!" murmured Grace, as the boat drifted onwards.

———

CHAPTER XXXIV.

RETRIBUTION.

A MONTH has passed since the events narrated in the last chapter took place.

The buccaneers have long since got over their anger

and disappointment at the escape of our hero and his two companions.

Determined not to be baulked of their diabolical plans, they had wreaked their vengeance on the other wretched captives.

They had gloated over their agonies, greeting their cries for mercy with shouts of laughter, and sparing neither man, woman, nor child of the company which only a few months before had set out from England, full of hope and happiness.

The infamous notoriety of Drake's band was now well known.

So much were they dreaded, that no steamboat dared venture up the river alone; and even when accompanied by others, the island was passed with many nervous backward glances, to make sure the dreaded buccaneers were not putting off in pursuit.

Food was getting short among the pirates.

The only thing to be done was to plan an excursion in search of provision and plunder.

Drake proposed a raid upon the sea-coast, and his idea was received with delight by the buccaneers, who were all heartily tired of the life of inactivity they had been leading.

In accordance with Drake's directions, the Black Cloud was got ready for sea.

He had determined, and all his men concurred in his decision, to try his luck in a short sea-cruise, and then look out for a new stronghold.

A number of hands set to work willingly, and before long the Black Cloud was reported ready for sea.

At the very moment she was about to be towed out into the river, from the creek where she lay concealed when not in use, a large steamer rounded the point, and came slowly up the river.

Anxiously the buccaneers strained their eyes, in expectation of seeing her followed by others, but no other appeared.

She was alone.

It was too good an opportunity to be lost.

Drake ordered the small boats to be got ready to attack her, and about half his band were told off for the service.

Drake did not go himself, deputing the command of the party to his lieutenant.

The steamer, apparently unconscious of danger, came slowly on, and even when the pirate boats put off from the island, and rowed towards her, no alarm was manifested on board.

The buccaneers, anticipating an easy victory, rowed on exultingly, and it was not till they were within hail of the steamer, that their presence appeared to be noticed.

"Boats ahoy!" shouted a man from the bow of the steamer.

The pirates rowed in silence.

"Boats ahoy!"

Still no answer.

"Stop her!" shouted Bill Buddock, who commanded the expedition.

"What do you want?"

"Want to come aboard."

"What for?"

"We'll tell you directly."

The steamer's engines were stopped, the boats drew up alongside, and the pirates scrambled up pellmell.

They were unprepared for the reception they received.

The moment they were fairly on deck, a detachment of soldiers started from behind the bulwarks and poured a volley of shot into the advancing pirates.

Completely taken by surprise, they were all but helpless.

A few random shots were returned, but a second volley thinned their numbers; and, after a feeble resistance, all those who remained alive were driven overboard at the point of the bayonet, while a wild hurrah of victory rose from the deck of the steamer, which had been sent expressly by the Government to rout out the nest of pirates, and to destroy their stronghold.

Drake had watched the attempt to board the steamer through a telescope; but no sooner did he perceive the trap into which his men had fallen, than he dashed the glass to the ground, and paced the ground in impotent rage, muttering fierce oaths.

Then, again taking it in his hands, he looked eagerly towards the steamer.

"Not one spared!" he cried. "Come, lads," he continued, turning to the buccaneers, who, furious at the treatment their comrades had received, gathered round him to hear what he would do—"come, lads, the Black Cloud is ready for sea. Get everything you want on board. I give you five minutes to do it; and then off we go!"

"To attack the steamer?"

"Fool! Don't you see she is a Government vessel, sent expressly, without doubt, to exterminate us? See—even already—the steamer is coming towards the island!"

It was the fact.

The Government steamer Warhawk, having made short work of those who had presumed to attack her, was about to carry the war into the enemy's country.

Thanks to the former expedition which had been proposed, the Black Cloud was quite ready for sea; and in less than ten minutes from the time Drake had given the command, all the buccaneers were on board, together with the greater part of their treasure.

The island hid the tall, tapering masts of the pirates' schooner from those on board the steamer till she was fairly under way, and some distance down the river.

It seemed a hopeless matter for a sailing vessel, however fast, to escape from a steamer; but Drake answered all such observations with a savage growl, and a desire to the speaker to hold his tongue.

Drake lay extended at full length upon the deck, his eye ranging along a large and beautiful swivel gun.

As the steamer drew nearer his gaze became more fixed.

He altered the position of the gun slightly.

"Steady!" he sung out to the helmsman.

Then, with one careful glance, to make sure the aim was correct, he applied a match to the touch-hole.

With a loud report, the powder exploded.

For some moments the smoke prevented his seeing whether it had told as he intended; but as it cleared off, he perceived the starboard paddle-box of the steamer in pursuit had, as was his intention, been completely shattered by the shot.

A wild cheer broke from the buccaneers.

The Warhawk's engines were stopped, and the Black Cloud, with a jeering laugh from her crew, turned the point, and sailed rapidly before the wind down the noble river.

There is an old proverb about not crying till one is out of the wood.

The joy of the buccaneers was slightly premature.

The Warhawk, though much injured by Drake's well-aimed shot, was not altogether helpless.

A temporary paddle was rigged up with as little delay as possible, and then she started in pursuit of the pirate schooner.

It was not until they had reached the mouth of the river that they saw the Black Cloud.

She was a long way ahead of them, and standing out to sea.

The Captain of the Warhawk deliberated with himself whether, in the dilapidated condition of his vessel, he might venture to sea.

The temptation of the possibility of bringing the Black Cloud back with him as a prize was too great to be resisted.

The Warhawk started in pursuit.

It was not a long chase.

The Warhawk soon ranged alongside the Black Cloud.

A broadside from the light guns of the pirates' schooner did little or no mischief, but the heavy ones of the steamer told wherever they hit.

Drake saw how little chance they had of escape.

"Men," he cried, "who is for surrender?"

"None—none!" they cried, unanimously.

"You prefer death?"

"A thousand times!"

The Captain of the buccaneers went down into his cabin.

He wrote a few words upon a piece of paper.

He put the paper in a bottle.

He corked the bottle.

This done, he threw the bottle into the sea from his cabin window.

Without pause or hesitation he walked to the magazine where the gunpowder was stored.

Opening the largest cask, he drew his pistol from his belt.

"Good-bye, old ship!" he muttered. "I've had some happy days on board of you!"

So saying, he discharged his pistol into the centre of the cask of gunpowder.

There was a sudden flash!

A dazzling, blinding, blaze of light!

A roar, as the fire found vent!

A terrific explosion!

High up in the air went fragments of the Black Cloud!

Blackened, scorched, and mutilated bodies were flung up high by the terrific force of the explosion.

A few minutes after, an eddy in the sea, and some floating pieces of wreck, were all that remained to tell the fate of the Black Cloud, and the band of buccaneers who had manned her under the command of Captain Drake.

The Warhawk had escaped almost miraculously.

Pieces of the pirates' schooner had been blown about in every direction; but, with the exception of a few accidents too trifling to particularize, she had come off scatheless.

The Warhawk put back towards land.

There was upon the sea-coast, and at no very great distance from the mouth of the river, a small collection of huts, and a few buildings of greater pretensions.

This village, if it may be so called, possessed a safe and commodious harbour, which, in after years, made the name of the semircircle of houses round it one of the best known in the whole of the vast continent.

To this village—or, rather, to this harbour—the Warhawk steered.

Some slight injury, however, which the engines had received, rendered it necessary for the steamer to stay her course for a short time while the necessary repairs were being made.

One of the officers leaning over the bulwarks remarked a bottle tossed hither and thither on the crests of the waves.

"By Jove, Tom!" said he, to his companion, "those pirate fellows always have first-rate liquor, and this bottle must have escaped the general smash. We may as well try for it."

It was said in a half joking manner, but the two officers were young and idle, and it offered an opportunity for much amusement, and a good deal of betting as to who would be successful.

At length the bottle was caught, and drawn on board.

The oilskin cover was removed.

The cork was withdrawn; but, when the bottle was tilted, instead of liquor, there came from it a small roll of dirty paper, in which a few words were written in an almost illegible hand.

This promised some excitement, and many gathered round to hear the contents.

They were as follows:—

"On board the Black Cloud.

"There is no chance of escape. I have resolved to blow up my ship; but ere I do so, wish to make what reparation is in my power for a deed I did, of which I have since repented. Owen Redgrave, who was transported for a crime of which I accused him, was *innocent*. I was the culprit.

"DRAKE, Captain."

"Who the deuce is Owen Redgrave?" asked the disappointed officer, and his companions echoed the question.

Arrived in harbour, the Warhawk and her crew were received with enthusiasm.

They had ridden the country of one of its greatest plagues, and were looked upon as national benefactors.

In relating their adventures, mention was made of the incident of the bottle and its contents.

The news spread rapidly over the village, and in one of the better houses the account of the words Drake had written caused more happiness than can be well described.

Lying upon the bed in this house was the hero whose adventures we have followed through so many lands, and in such varied scenes.

Owen Redgrave was dying.

The wound he had received in escaping from the island was not mortal, but he had lost a great quantity of blood.

The boat in which they had made their escape had been picked up by a steamer, and Owen, together with Grace and the lawyer, conveyed to the village.

Here, partly owing to the ignorance of the sole medical attendant of the place, Owen sank into a low fever.

For days and days he lay in a state of semi-consciousness, recognising no one but Grace, who watched him with a wife's tenderness.

It was not till the news of the destruction of the Black Cloud and all her crew was narrated in his hearing, that his mind seemed to regain its activity.

The narrative concluded with the account of the picking up of the bottle and its strange contents.

"Thank God!" cried Owen, fervently; "I am freed from that charge."

He fell back as he uttered these words.

The exertion had been too great for him.

Owen Redgrave would never speak more.

He was dead.

Reverently Grace drew the sheet over his face—so handsome in life, still more so in the stillness of death.

This done, she cast herself upon her knees at his bedside, and prayed with the whole ardour of her heart and soul, that the sins of the erring, sinful man she had loved so truly through everything, might be forgiven.

Who can dare say her prayer was not granted?

THE END.